Kane's Cross

Witchfinder, Volume 2

E.M.G Wixley

Published by E.M.G Wixley, 2017.

KANE'S CROSS

First edition. April 26, 2017.

Copyright © 2017 E.M.G Wixley.

ISBN: 979-8224064885

Written by E.M.G Wixley.

Dedication

This book is dedicated to my dear friend Melanie for her kindness and unending support. I would also like to thank my family, who have supported my dreams with patience and understanding.

Chapter One

"Hi, Dad, how's it going?"

"Yes, it's okay here, but the job pays badly. I've run out of money and food, and it's a long way from payday."

"I know you're skint. I just wanted someone to talk to."

"Don't fucking bother! I asked you to phone me yesterday, but as always, I'm the last person you think about."

"Why did I bother making up with you – it's the same old shit."

"I would rather you beat me growing up than this shit. Just thinking of yourself as always."

"When was the last time you showed me you cared - you act like a child!"

"I tell you I'm about to kill myself, and even then, you don't put in the effort."

"I'm gonna hurt you as much as you've hurt me!" Kane slammed his phone on the bar and glanced around as his audience bowed their heads, making out they weren't listening. *I'll give you entertainment,* he thought and once again picked up his mobile.

"You have fifteen minutes to phone, or I'm plastering the internet with shit about you, and I won't feel any guilt after the way you have treated me. What do you think you're achieving apart from making me hate you more and burning all bridges?"

"You want to torture me over and over mentally. You give me no choice but to get angry. Then you use that as an excuse to say I'm crazy. I'm this mad because it's like talking to a brick wall."

"Check your computer, and I've messaged your slag of a mistress, and it's gonna get worse."

"You can talk to everyone else but not me."

"If you're going to ignore me, I'm gonna come back and make sure you can't ignore me."

Kane's phone died; he stuffed it in his pocket and slouched forward on the bar. Sunk in thought, he played with the dog tag hanging from a chain around his neck. Opposite, the barman was standing, drying glasses and staring down at his angry and morose patron.

"Mate, this is a quiet pub," he said in a stern, lowered voice. "I'm going to have to throw you out if you don't calm down."

"There are other pubs," Kane slurred.

"Drinking in the middle of the day, every day, isn't a good thing," the barman said and, without waiting for a reply, continued. "You've been hanging around this place for a few weeks," he paused to place some of the glasses under the counter. "Look, don't take offence - I wouldn't normally say anything, and mostly, I'm only too happy to take my customer's hard-earned cash, but I can see you're a member of our armed forces."

"Was," Kane replied. "The booze stops the tremors but isn't great for combat situations."

"Oh, I see," the barman uttered.

Kane rubbed his weary eyes and glanced up. "Another Jack, please, mate," he said, dropping his gaze.

"I don't want to serve you," the barman said, his brow knitting with a mixture of pity and annoyance. "Go home, back to your family. You have a northern accent - I've been told they are friendly up there, better than this bustling City."

Kane shed a few silent tears on the back of his hand. The barman looked at him, stunned. He stretched his arm over the bar and placed his hand on Kane's arm.

"It's time to go home," the barman said softly, "back to your own town."

"If I had come home with no legs or arms, people would understand as my injuries would be visible. As you heard, my folks think I've gone mad," Kane whispered through his snivels. "My wounds are internal - constantly oozing. I don't understand what's happening to me, so there's no way anyone else will."

Kane stared up at the barman, his eyes loaded with sorrow. "Tell me, how do I explain the shaking, the night terrors, confusion and, of course, the drinking? Besides, I can't handle any relationships right now. It's enough trying to get through the day."

"I thought there were places the army could send you for help," the barman said, looking in the direction of an anxiously waiting customer.

"We're taught to suck it up to control our emotions and not to reveal any weaknesses." Kane wiped his tears away and took a deep intake of air. "Please, another drink, mate," he pleaded. "I swear this is a temporary thing. I can sort it myself."

"I will serve this other customer," he nodded in the direction of a well-dressed man who was looking more annoyed. "Then I will get your drink, but it will be your last."

Kane waited in restless silence. *This was terrorism at its best,* he thought. *The enemy has gone, but I'm still locked in a cell being tortured. Twenty-one, and my life's over.*

"You can't come in here! You're too young!" the barman's deep, stern voice shouted across the room.

Kane pivoted around on the barstool and saw a vulnerable, diminutive, pathetic looking girl standing in the doorway. *It's Sandra!* Kane thought, feeling briefly elated. His sister, who was also small with dark hair had vanished from home a week previously. Kane's distressed mother had begged him to travel north to join in the search.

"Please, son, come home," she'd sobbed down the phone. "She's just vanished. We were at the club - I saw her on her phone, and then she was gone. Nobody has seen her since. The twins don't understand and keep asking where she's gone."

"Mum, I will come back as soon as I can, I promise," he'd replied, feeling torn. When the phone went dead, he'd quickly downed a few whiskies to suppress the shock of the terrible news. Then, he'd made plans to leave and had been determined to catch the next train. Instead, feeling heavy and tired he'd stumbled back to his flat and fallen asleep in the chair. Each day since, he'd told himself he would return soon but remained stationary. He could not motivate himself – he needed to be dug from his pit by caring hands before he could help anyone. Still, everywhere he went, he searched, hoping to bump into her around each corner.

Kane took a closer look at the girl who hadn't moved from beneath the door frame, and although she resembled his sister, there was something very peculiar about her persona. Her diminutive frame was, swamped by a grubby grey, long smock dress, and her long hair appeared greasy.

Kane watched as the barman rushed from behind the counter and began pushing the girl towards the door.

"Wait a minute!" Kane snapped back as he saw the defeated girl turn to leave. "She has come to speak to me," he said, taking some nicotine chewing gum from his coat pocket and stuffing it in his mouth to try and kick-start himself into life.

"Well, I wouldn't get too close. It looks like she could do with a bath," the barman said, as the girl swiftly disappeared - the door swinging behind her.

Kane eased his six-foot-five frame off the stool and, holding himself straight, stiffly walked out of the pub to the sound of people chuckling and gossiping about the strange girl.

Chewing vigorously to get the most nicotine from the gum, Kane focussed his attention on the girl. His heart was pounding, goosebumps sprung on his arms, and he sweated in the sudden heat. She was moving quickly, and he was frightened she would disappear.

"Wait!" he shouted, but a motorbike roared by and drowned out his voice. The once fit soldier found his legs and increased his pace.

He caught up with the girl just as she was about to turn the corner into another street. Daringly, he approached her, hoping she wouldn't run away.

Kane placed his hand on her shoulder and felt her jump with alarm. "I don't mean to bother you, but you look lost," he said with a voice thick with booze.

"Yes, I am. I've left home and don't know my way around," she said, as tears of helplessness flowed down her face.

"A word of advice: you need to be very careful who you say those things to. There are people around who will do terrible things to someone on their own."

Kane saw the girl's cheeks go crimson, and she glanced at her feet.

"I hope you don't mind me asking, but how old are you?" Kane felt uneasy, as the girl looked very young. She reminded him of a North American Indian and resembled his sister with her long, black, straight hair. "If you've argued with your parents, I can assure you it would be far better to sort your problems out. Hanging around the streets is dangerous."

"I'm seventeen - and I can't explain, but I need help – I can't go back home," she whispered, still staring at the ground.

"Okay, then you can come back to mine for a while until we can find you some proper help. I promise you will be safe with me."

"How do I know I'll be safe with you?" Abruptly, she looked up and held his gaze with a deeply perturbed expression in her dark eyes.

"You don't, but in truth, it looks like you're going to have to put your trust in someone," Kane said softly, running his hands over his shaved head as his internal voice asked, *should you really be doing this?*

Together, they stood frozen, pondering the situation. A group of drunk youths stumbled through the pub doors and out onto the street. Kane heard voices and footsteps rapidly approaching from behind. He looked down at the girl, and she flashed him a look of panic.

"Hey mate what you doing with that crazy girl?"

The group surrounded Kane and the girl as they went to move past. One youth deliberately knocked the girl, and she fell hard onto the pavement. In an instant, Kane had grabbed the youth's collar and was striking the side of his face with blow after blow of his fist. The youth's skin split open, and he stared stunned through a crimson mask and collapsed to the ground. Kane kicked him with a rage for which even he was not prepared.

"Stop! Stop!" the girl cried out.

Kane glanced over at the girl who was scrambling to her feet. Automatically, he bent over and held out his hand. He connected with her small clammy palm and instinctively began to run at a speed she could manage. When finally, he noticed, the group had gone, their pace dwindled.

"I'm sorry about that, but they're just the kind of people you need to be careful of," he said, aware of the tremors which had returned to his body. "What's your name?"

"Poppy," she replied in a sulky voice, "Poppy Morgan."

"Well, that's a pretty name. I'm Kane Rivers."

Poppy followed Kane in silence back to his flat. For three days, she remained huddled in the corner of his front room in a staring silence, only washing or eating when he went out. On his return, he would hold an endless one-sided conversation with her while preparing food or watching television programs.

Poppy was a complete puzzle to Kane. It was as though she had been hiding in a dark crack her whole life. He bought her shorts and T-shirts to get her out of her stinking dress. One day, he came home, and she was sitting in a chair, wearing her new clothes. Over time,

Poppy's manner became increasingly warm and lively. She began hesitantly to explore objects in his flat as though she was seeing them for the first time.

When he took her out to show her the sights, she became animated, overexcited, like a claustrophobic who'd been released from her prison cell. Once she'd gained her confidence, she would talk endlessly about the wonders of everyday life, the splendour of buildings, and her amazement at how well the chaotic system of town life worked. However, there was never any mention of her background or life experiences. When pressed for answers, her mood would become more pensive; her lower lip would quiver and her eyes water.

"Please don't ask me. I can't tell you, and I don't think you could understand," she would say and swallow back her tears, "this is my life now, with you."

There was no understanding of the girl, and he couldn't help but wonder if she had escaped from a mental hospital. After a week, her mood grew grimmer again, fretful, and she paced the small flat as though she was struggling with an internal dilemma.

"What's the matter?" Kane had finally asked. "Please tell me I might be able to help."

"I need to get as far away from this crowded City as possible," she said, staring at him with eyes wide and fearful.

"Well, next spring, I will be starting a computer programming course in London. I intend to start getting serious about life. Get myself a proper career," he smiled, anxious to prevent the tears from flooding down her cheeks. "We could take a holiday to Cornwall. That's as far south as we can go without passports."

"What's a passport?"

"It's a document you need to go abroad," he replied, puzzled by her ignorance.

"Oh, I see. Cornwall sounds good," she said, the brightness instantly returning to her eyes. "Tomorrow then?"

Stunned, Kane smiled dumbly and nodded his head. He couldn't tell her that he had hardly any money in his bank account and that surviving would be rough.

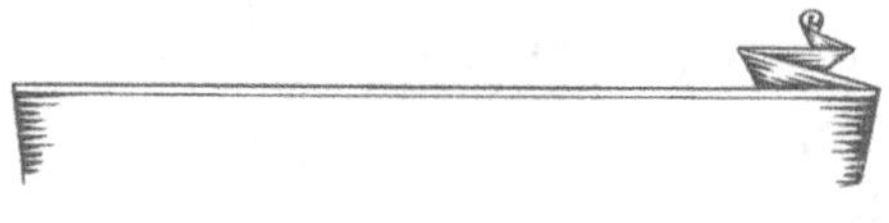

Chapter Two

It was May and unusually hot and dry. Before they had left home, the news had all been about global warming, how the country would need to adapt to the new hotter springs and summers. To Kane and Poppy, as they stood by the motorway thumbing a lift, the brightness and heat added to their excitement.

"I'm free! I'm free!" Poppy said repeatedly. Then she hummed an unidentifiable tune over and over.

Kane watched her jumping around like a puppy dog. She wore no makeup, and the shorts and t-shirts were her only items of clothing. He had never met anyone so animated before. If her body wasn't constantly moving, then her mind would be coming up with stories and ideas. He was charmed by her humble innocence, the way her speaking and joyous actions seemed unconscious and her manner unaffected. He found all these qualities endearing, and he'd felt a brotherly love for her from the start.

"We've escaped. I'm so happy," she said, fanning her blushing cheeks.

"Yes, now all we need to do is get a lift." Kane smiled.

"Perhaps I should lift my leg and show some thigh," she laughed. "How long will it take to get to Cornwall?"

"One, maybe two days, depending on how good our rides are."

"Thanks for doing this for me."

"No problem. You cried help, and I came running," he smiled. "I thought you were a deserving cause," Kane said, taking a quick swig from the bottle he'd put in the front pocket of his rucksack. *I don't want the tremors now,* he thought.

A car stopped, and the young couple scrambled in and immediately thanked the driver.

'No trouble, I'm Mark," he twisted around awkwardly and shook their hands. "I'm in sales. I'm hoping your company will keep me awake. Where are you heading?"

"Cornwall," Kane said.

"Well, I can take you as far as Bath," he said, smiling broadly at them in his mirror. "It's a long journey from Canterbury down to the south-west," Mark said.

"That would be good," Kane replied, realising he was embarking on a mystery journey, leaving the City that had held him captive for the last year. Since the abrupt end of his Army career, he'd drifted from one southern town to another, avoiding his northern home of Middleport. His life had been vague, empty, and meaningless, but now he was moving again and felt more solid.

As they sped along the motorway, the ugly landscape of overlapping roads, cars and industry flashed by in a shimmering silver, metallic haze.

Eventually, as the light began to die, they found themselves slowly driving past Stonehenge in a Rolls Royce. Their driver an elderly gentleman with a handlebar moustache had made the detour just to show them the monument, which Kane had never seen. Their surroundings were now more picturesque, and everything had become dark greens and shadows in the half-light.

Finally, the driver drove down a quiet side road and dropped them off by a meadow. He said his farewells and disappeared into the darkness. It was late at night by the time they'd pitched their tent. Kane watched as, without any shyness, Poppy undressed. He had dreamt about her every night since they had met, and now here she was naked. She climbed into the sleeping bag with nothing on except for what appeared to be a flint spearhead on a gold chain, which hung around her white throat.

They lay side by side, listening to the silence, lost in their thoughts. *Would she ever tell me her secret?* Kane pondered.

"Why was it so urgent for you to leave home?' he finally asked.

"If I tell you, you will end up dead," she laughed, but Kane could sense that she was serious. "You wouldn't believe me anyway."

"Are you expecting us to be followed?"

"Not sure. I think we're safe."

"Was it your parents? Were they bad to you?" Kane bravely asked.

"Definitely not," she lifted herself on her elbows, turned and looked directly at his face. "I'm sorry, but I can't say anymore. Please trust me."

Her seriousness was such a contrast to her cheerful mood of the day that Kane immediately fell silent.

"Just hold me, please."

Kane wrapped his arms around Poppy and drew her close. He held her tight the whole night through until dawn.

The next day they arrived at their destination. Watching Poppy's reaction to her first sight of the sea was as magical as witnessing a child's first steps.

"I have never seen anything like this before," she said, falling to her knees on the sand. Everything is free and moving." Poppy ran down to the waves and then back up the beach, studying the sky, feeling the sand, and breathing in the air. "It's all so bright."

"It isn't always like this," Kane replied, feeling bemused by her overwhelming enthusiasm. It was as though she'd lived in a rigid, black-and-white world, which had now melted away, and for the first time, she was experiencing colour and perpetual change.

Finally exhausted from running up and down, she stood beside Kane, breathing hard. He took hold of her moist hand.

"What do you most wish for?" he said.

"To be re-incarnated into your world," was her immediate reply. "What's yours?"

"To always make you happy and keep you safe."

Chapter Three

They pitched their two-person tent at the far end of the town's beach, next to boulders, which helped to support a railway line. On the other side of the track was a road and, beyond this, a small campsite. Kane had already decided that they could sneak in there for showers.

On that first night, they had settled down in front of a driftwood fire, which had provided them with their only light since Kane's battery had died on his phone. In silence, they ate bread and cheese, allowing their thoughts to stray as they stared into the flames. The fire spat, sparks flew, and smoke filled the air.

Later, exhausted Poppy sunk into a deep sleep. Kane lay awake, snug beneath the sleeping bag, listening to the night's noises, the crashing sea's rhythm, and the sighing breeze. Slowly, he became aware of creeping anxiety. Outside was the almost imperceptible sound of animal movement. Something else was alive in the darkness. Listening intently, he cautiously stuck his head out of the tent. There was no moon, and the dark was thick. Whispering but distinct voices came from the direction of a cave, which lay further down the beach. Kane stared hard but couldn't make out any movement. Uneasily, he climbed back into the warm cocoon and stiffly lay until the fizzing bubbles of exhaustion confused his rational thought, and he fell asleep.

After a few days, they'd settled into a routine. Dawn broke with the seagulls crying. Poppy awoke and greeted Kane with a dazzling smile. They would wash and clean their teeth in the sea. Then Poppy would become restless and anxious to be away exploring her new golden universe. Kane would leave her to walk into town to buy food and have a few necessary pints. He would watch her as he walked along the coast path, curiously examining everything she came across with enduring delight.

On his return, he would often find her on the edge of the waves, whether the sea was seething or calm, splashing around with the spontaneous joy of a child. At night, Kane slept with a knife under his pillow, waiting for the disembodied voices to begin their whispering. He would be ready to attack if whatever was lurking tried to pull them out of their tent and into the shadows.

Kane felt unable to express all these fears to Poppy, as he didn't want to deflate her buoyant mood. He was desperate to keep everything light. He didn't want her to have access to his soul and to set eyes on his ugly internal world. It was enough to have a new purpose: to protect and watch as she grew.

After two weeks, Poppy awoke to find the tent empty. She sensed something was wrong and spent the morning studying her collection of items, which she'd found on the beach. Then, she uneasily flicked through a magazine. By lunchtime, she was keenly feeling Kane's absence. She crawled from the tent and began to search every part of the now-familiar beach. Gradually, she began to walk towards the town centre. The crowd thickened, and she felt uneasy as she stared into strange faces and met a multitude of expressions. The bustling, noisy streets were painful and too busy, and she was unsure as to where to look. Defeated in the still-parching afternoon heat, she drifted back down the hill towards the beach.

Poppy returned to the tent, sat peering through the open flaps and waited anxiously, aware of her increasing thirst. In the ghostly light of dusk, she saw a tall figure stumbling towards the tent.

Kane felt guilty, staring down at Poppy's furrowed forehead. "I'm sorry I got nicked. I have to appear in court in a few months." He smiled at her pitifully, always ensuring his voice was extra gentle when he was drunk. "I tried to steal us some food. I suppose wearing a big coat in this heat was a giveaway." Kane tried to smile but felt it die on his lips. He dropped to his knees and crawled into the tent. Poppy followed.

They kneeled in the small space face to face. Kane cleared his throat, and the smell of alcohol filled the air.

"I have a confession to make." Kane paused and coughed again nervously. "I have run out of money. We have no way of getting food."

Kane wanted to avert his eyes from Poppy, who stared at him steadfastly as if she were struggling to process the new information. "What about that card you put in the wall?" she asked.

"Well, put it this way. My box is empty."

Ashamed, Kane looked away. He couldn't control the wilt of his body, the droop, of his mouth and his eyes from glazing with tears.

"Don't worry, we will find a way," she said.

"Some protector, I am," Kane muttered, feeling a pang of sorrow at Poppy's attempt to soothe away his pain. "Please, no pity. You don't understand," he said, sighing dramatically. "If I hadn't wasted it all on booze, we could have lasted a good few weeks."

"Why do you drink alcohol? We're not permitted to drink where I come from, as it poisons the mind," Poppy said in a matter-of-fact way.

Kane saw Poppy, studying his face. Tears filled his eyes, and his Adam's apple danced in his throat as he tried to swallow them back. Kane then collapsed onto the inflatable bed and covered his eyes with his arm.

"You found the wrong person to help you. My life is nothing; it's out of control," he said in a thick voice. "You came too late for me."

"Perhaps it's my turn to help you," Poppy said calmly. "I needed time to adapt, that's all."

"If we don't die of thirst, first, then we will have to return to my hometown."

"I will sneak into the campsite over the road and get us some water. You sleep," Poppy said and disappeared before Kane could utter another word.

Kane shut his eyes, feeling disgusted with himself. *She's caring for me when I should be helping her,* he thought and fell asleep feeling useless.

Chapter Four

The next morning was a Saturday, and they awoke late to the many voices of people who had rushed to find available space on the beach. When they looked out, they saw sun-seekers lying prone, hungrily, eating up the rays of light as the sun burnt a golden hole in the sky. Children laughed, played, and ran towards the waves to cool off, free from the constraints of their parents.

Kane squinted in the brightness. He felt unwell and conscious of his alcohol-induced fever. Typically, he would have made excuses and rushed to find something to alleviate his agony. Then he remembered he still had some dregs in a whiskey bottle hidden in his bag. When Poppy climbed out of the tent to clean her teeth, he swallowed the last mouthfuls.

"Follow me," she commanded as she poked her head back through the tent and dropped her toothbrush in the corner. "We will get some food."

Kane felt too rough to argue and climbed into the dazzling, sickening light. Poppy actively ignored his signs of distress and, in her normal bouncy mood, walked ahead. In a cloud of melancholy and self-pity, Kane watched her as he stumbled behind, aware of his whole body trembling. It looked as though Poppy was on a mission, ignoring the crowds and heading for the nearest beach kiosk. *Had she found some money?* Kane thought as he increased his pace, aware of the gnawing in his stomach.

When they arrived at the kiosk, Poppy joined a queue of five people. Kane waited to one side a few feet away, feeling self-conscious about his dishevelled appearance and his inappropriate attire of black trousers and a long-sleeved shirt. *At least the tremors have stopped,* he thought, as he noticed the odd glance in his direction.

Kane's eyes strayed towards the sea, where people rode the waves and shrieked with delight. Movement in his peripheral vision and a familiar voice prompted him to turn back. Poppy was taking her turn at the kiosk. Kane watched intently, wondering how she could pay for anything.

Although Kane was standing back, he was facing the queue and could see Poppy's face. She stared directly at the man with eyes wide and blazing. Then she tilted her head to one side and began to speak emphatically in an unidentifiable foreign tongue. The man behind the counter appeared unaware of Poppy's presence and talked as though addressing another invisible customer. People standing behind Poppy were also reacting as though she wasn't there.

Stunned, Kane observed Poppy reach out with both arms and scoop up items within her reach, mostly sweets. As she turned and calmly walked away, she looked up and exchanged a smile with Kane.

Once she was at his side, Kane relieved her of some of her burdens.

"Shouldn't we be running?" he said.

"No! Don't worry! I've just altered his perception – he won't have seen me or anyone else," she smiled. "The people in the queue and the assistant's mind will be someplace else for a while."

"Perhaps you could reset my view of the world," Kane laughed, thinking that he was responding to a joke.

"I told you I couldn't do it for long periods of time," Poppy said in a serious tone. "At least, not without the others."

"What others?" Kane asked, finding it hard to follow her meaning.

"Oh, nothing - I'm good at stealing things and obviously better than you."

"I couldn't go back to how I was anyway—that man no longer exists," Kane mumbled, confused.

As they walked on silently, Kane wondered if he hadn't stepped over the line into madness. Maybe all his drinking had finally taken a toll on his brain.

"Take these off me," Poppy said, handing him her softening sweets. Kane complied, stuffed what he could in his pockets and watched as her eyes scoured the ground. Suddenly, she bent down and, digging in the sand, retrieved a two-pound coin. This process continued all the way back to the tent. Her eagle eyes picked out every disturbance and detail between each grain of sand. Kane watched in disbelief as continuously she swiftly bent down and with agile fingers searched until she found gold and silver.

"Who needs a metal detector," Kane said aloud to reassure himself he was conscious.

By the time they arrived back at the tent, they had acquired seven pounds of coins.

"This should keep us going while we pack and travel back to your home," Poppy said, throwing everything onto the airbed. It's time to move again, anyway."

Chapter Five

Oliver Baker was on a precipice looking down. In a state of dread, he scrutinised the depth and fragility of the hole. It looked like the entrance to the bowels of the earth, and he wished his first assignment as a qualified archaeologist had taken him to a muddy field. Oliver breathed in the stagnant air and began to climb down the flimsy rope ladder. He had always been nervous of heights and confined spaces but kept his fears hidden, as he knew he would be required to work in those environments.

Feeling a sense of relief, Oliver finally placed his feet on firm ground. He cast his eyes around and saw that he was in a vast chamber, the hub of a wheel with tunnels leading in all directions. A string of three dull light bulbs hung from the ceiling, producing inadequate light, but from this, Oliver could see that most of the passageways were blocked, and only one appeared accessible.

Oliver spotted the hunched figure of Professor Rupert Roehampton at the far right of the cave. On his head was a hard hat with a powerful lamp attached. Oliver could see the professor was lost in thought, inspecting the wall intently. He was humming to himself and seemed unaware of Oliver's approach.

Oliver felt like an intruder standing at the professor's side, his nose dripping from the cold, and unsure if he should speak or remain silent. As he fumbled in the pocket of his high-visibility jacket in search of a tissue, the professor became aware of his presence.

"I suppose they've sent me another scrawny geek," he mumbled almost inaudibly.

Oliver felt irritated as his keen hearing had picked up the vital words. The professor turned, peered over his glasses and smiled up at Oliver.

"Are you what they call a 'gamer'?" The professor asked scornfully.

Oliver felt himself blush and, feeling uneasy under the professor's gaze, lowered his eyes to the floor. As a teenager, he'd been an avid fan of computer games but hadn't played for a good few years.

"Oh, don't take offence. The last graduate they sent me wasn't up to much. It turned out his interests lay in the virtual world rather than reality."

"I can assure you my feet are firmly planted in this world," Oliver said.

"Ah, good! Good! I'm presuming you are my new assistant, Oliver Baker." The professor rubbed his hands together to remove the dust and then held his hand out in greeting.

"I'm pleased to meet you, Professor," Oliver said, shaking the man's cold hand.

"Oh please, call me Rupert," he smiled, revealing yellow stained teeth within his beard. "I have so much to show you," he added with bubbling excitement."

"I'm amazed that someone had this place beneath their house without the building collapsing," Oliver said as he looked into the shadows.

"Mr Clements knew about all of this - he had his house deliberately built over it and ensured the foundations had added support. He was an extremely wealthy industrialist, a philanthropist, and, they say, a devout Christian. He never married – he passed this place to his nephew, who also never married." Rupert paused, took a bottle of water from his pocket and took a few sips. "We can talk about all that later. Come over here," he said, directing Oliver to look at an image on the cave wall, highlighted by his flashlight. "What do you know of these?"

"It's a hand stencil, and they have been found in about eight caves in France and Spain," Oliver confidently answered.

"And, Argentina, Africa, Borneo and Australia," Rupert added. "I have been studying cave art for almost two decades now and visited most of the sites. Still relatively little is known about the people who created them."

They both fell silent and meditated on the images. Surrounding the hands were pictures of game animals, bison, reindeer, horses and woolly mammoths.

"I read that the current thinking was that female shamans probably made these pictures. They would come into the caves and, in some trance, connect with the spirit world," Olive said, feeling a need to break the profound silence and show off to the professor.

"Yes, indeed," Rupert said, still lost in contemplation. The Palaeolithic world reached out to touch the hand of the future, an ancient way of saying, 'I was here!'

Suddenly, Rupert glanced up at Oliver half-turning and clutched his arm. Oliver captured an indescribable expression on the man's face, perhaps fear or desperation. The icy air caused Oliver to shudder.

"These pictures were not my main reason for asking you down here," Rupert said, relaxing a little and smiling. "We will need to go into the tunnel. You had better put your light on," the old man instructed, leading the way into the darkness. "So far, you are the only person I have shown this. I feel I need to understand more about what we're looking at before I reveal my findings to the world." Rupert stopped at the entrance to the tunnel and rambled on as if he suddenly needed to explain everything in a hurry to the younger man. Oliver gazed at Rupert's face and tried to listen, but he was aware of the cold gnawing at his body.

"Of course, the house has been derelict and boarded up for some years, but now the council plans to keep the shell and turn the interior into luxury flats. All this would have to be covered and stabilised," he said, looking over his shoulder at the circular space.

"As an archaeologist, I was called away from Oxford to investigate the house's history and Mr Clements. It was no big deal; I was here to provide a historical document on an exceedingly wealthy but mysterious man for future posterity. I had a professional photographer come and take photos of the rooms, as they intended to strip out the old fireplaces and remove the décor."

"How did you discover this underground world?" Oliver asked.

"My time had run out; my investigation was officially over, and the builders were to begin their work in a week. I was having a last look around," Rupert said and paused to take another sip of water. It was clear to Oliver that he was anxious to tell his story as quickly as possible.

Rupert cleared his throat and continued. "I noticed an electrical wire running down the wall. When I followed it, I saw it went into a hole in the concrete. I chipped away at the crumbling floor and found a sheet of metal. I was curious. I should have informed the university, but something stopped me."

Rupert fell into silence, and Oliver noticed lines of anxiety cross his brow. "How did you clear the concrete?" Oliver asked.

"I paid the men who were working on my house to break through. They removed the concrete and the metal sheet, revealing a large hole. I didn't know what else I would find."

Oliver and Rupert entered the tunnel, and the temperature dropped considerably from a chill to icy. Straight away, their lamps lit up the cave walls covered with ancient art.

Oliver moved closer, bent forward and positioned himself to get the best look. The hands were not stencils but detailed prints, and instead of the game animals, there were symbols and pictograms.

"These images are far more advanced than the others," Oliver said as he straightened. "They are fascinating!"

"Yes, indeed. It is widely known the images were modified over thousands of years, but this is more than that, as you can see." Oliver nodded dumbly. "I have taken photos and recorded all the details for further study," Rupert added.

"I suppose Mr Clements knew all about this place," Oliver said.

"I presume it was him who fixed the ladder and installed the electricity. Why Mr Clements put so much work into preserving this place and to make the floor above stable enough to build his home on, or why he'd kept it a secret from all but his nephew, is a question I can't answer."

"Rupert, you wouldn't suppose Mr Clements faked the paintings."

Oliver looked directly at Rupert and saw his forehead creased into a stern frown. "Definitely not! Would I bring you down here if that were the case?"

"I'm sorry, it seems so improbable. I've never seen or heard of anything like this before," Oliver said, in an apologetic manner.

"I suppose I came to the same conclusion at first. As I said, I have studied cave paintings for many years, so I know something about the reasoning behind them and know when they're genuine."

As Oliver leaned forward again to study the images further, Rupert continued to speak.

"Besides, I took samples of the paint, animal bones I found, soil, rock, everything I could and sent them away for radiocarbon dating."

"Well, I know the caves in France and Spain were about 12,000 – 40,000 years old," Oliver muttered.

"Yes, that's correct, and the earliest evidence for Homo sapiens in Europe is 37,300", Rupert said.

"So, what period are we looking at?" Oliver asked as he traced along the wall deeper into the tunnel."

"We are looking at something much earlier than the first humans."

"Neanderthals?" Oliver shouted, stood up straight, turned and stared directly at Rupert. He could feel his heart pounding and his eyes popping with disbelief. "You are kidding me. There is no evidence on this planet that they could produce anything like this. If that were true, it would turn our early history completely upside down."

Suddenly, Rupert rushed ahead of Oliver, bent close to the wall and began brushing away at the rubble and dirt. "Come and look at this!" he shouted.

Oliver rushed over and crouched at Rupert's side. He tilted his helmet light so it illuminated the object. In absolute astonishment, he stared at the rock, which had been tooled into a flat disk. On its surface was what appeared to be a form of writing, and at the top was a perfectly carved acute heptagram.

"Isn't that the seven-pointed star used in witchcraft?" Oliver said, aware that he was shaking with the cold and excitement.

"Well, it is now, but who knows what it meant then," Rupert replied. "There are also signs that this cave was not only used for ceremonial purposes. As hard as it is to access, there are signs of habitation."

"When do they start building work?" Oliver said, overwhelmingly enthralled by Rupert's discovery.

"Next week, that is my dilemma. Is the world ready for such a find? You see, I came across something like this cave years ago but was sworn to secrecy. I was about your age and had forgotten all about it, but then I remembered my old professor who had written a paper on his findings. Unfortunately, he died, and I moved on to fresh ground without giving it further thought."

"Yes, but you must inform the univarsity so it will halt the building project."

"I have to return to Oxford tonight and find those papers," Rupert said, almost to himself.

"I wasn't sure how long we would be here, so I booked my train for the day after tomorrow," Oliver added.

"Come around to my house as soon as you can, but while I'm gone, stay away from this place. I've also been receiving some unwanted emails." Rupert looked around nervously. "We can go over the evidence together, and if you think I'm not a foolish old man, then we will take it to the board."

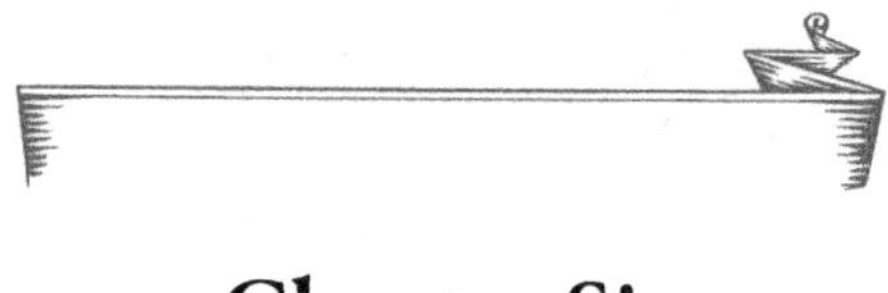

Chapter Six

With a glass of red wine in his hand, Adam walked towards his dressing room. Each time he thought of Dylan, his stomach knotted, and his heart began to thump. He waited impatiently to set eyes once more on the enigmatic man he loved. Gulping at his wine to steady his nerves, he idled along in a dream, oblivious to background noises and all the preparations for his performance.

On the surface, it was an unlikely match. Dylan was a mild-mannered, very shy man and a priest who belonged to a mysterious order. *Perhaps it was the forbidden nature of their relationship that made the man so attractive,* Adam thought. His complacent blue eyes were unable to look anyone directly in the face, and he would look to the side to talk or to the floor. The constant smoking was a distraction, which enabled him to occasionally glance in a speaker's direction. However, their mutual illicit, pleasurable encounters left them both rapturously happy.

Adam turned the door handle to his dressing room. Lately, everything in his life had added to his buoyant mood. The dark shadows of his past had successfully been painted over. Not only was he a highly-acclaimed violinist, but now also a composer. The sublime music he created soaked into his soul from the ether, and he loved the mesmerising effect it had on his audiences.

"Adam, you have half an hour," the stage manager called out.

"Okay, I will be ready," Adam, said, turning and flashing a smile in the man's direction.

Adam stepped into the small dark room and flicked the switch. Instantly, any joy was obliterated as a grotesque image jumped into his vision. The glass exploded in his hand as he set his eyes on the doll sitting in his swivel chair, which had been deliberately turned to face the door. He stared directly at the diabolical object with a hateful expression as he tried to ignore the hysterical thoughts screaming in his mind. Then, an image flashed before him of his previous encounters with the doll, ending in him smashing it up and releasing the spirit of Mathew, the man. *How can this thing still exist when I destroyed it with my own hands? Is this an illusion created by the real Mathew? Was this Mathew's calling card or a boy's tool for finding witches? Whatever it's for, one thing is clear: Mathew has come to claim his debt,* he considered, as he turned to leave the room.

"There, be witches," the Mathew doll said in his deep raspy voice.

Adam froze and then, shutting the door behind him, walked into the dull light. He plucked the doll from his chair and held it, squeezing its soft middle tightly. The wide scarlet lips on the white porcelain face turned up at the corners in an ugly grin, and the oversized eyes stared motionless, shining with evil intent. Adam longed to tear its ugly head off but feared the consequences.

"Mathew watches over your life," the doll said. His head spun around a full three hundred and sixty degrees, and when he faced Adam again, he held his attention with his menacing black, glassy eyes. "You had a deal, which must be kept. You find them and bring them to court. Mathew will be judge and executioner," the doll said, reminding Adam that his nightmares were real.

"The musical talent you possess was liberated for you from the heavens. Mathew has the power to suck it up and put it back in the spiritual box." Mechanical eyelids dropped over the doll's eyes as if he was suddenly sleeping.

A fear mounted up inside Adam, which he was unable to suppress. He nodded dumbly. His claustrophobic room felt deeply silent, but he was aware of the orchestra tuning up their instruments above his head. Filled with panic and drowning in a cold sweat, he took several deep breaths.

There was a knock on his door. "Are you ready, Adam?"

"Yes, I'm coming," he said and stared hard at the hostile intruder, placed him back on his chair and rushed out of the room. It felt like a long walk up the worn steps to the wings. He tried to push the knowledge of his returning madness out of his mind. He knew what Mathew was capable of and whether real or imagined he acknowledged that all though he was a reluctant accomplice, he would agree with all the witchfinder's demands.

Adam felt exposed and emotionally raw as he stared out into the settling crowd. Nothing appeared to have changed. He felt the heat of the lights and listened to the mutterings and shuffling. Then, the audience was expectantly looking in his direction. Adam couldn't prevent his eyes from rummaging amongst the blur of faces for Dylan, the man whose passion had kept his soul rooted in reality. Suddenly, the audience melted away, and Adam's eyes locked onto Mathew. He cringed at the sight of the black hat, straight long silver hair, strange clothes and a hooked nose. He tried to hold his adversary's gaze, but Mathew's eyes pierced right through him, causing him to become further agitated. He looked at the floor and considered the possibility of running. Instead, he placed his violin under his chin and, with his eyes half-shut, hid in the universe of music. Adam's fingers and bow danced over the strings, and the mystical key of his talent unlocked the doors to the divine. Everyone in the venue, including Adam, quickly fell under a spell, released from gravity and transported into the heavens.

Adam then spotted the familiar figure of Dylan pushing his way past a row of passively annoyed people towards an empty seat next to Mathew. As he watched the two men shake hands, Adam realised the terrible significance of their actions. Their meeting was not an accident.

Adam felt his heart wilt at the sight of such a bitter betrayal. His music wavered as he stared with yearning at the grey head with its faded blonde streaks. Tears rushed into his eyes. He dropped his lids and increased his efforts to finish his piece with dignity.

The crowd applauded rapturously, desperate to show their appreciation for being lifted from their everyday lives. Adam wanted to extend his stay in his sanctuary, but the curtain was falling, and he knew his visitors would be seeking him out. Hastily, he left the stage. He had decided he would run and go far away out of Mathew's reach. He dashed down the stairs towards the stage door.

Adam could feel their pursuit through the mingling crowds and heard their footsteps. The door was in sight and open, beckoning to him to step over the threshold. Incantations rang in his ears, and he could smell incense. The door abruptly banged shut. With his pulse racing, Adam struggled to open the door.

Someone touched Adam's shoulder. He turned around to be confronted by Mathew's stern and intimidating face. Beside him, Adam saw Dylan reaching into his pocket for his cigarettes and refusing to make eye contact. Tears of despair ran down Adam's face.

"Please, I can't do this anymore," he said, pleading, unable to retrieve all the strong words lodged in his constricted throat. For once, I was enjoying life."

Mathew grabbed hold of Adam's arms and bundled him towards his dressing room. He didn't have the strength to fight back. Adam was thrown down onto the concrete floor. The doll laughed, and his head spun around.

Adam lifted his face towards the men, "I'm not a murderer."

"We have all been summoned. Our crusade won't be over until all the black hearts are extinct," Mathew's voice boomed.

"But you have managed without me for all these years."

"They have lain low like dormant rats. Our world will swell with disease as their dark energy takes hold," Mathew said, staring down at Adam with thunderous eyes. "We heard the rumble and felt the tremble of the Earth and, following the signs, discovered their hole. They had eliminated themselves before we had a chance to take them in front of the Inquisition. We were unable to extract any information on any other hiding places. This has been their method throughout history: sacrifice a few while others escape and continue."

"Why me?" Adam protested, not daring to move from the cold floor.

"It's your destiny. Centuries ago, you put yourself up as a witchfinder. From that day forth, your role is set until the last witch is eliminated."

"And you, Dylan, what's your part in all this?"

"We will be collaborating with the order of the Mannerband, under the direct command of the Pope. Dylan here needs to make reparations, or he will be the first at the doors of hell. Throughout history, they have worked tirelessly to keep any traces of these perverse creatures away from human knowledge." Adam saw froth at the corners of Mathew's mouth, making him look like a hungry beast.

"This world is for Homo sapiens, the sons and daughters of Adam and Eve, God's children, not for Neanderthals or any other forms of intelligent apes. We have ruled since the beginning of time," Mathew stated with conviction. "You are doing God's work. Be of peace, son; you have the blessings of the highest authority," Mathew said, reaching down with his hand to help Adam to his feet. "You must alter your thinking," he smiled warmly. "This is a good thing that you do. You belong to us." He rummaged around in his coat pocket, pulled out a card and handed it to Adam. "Come to one of our meetings at the abbey, and you will understand."

The two men turned and calmly walked towards the door. Mathew seemed to vanish, but Dylan turned and smiled again and, in a soft voice, said, "I'm sorry, Adam, but this thing is bigger than either of us. You will soon appreciate that you're in an honoured position."

Chapter Seven

Kane enjoyed driving the armoured truck through the desert. Their vehicle was the last in the convoy. An easy banter flowed between the four men. Arron, his best friend since childhood and his closest mate in the army, was sitting beside him regaling them all with his bizarre love life. The laughter grew until it was hard to remain vigilant.

"Shut up, Arron!" Clive, who was sitting behind Kane, shouted. "Ginge and I are supposed to be keeping watch."

Arron deferred to the older man and turned his attention to Kane.

"I can't wait for leave. I swear this one's the real deal," he said, grinning up at Kane like an excited schoolboy. "It's not her body I'm interested in; she's clever too, a nurse, but she does have a pair of great knockers.

"You only met her twice," Kane said.

"We've been face-timing - and what a face. In two weeks, I will be tumbling into her bed, and I can't wait."

"I suppose he will have to find out one day," Clive said, laughing from the back.

"What do you mean?" Arron said.

"Well, the ones who hang around barracks are not that fussy."

"She's not like that!" Arron twisted around in his seat to confront Clive.

Kane took his eyes off the road and turned to pull Arron back.

"Don't be an idiot. He's only joking," Kane said.

As Arron turned back, he glimpsed a figure dressed in black step in front of their truck.

"Watch out!" he screamed.

Kane slammed his foot hard on the brake. There was a loud thud, and the truck came to a halt.

"He just walked straight in front of us," Arron said in disbelief.

"We should check under the vehicle for a device," Clive said.

"I'll do that," Kane said. "You guys keep watch and shoot anything which moves."

Kane was about to exit the cab when he saw a man dressed from head to foot in black and bent double stagger over to the side of the road. Rapidly, he slipped from his seat and slid out of the vehicle. He heard a door click open on the opposite side. He poked his head above the bonnet and saw Arron strolling towards the injured man.

"What the fuck!" Kane shouted, "Arron, get back here!"

Clive pushed his head through the window. "Kane, don't call out. You will wake the enemy," he whispered. "I will go and get him."

The next thing Kane saw was a blinding flash. A deafening boom sent his ears ringing, the air cracked, and a blast of heat and dust whipped into his face. Following his instincts, he fell to the ground, crawled around the truck, and towards the billowing cloud. At the side of the road, he straightened and, breathing the odour of almonds, immediately understood what had occurred.

Kane no longer cared that he was exposed to enemy fire. As the smoke cleared, he stood petrified, dumbfounded, staring down at the hideous sight. He saw blood, skin ripped from the flesh, bone fragments mingled with dirt, and limbs torn and scattered. A ball shaped object lay a few feet away, and with his brain still numb, he went to investigate. Arron's head stared up at him with shocked, accusing eyes, and his mouth was open, locked in an agonised last shout. Kane turned and spewed into the dust. The lack of dignity and humiliation sent a fire of rage shooting through his veins. His friend deserved better than this.

Kane had only been half aware of the murmured cries for help. Slowly, he straightened and walked towards Clive. The man's legs were mush, and he'd never seen anything bleed so profusely before. Kane crouched down by the man's head.

"I'm so cold," Clive said through chattering teeth. "How long will I live?"

"Until you are old and grey," Kane said, struggling to find words of comfort. "Help is on its way."

Kane stroked Clive's brow and saw the sharp pain twist his mouth.

"Get back here before they start shooting," Ginge called out.

"This is going to hurt, but we need to get you to safety."

"Leave me, I'm dying anyway," Clive said as tears made tracks down his dirt-covered face.

"No, you're not," Kane said as he dragged his friend over the rubble-covered ground.

The two men lugged Clive into the truck. Quickly, they set about bandaging Clive's wounds and making him as comfortable as possible.

"We can't wait for help to come. I'll drive us back to camp," Ginge said, climbing into the driver's seat. "You keep him talking. Don't let him sleep."

Kane cringed down next to Clive with his finger twitching on the trigger, waiting to be ambushed. Beads of sweat from the intense heat and panic continually dripped down his face. Endlessly, he rambled to his patient, and when there was no response, he gently shook him until at least he heard a moan. He remained frantic and on high alert until they passed through the gates of the camp. An hour later, he was told that Clive had lost his battle for life.

Kane's screams rang out uncontrollably, waking the whole house. Even his father, Brian, who was partially deaf, came rushing into his room.

"Son! What's the matter!" He walked over to Kane's bed and rested his hand on his shoulder and felt Kane stiffen under his touch. "Wake up, son!"

Kane sprung into a sitting position, clutching his head and sobbing. "I can't stand these endless night terrors. It was so real."

"It will get better, son."

"No, it won't be Dad," he snapped. Kane didn't want his father awkwardly hovering around him and so swallowed back his tears. "Dad I'm okay now. Go back to bed."

Brian turned his tortured face towards Poppy, who was sitting up in the chair she had been using as a bed ever since Kane's night terrors had become threatening.

"It will be alright, Mr Rivers," she said.

The old man's mouth dropped, and solemnly, he left the room.

Kane flopped back down, turned and stared at the wall, too scared to go back to sleep. Poppy sat up and watched over him; his body was trembling uncontrollably, and she was aware of a heavy silence between them.

"You could end this by getting me a drink," he finally said through his tears.

"We agreed that you would stop drinking," Poppy whispered. "It only masks your pain."

"It was after my friend's death that the shaking started, random twitching and cold. I'm always so cold, even when it's hot."

"You were younger then, and I'm sure you did everything you could," Poppy said in her most soothing voice. "Your friends would be upset to know you were still agonising over their deaths. This is not what they would want for you."

How can I tell her I'm grappling with guilt every minute of every day? I should have driven more carefully and predicted what might happen. Use my knowledge to see into the future. There is no doubt I was negligent, he brooded.

"A few months before Arron's death, we had both witnessed a road accident. The body was unclaimed - it lay beside the road rotting. Arron hated the thought that nobody cared enough to bury the poor man. I should have known he wouldn't be able to allow another person to die alone," Kane sobbed. "He was too soft for the army."

"It's normal to feel as you do, but you can recover. Don't allow yourself to be high-jacked by bad memories. Use your imagination to focus on the good things. That's what I do. I push the flashbacks away," Poppy tried to reassure.

"Part of me feels I must hang on to what happened. If the memories fade, then they will truly be dead."

"Do you want me to come and keep you warm," she said sweetly. "Promise me if you fall asleep, you won't try and kill me."

Poppy climbed into the single bed next to Kane and lay on his unyielding body. He lay rigid, unable even to put his arm around her shoulder.

"I wish I could float away on the breeze into a nightmare-free existence," he said before he fell back to sleep.

Chapter Eight

A week later, the image of Kane's dead friends still throbbed in his head, but now he was more able to push the intrusive thoughts away. He reinforced his memories of happier times by sharing antidotes with Poppy. She was robust and resilient and was not afraid to listen to any subject.

They were walking through the park on the edge of the town to his mother's house. His parents had divorced when he was a teenager, and his mother had since had twin boys from another relationship, which was off more often than on. Despite his mother's troubled life, he admired her and wanted to introduce Poppy to her and his brothers.

"You might find the twins a little strange. They have high-functioning Asperger's Syndrome," he glanced at Poppy, uneasily aware that he was throwing another drama in her direction. All that means is that they get locked on certain subjects and don't want to talk about anything else. Also, they misread things like expressions and feelings."

"Don't worry. I'll be pleased to meet the rest of your family."

"Well, you will like my mother. She's an amazing person," he said smiling, "although I've given her a hard time in the past."

They sought out the tranquil, cool tunnel of dense trees, which provided relief from the sharp heat of the midday sun. As they strolled under the canopy, Kane hit out at the buzzing insects, which reminded him of flies hovering over a corpse, and the sickly, yellowing grass made him feel uneasy. He paused to kick an ant's nest and watched the creatures scatter.

"What's the matter?" Poppy said, noticing his aggravation.

"I would rather it rained," he flashed a half-smile. "This heat reminds me of when I was away. The thing I missed the most when I was on active duty was green; dripping, luscious, rain-drenched green."

Poppy laughed and said, "Well, I can hear a fountain." She pointed in the direction of the sparkling water, which was spitting up towards the sky. "I will race you there," she said, looking up at Kane with her dark eyes. Then she turned and sprinted away.

Kane felt compelled to chase her. He knew that forcing him to live in the moment was her way of chipping away at his melancholy - a deliberate ploy, distracting him as though he were a child about to cry.

Kane saw Poppy's pace slow; she bent over, holding her knees and gasping for breath. Kane caught up and went to grab Poppy around the waist. She twisted fast out of his way and laughed. He seized hold of her for a second time. Gently, he pulled her to the ground, where she wriggled and fought back. Then they wrestled close. Kane allowed Poppy to be the stronger opponent. Her feeble punches left no impression, so as Kane lay on his back, she sat astride of his belly and tried tickling.

They both enjoyed the non-threatening play and the effect it had on any passers-by, who lingered curiously and shot them looks of disgust. In an exuberant mood, they tired and pulled apart. They continued their walk and reached the fountain. They removed their shoes, sat on the low perimeter wall, dangled their feet in the refreshing pool and watched tiny birds bathing and preening their feathers.

After some time, Kane said, "I want to show you something before we have to go." He twisted around and began drying his feet on his socks. "You can use my socks to dry your feet, or they will slip in your flip-flops," he said, smiling.

Kane grasped Poppy's hot hand and led her along a path through a rose garden. He watched Poppy breathe in the fragrance with delight.

"These flowers are so beautiful. I want to look at each one."

"Not yet," Kane said, as he saw her spot the façade of the mansion house appear above the tall privet hedge.

"Wow! What an amazing house," Poppy said, staring in awe.

"It was when I was a boy, he said, looking Poppy in the eyes and smiling warmly. "It's derelict now, an empty shell, but I had many happy hours playing amongst the ruins."

They stepped from the gardens onto a gravel drive.

"This is where rich guests would park their cars," Kane said as they walked up to where the front door would have been.

To Kane's disappointment, all they saw was screened Harris fencing. He saw Poppy's face darken, and he felt as though he'd let her down. Together, they stared through a green mesh, trying to make out the details.

"I wanted to show you it as it was." Kane felt his face drop with disillusionment and a pang of sadness at the loss of another happy memory. "I had heard someone had bought the land and was planning to build flats or something. I suppose it's gutted behind the barrier."

"Don't be sad," Poppy said, "You can tell me what it was like for you inside, and I can imagine it as it was."

"I'm not – it just that it was a special place to me. If we're ever separated, or you get lost, look for me here. This can be our place, this park, this house. I will take some pictures on my phone in case they decide to knock the whole lot down," he said, ignoring the heavy anchor of darkness that was pulling at him trying to ruin their day. "Why don't you sit on the bench," he said, pointing to a seat which looked from the gardens over to the house. "I might try and sneak around the back to see if it's the same."

By the time Kane returned, his darkness had once again melted away. He looked over to where he'd left Poppy sitting. Something about her held his attention. He stood watching intently. Poppy was frozen; her vanilla skin was marbled white, and her eyes were staring into the void, distant and afraid. He turned to see what had her transfixed but saw nothing unusual. He took a deep breath and slowly approached. Poppy appeared utterly unaware of his presence.

Unnoticed, Kane sat beside Poppy and looked hard in the same direction where she saw something. From out of nowhere, he heard an object drop to the ground and looking down saw a round stone moving on its own volition towards Poppy. It stopped at her feet, and Kane watched as she bent forwards and retrieved it while remaining in a trance.

Kane felt his skin crawl. He began to chatter about mundane everyday things, hoping it would click her back to life.

"We should be making a move. Mum will have tea on, and I want you to meet the twins before they go to bed." Poppy remained motionless, meditating on the stone. Kane stood up and grasped her arm. "Come on, move, please. It's getting late."

Poppy stared up at him with dark eyes brimming with tears. Then she rose and allowed Kane to direct her towards the park gates. As they hurried along, Kane felt the sensation that they were being watched. In his peripheral vision, he thought, he saw a girl flash past them. She was about the same age and build as Poppy, with long straight black hair, just like Poppy's.

Chapter Nine

Kane and Poppy walked up to the front door of the ordinary and slightly scruffy-looking council house. Poppy was troubled by doubts, and her mind was racing as she wondered if she would be liked and accepted. Meeting new people filled her with horror - all the questions for which she had no answers. She knew she had no choice as Kane was hankering to see his mother, Judy, to feel the embrace of normal family life, and temporarily escape the cloying morose nature of his father.

As Kane knocked on the door, Poppy felt she was about to experience something unpleasant, even perilous. She listened to the symphony of laughter and happy voices coming from the hall. Soon, a woman in her forties answered and held her arms out to Kane. Poppy watched them embrace.

"I'm so glad you've come home son," Judy said, in a gravely but kind voice.

"This is Poppy, mum."

"And you are very welcome too, Poppy. I have heard all about you from Kane's sister, Sandra." Before Poppy could say she'd never met Sandra or heard her mentioned, the woman had wrapped her arms around her and kissed her cheek. Poppy stiffened. She wasn't used to being hugged, especially by strangers. In her home of Cailleach Veil, only close family and lovers embraced, and that was rare. Judy stunk of smoke, and when she broke away, Poppy noticed her thick neck and wrinkled, unhealthy-looking skin.

"I'm off to the pub then, love," a man said, leaned over, kissed Judy on the cheek and pushed past the guests. "Nice to meet you both," he added, nodding in their direction.

"Come in, come in," Judy said, inviting them into a cramped hallway. Poppy stared at the walls stripped of paper as though they were in the process of re-decoration. Then she glanced at two blonde-haired boys, who grinned mischievously and scurried off into another room. "Don't worry about them. They're not shy once they get to know you."

They all followed the boys and entered a shabby front room.

"This is Joe and Jim - both were ten in March. They're identical, mirror twins. Joe's left-handed, and Jim uses his right hand." Judy said, introducing the twins, who had jumped onto the sofa and were half falling off again. "Say hello to Poppy."

"They look so much alike," Poppy said and sat on the sofa beside them.

"I know, I can hardly tell them apart. Joe is slightly bigger, and Jim is quieter. They're my little princess," Judy smiled, indulgently.

"I love 'Star Wars'!" Poppy said, picking up 'Darth Vadar and Luke Skywalker,' figurines from the carpet. "It was one of the only films I was permitted to watch."

The twins grabbed the toys from her hands and showed Poppy how they fight. "The force is strong with this one," Joe, being 'Darth Vadar', stated.

"You are not my father!" Jim shouted in a stern voice.

Poppy grasped a 'See-Threepio' that was sticking out beneath a cushion and began to play, but she found she was, mostly ignored. Kane flopped into an armchair and fiddled with the TV remote.

"I'm afraid there's not much for tea," Judy said as she laid the table. "Still, it's payday next Friday."

"Looks like you've been decorating mum," Kane said as he gawked at the large screen, which dominated the room.

"When I've finished the hall, I will do the boy's room." Poppy twisted around to show that she was listening. "I'm going to try and find someone to paint a mural. You were always good at art, son. Do you remember that chess set you made out of clay?"

"Yes, I still have it at Dad's house," Kane said, still distracted by the images flashing up on the screen.

"I would love to do it or help," Poppy interjected.

"Star Wars!" the twins shouted in unison.

"Why don't you take Poppy upstairs and show her your room so that she can get some ideas."

Poppy was glad to be whisked away by the children as their questions were more palatable, and as they all clambered up the stairs, she felt like a child again.

The only light in the room came from two weak bedside lamps. Poppy noticed a bare wire hanging from the ceiling. The walls were empty of decoration and roughly painted in night blue.

"Well, the background colour is perfect," Poppy said, standing uneasily in the doorway. She noticed felt pen marks by the beds. "It looks like you have already started decorating."

"Mum said we could draw on the walls, as long as we promise not to do it after," Joe said as he bounced on the bed. "This is my bed, Joe's bed," Joe said with delight.

"And this is mine." Jim said, diving on the mattress, which was pushed up against the opposite wall."

Then Joe pulled some magazines out from under his pillow, rushed over to Poppy and bounced down onto the floor.

"Look at my train magazine," he instructed. Poppy felt obliged to join Joe, who had an edge to him, which made her feel as though he would erupt with rage at any sign of non-compliance. She crouched on the carpet next to the bigger, more dominant personality and feigned interest.

"This is my favourite. It's a British Rail 20 diesel," Joe said excitedly. "It's a 1000-horsepower English Electric Type 1. It hauls freight." Poppy watched bemused as Joe thumbed quickly through the pages, only stopping to point out other desired engines.

"Okay, Poppy, which one was my favourite?" he said, closing the magazine.

Poppy hadn't been paying attention and knew she couldn't answer. "I don't know, Joe; I'm afraid they all look the same to me." Poppy glanced nervously up at the boy and saw his face go red and crease with rage as he stared down at the magazine.

"Wrong! Wrong!" He screamed. I told you which one. Find it - you must know," he whined with growing frustration.

Jim sidled up to Joe's side and, without being able to gauge his brother's mood, began talking to Poppy about his Millennium Falcon.

"This Millennium Falcon has warp drive, Poppy," he said holding the plastic spaceship up in his right hand. "I will explain how it works."

Suddenly, Joe bashed his shoulder into Jim's leg. "Stop interrupting. I'm showing Poppy my trains," he said and furiously began flipping the pages.

"That's your train," Poppy interjected, relieved that she'd remembered the page number.

"You're correct, Poppy," Joe said, immediately becoming calmer.

Jim continued interrupting, and each time, Joe shouted at him to wait his turn. Poppy kept trying to steer them towards imaginative play, but they remained inflexible and continued to bombard her with information until she was left feeling bored and exhausted.

"Boys! Wash your hands and come down for tea," Judy shouted up from downstairs.

Bubbling with excitement, the twins hurried towards the door. "You can look at my magazines if you like," Joe said as he pushed past Poppy. "But make sure you put them back after."

Alone, Poppy picked up the publications and warily proceeded further into the room, avoiding stepping on discarded toys strewn over the carpet. She gingerly placed Joe's treasured possessions back under the pillow. She felt a sinister movement in the air, a presence as though she wasn't alone. An object was jutting out from beneath Joe's bed. A pain slowly twisted in her guts as she focussed on the dark shape. As she bent down to investigate, an obnoxious smell snaked through her nose and mouth, causing her to retch.

In an instant, she grabbed the object, pulled it from the darkness and saw that she was holding the leg of a doll. As it hung upside down, she briefly looked it over. It appeared to be a strange doll for a child, larger than normal and dressed all in black. Handling the doll carefully, Poppy flipped it the right way up and, for the first time, was able to see its ugly face. It had a large hooked nose, like a 'Punch doll'. Mechanical lids covered its eyes, and straight grey hair stuck out from beneath a dark hat. It wore a raven black, peculiar type of suit and old-fashioned shoes with large silver buckles.

Unexpectedly, its lids sprung open, revealing black living eyes. Then its mouth dropped open. A dark shadow oozed from the parted scarlet lips like an insect's swarm. Poppy watched, transfixed, as the cloud settled on the wall by the bed. It grew into giant proportions and transformed into the silhouette of a man, which clearly resembled the shape of the doll.

Poppy jumped as something touched her shoulder and blurted out, "Who's there?" The doll laughed deeply. She dropped it and kicked it back under the bed so that she wouldn't have to see its hideous expression.

"Don't be afraid. It's only me." Poppy turned and saw Kane's untroubled face smiling at her. "I was beginning to wonder what had happened to you. Teas ready."

"Can you see what's on the wall?" she whispered, too scared to turn and view the image again, "the shadow looming over Joe's bed."

"Oh, you've spotted the black mould," he said, moving around her to take a closer look. "I've just been talking to my mother about it. Apparently, it is slowly creeping through the house. It happened when the lodger moved into the box room. After a storm, the roof began to leak. We will need to paint the walls with anti-fungal stuff before we paint. Still, I can't see any in here," Kane mumbled his thoughts aloud.

"Look, you can't miss it!" Poppy said exasperatedly, but on turning, she saw that the shadowy swarm was no longer visible. Well, I thought I saw something; perhaps I was wrong."

"I must explain to Mum how dangerous mould can be. They fixed the roof and painted the small room with special stuff, but I bet it comes back."

The twins were already seated at the table when Kane and Poppy entered the dining area of the front room. They seated themselves opposite the twins, and Judy sat at the head of the table with her back to the patio doors.

"Aren't you going to turn the TV off, Kane?" Judy inquired.

"I've just got it on for the weather. I wanted to see if there was any chance of the heat breaking. I'm getting tired of the sun."

Hands pulled at the thick slices of bread piled high on a plate placed at the centre of the table. The twins tore chunks off and dunked them into their stew.

"Don't mind them. They have no manners," Judy said, pulling the plate away from Kane and offering it to Poppy. "They say your children return to their childhood state when they come home," Judy laughed.

Poppy smiled, took a slice of bread, and put it on her plate. She kept noticing Kane glancing in her direction with a concerned expression. The experience in the bedroom left Poppy with no appetite, but knowing it would be rude not to eat, she held the spoon to her mouth and sipped. "This is delicious," she said and watched Judy's face light up.

"It's not much, but I pride myself on being able to create something edible from nothing," she said. Then she turned to address Kane, "You know your greedy father will demand rent soon."

"We're only staying until the new year when my course starts," Kane said.

"Well, you know what he's like. Even for a short time, you will both have to work. I could probably get you a job at the factory, Poppy," Judy looked directly at Poppy, who felt suddenly uncomfortable under the scrutiny of her piercing pale blue eyes.

Poppy lowered her gaze and listened to the news, which was playing in the background.

"Will you play with us after tea?" Joe asked Poppy.

"If you want me to," she replied with a straight face, unable to disguise her lack of enthusiasm.

"Stop troubling the girl. Anyway, you have school tomorrow," Judy interjected.

"I was looking at some of your toys earlier and found a strange-looking doll. It was creepy," Poppy ventured, feeling her cheeks flush.

"We don't like it either. That's why I hid it under the bed," Joe said.

"Adam gave it to us," Jim added.

"Adam's our lodger," Judy said, pushing her empty bowl away. He's very good—pays top whack and is always on time. We couldn't manage without him, plus he is rarely here, so he doesn't take up much room."

"The mass suicide was only discovered when a child from this secretive community was found wandering around the village without his parents."

Quickly Poppy muffled her gasp of shocked horror with her hand. It felt as though the ground was shaking and the walls were crashing down. *If they spot my expression of terror, there will be endless questions, and my differences will be exposed,* Poppy rapidly considered. She began to loudly cough as though she was choking on something, partly to drown out the news and partly to provide an excuse for her discomfort. Kane immediately patted her back and offered her water.

"I'm fine now, thanks. I think a piece of bread went down the wrong way," she muttered breathlessly. She made sure they fussed over her until the news had moved onto another subject.

Poppy felt a sense of relief when, finally, they could make their excuses and leave. Standing outside the house waiting for Kane to say goodbye to his mother, Poppy listened to the chatter and laughter sprinkle down from the open window of the twin's bedroom. The sound was no longer pleasing, it felt like a tickle, which had gone too far and becomes painful. She associated the twins with something ominous, unidentifiable and bad.

The gate squeaked open. Poppy turned to see a tall, handsome man carrying a violin case walking up the path. He smiled and said, "good evening" in a deep syrupy voice. Once he'd passed he glanced back at her his lips had dropped downwards, his face was stern, and there was an acid glint in his eyes.

Finally, Kane stepped out into the warm night air and waving goodbye they strolled down the street. Poppy sensed that Kane was hungry for answers. She had noticed him reading her every expression. He hadn't been fooled; he had gone along with the choking scenario trusting that her performance was for good reasons.

"What's the matter?" He said, grabbing her arm and forcing her to stop. "From the moment we entered the house, the normal joyful Poppy faded and died. I know my mum can be a little rough around the edges, but she means well.

"It's not that. I think I'm being pursued again," she said, holding his gaze with her wild, desperate eyes.

"We can't move yet. If you told me what was wrong, we could face it together and fight this thing," he said, looking downcast.

"I will, I promise," Poppy said, realising that the time had come to tell him her crazy story and hope that he would believe her. "I'm not the only one with secrets."

"What do you mean?" Kane said.

"You didn't tell me that you have a sister,"

"Did. She used to live at my mum's house, in the small room, but about a week before I met you she went missing. Everyone except my mother thinks she's dead. She reckons that Sandra can communicate with her from wherever she is. Strangely, she never tells my mother what has happened to her. Mum will never accept it and always speaks as though she's still alive. She feels guilty for splitting from my father, but it was him having an affair."

"What happened?"

"Sandra was older than me. All I know is that she had a mysterious boyfriend and went missing. Her body hasn't yet been found, but the Police are convinced she was murdered."

Chapter Ten

An elderly woman showed Oliver into the front room of the large Georgian house.

"I'm Professor Roehampton's housekeeper," she smiled warmly. "I will fetch him for you," she said and scurried out of the room.

Oliver cast his eyes about at the beautifully proportioned room, the high ornately plastered ceilings and the tall windows, which ran almost from floor to ceiling at either end of the room. Dust particles danced in a shaft of light, which cut across the cream-coloured carpet. His eyes alighted on a large glass sphere placed on the floor by the marble surround of the fireplace. Oliver shuddered with disgust as he saw that inside the container was a massive, un-moving spider. He stood uneasily with his eyes firmly fixed on the creature. Suddenly, the room seemed airless, hot, and he longed to open a window.

As his eyes quickly scanned the windows to see if he could open them, at the far end of the room, he spotted more glass containers, each holding the coiled shapes of snakes or the flashing movements of lizards. Oliver felt his heart go into palpitations, his hands fretted at his side, and his impulse was to leave the house immediately.

"Oh, I'm so glad you could make it," Professor Roehampton said, announcing his presence. "My good man, you don't look at all well!" he said as Oliver turned to face him.

"I prefer old bones to living creatures," Oliver said, forcing a smile onto his lips.

"The living hold many clues to our past," Rupert stared at Oliver with earnest eyes as if he was again unsure of his young assistant's suitability. After an awkward pause, he said, "Well, I will be retiring soon, and I will need a hobby." He flashed a half-smile.

"I'm fine with mammals; it's just reptiles and creepy things. I have considered hypnosis as I know my fears will be a hindrance to my career."

"Do you have any other phobias?" the old man took his glasses off and wiped them on his shirt.

"Heights!"

"Before you leave, I will give you the number of a very good cognitive therapist. He's been known to cure people in only a couple of sessions," he said, examining Oliver quizzically. "Let's go to my study. I can assure you there are no living creatures there, but you will have to climb many stairs as it's at the top of the house," he said, turning and leading the way.

Oliver remained vigilant and kept his eyes focused on Rupert's bent back as they left the room. He trudged up the stairs, not convinced that he wouldn't spy more creatures in his periphery vision.

"The thing is, I need someone I can trust implicitly, a person of resilience," Rupert mumbled as he slowly moved his stiff legs. "We are going to be up against it when we submit our case to keep the site at the house open for longer."

Finally, they entered an attic room. Bookcases lined the walls, pillars of papers and journals sprouted up from the floor. Rupert gestured for Oliver to take the spare chair at the cluttered desk. Oliver complied, happy to be in a more familiar environment.

"I want to show you something which could be life-changing," he said, rummaging through a pile of papers on the large desk.

"The problem is, even the most dedicated scholars will shift things slightly to suit their own needs," Rupert said, throwing unwanted items to the floor as he searched. "There are restraints on even the most powerful minds - after all, we're all human."

"I'm not sure I know what you mean, professor," Oliver said, feeling baffled.

"Religious people need their ten commandments, and archaeologists and palaeontologists like their dates and timelines." Oliver watched as Rupert walked over to a bookcase. "This place is a shambles," Rupert sighed and began to allow books to fall to the floor. "I'm talking about the dates of the handprints not adding up. Believe me, most of those who hold positions of power in the universities won't be happy about our re-working of the human timeline. If I could find this paper, I could show you what I mean. Ah! At last, here it is. I hid it," he said, hurrying back over to the desk.

He remained standing by his chair. "It all started when I worked on a site with Professor Simon Briggs. As you know, the oldest fossil remains of anatomically modern humans ever found are the 'Omo' remains, which date back to 195,000 years."

Oliver nodded his head, "Yes, but there is much evidence which points to modern humans being around for 200,000 years or more."

"Yes, but for how long," Rupert muttered as he stroked his beard thoughtfully. "So far, no bone remains have been found - well, at least that's what most people think."

The significance of Rupert's last words hooked into Oliver's mind, and he watched the old man's sinewy hand hover and shake over the document.

"I was a much younger man back then and didn't understand the significance of what Briggs was trying to convey," Rupert said, nervously shifting his weight from one leg to the other. "An old scroll had turned up in the vaults of a collector's home and been given to the college for study. It landed on Professor Briggs's desk. There was a small mention of an ancient tribe of miners and a description of the mine's location. Briggs managed to get authorisation for a dig in the presumed location on Anglesey. The site was well hidden, as the entrance was on a cliff face. It was treacherous; even I was scared. You would have hated it." Rupert paused and looked up at Oliver, peered at him through his thick lenses and smiled.

"No, even with a harness on, I wouldn't climb down a cliff," Oliver stated.

"Well, you might have to."

Feeling uncomfortable, Oliver broke Rupert's gaze and looked down at the man's hand resting on the documents. Rupert seemed tired and eased himself down onto his chair and, deep in thought, began cleaning his glasses.

"We hadn't expected to find anything of significance, but deep down, we found a maze of tunnels. There were paintings all over the walls, symbols and a type of language. It was clear that these people were not only mining tin but also living underground. Shelves were carved into the rock walls, burnt ground, and signs, which indicated spiritual ceremonies had taken place."

"I won't explain all the details now. I will give you his paper to take away with you, and you can go through everything. The point is we found more than animal bones and some evidence of sacrifice."

Oliver watched as Rupert broke from his speech and looked around the room with concern written in his eyes as though he thought someone else was with them listening.

"What else did you find?" Oliver said, fearing Rupert was thinking twice about revealing his secret.

"We found bodies and strange bones," he said in a lowered voice. "These remains spoke volumes. Briggs had them carbon-dated and took his paper and evidence to the Royal Archaeological Institute. Their reaction was unexpected. They ridiculed the poor man and refused to allow him to publish his paper."

"What were they so afraid of?" Oliver said, aware that his stomach had turned to jelly.

"The unthinkable truth! They decided ignorance was the safest option. I must admit I was a coward. I dissociated myself from Briggs, fearing for my career, which had only just begun. I watched the undeserved assault on his reputation from the sidelines." Rupert dropped his head into his hands and contemplated his past in silent despair.

Oliver was dumbfounded but was hungry for more information. "Much time has gone past, and you have more evidence if what you discovered is the same people. I'm sure if we confronted them again, it would be a different story this time," he said, trying to reassure Rupert.

"Briggs killed himself not long after," Rupert muttered, raising his head. "I will submit the evidence again. I'm no hero, but I'm old and have little to lose. I want to give those people a voice. I want their bones to talk."

"I would have thought such an important find would have brought Professor Briggs fame and fortune?" Oliver said.

"So, did he. But the findings were all wrong because they didn't fit in with our known history. The bones were humanoid in many ways. There was no brow ridge, a large brain cavity, small-boned, and the mummified ones had big almond-shaped eyes with straight black hair. They dated back to roughly 2.5 million years, a time when there is no evidence of intelligent life. That is what is so shocking: the timeline. These unknown people were living underground in fear of something devastating above."

"Now you are living in fear," Oliver said, feeling for the first time that perhaps he was in the company of a madman.

"Oh, I'm too old to care about being thrown to the wolves, but I need help. You see, I don't believe Brigg's death was suicide. It is an unmentioned secret amongst scientists that there is a secret society called the Mannerband, which monitors what is released into the world. I need to find someone I can depend upon to help me leak these ideas into the universal consciousness."

"You can depend on me. After all, I'm the internet generation and know how to get secrets into people's minds safely," Oliver said, and the two men smiled knowingly at each other. "What about the new site, how can we persuade them to keep it from being buried under a concrete floor?"

"Take these papers and study them overnight, and by the morning, I will come up with a plan," Rupert said, handing Oliver the documents. "Can you see yourself out? I have some things I need to clear up here. We don't have much time. Meet me here around lunchtime tomorrow," Rupert smiled with a look of mingled excitement and relief.

Oliver rose from his chair and walked to the door, carrying his bundle. With his hand on the knob and the other, awkwardly holding the precious papers, he turned.

"One more question: what happened to the bones?"

"They were disappeared along with other evidence except, of course, what Briggs left under my protection," Rupert grinned, and Oliver saw a mysterious glint in his eyes. "Oh! Oliver, get help for your phobias. You will find the number of that therapist written on an envelope amongst those papers."

Oliver was not completely satisfied with Rupert's reply, but his head was buzzing with ideas, and he was anxious to get home and study the details for himself.

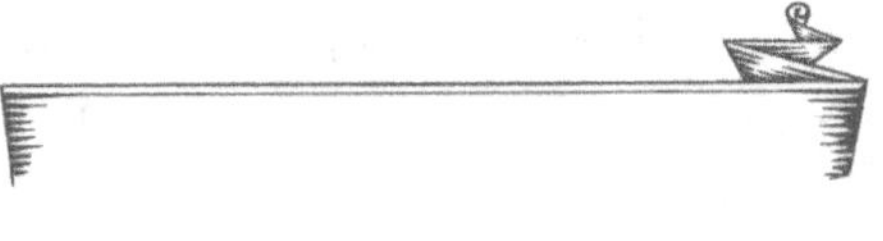

Chapter Eleven

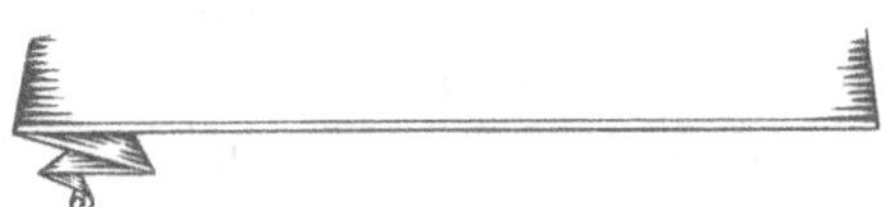

Oliver ran from his digs through the bustling streets to Professor Roehampton's house, situated in a quieter residential area. The precious documents were safe in his backpack. Excitedly, he weaved around people. The vigorous activity was relaxing Oliver and emptying the forefront of his mind while simultaneously at the back a crowd of ideas and questions jostled to be first in line for answers.

Standing, panting on the top step, Oliver absent-mindedly pushed the bell. While he waited in front of the large door, all his thoughts rushed through his brain at once. The first question he wanted to ask was why Rupert had given him an envelope with random numbers written on the front and why there were two keys in it, one of which was labelled basement. He was also desperate to tell Rupert that he believed him and wanted to be a part of whatever he had planned.

Oliver rang the doorbell again and waited anxiously to be admitted. Time stretched agonisingly without anyone coming to answer his call. He jigged on the spot. *Surely, Rupert had remembered their appointment,* he thought. He went to bang on the door, and it was then that he noticed that it was ajar. Cautiously, he pushed it open and stepped into the hallway. His eyes scattered around the scene, and he rapidly assessed that everything appeared normal. To his left, the door to the front room was open. *Perhaps Rupert had fallen asleep in the chair,* he considered.

The long, heavy curtains were drawn. A chink of light intruded into the darkness. Oliver stood in the centre of the room and peered at the dark shapes to get his bearings. He heard a rustling like something moving amongst papers. He froze listening hard. Then he heard it again, louder. Oliver cringed with the realisation that he was definitely not alone.

As his eyes grew accustomed to the half-light, he caught sight of a shape slithering out from under an easy chair. He felt the hair bristle on the back of his neck, and his skin crawl. With his eyes locked onto a flicking tongue, he backed away and stood pushing his body into the wall. He watched as other shiny shapes glided along the floor, scuttled, twitched their tails and smelt the air with their tongues. He felt a deadly terror clasp his throat. He was unable to breathe and was rooted to the spot.

Was this the Professor's warped idea of therapy? He thought, as his anxiety levels rocketed. He felt as though he'd been forced onto an extremely high fairground ride, and his mind was dizzy with the dilemma of whether to stay or run. He was aware of a semi-circular table beside him and, whilst keeping his eyes fixed on the movement, reached down and picked up a marble statuette of a goddess, which he'd admired the day before. Oliver felt safer with a weapon in his hand. Silently, he opened his mouth and gasped at the air. Then he wondered if the spider was also free. His instincts told him to leap onto the nearest piece of furniture, but he knew this would be a fruitless action, as the creatures could climb. Without another, thought he skipped towards the door, lifting his legs high as though he was hopping onto stepping stones placed over quicksand.

Once he was back in the hallway, he slammed the door shut and clutching the statuette tightly, uncertainly walked towards the stairs. He peered up into the darkness. Reluctantly he began to ascend, one fearful step at a time. His eyes darted into every corner, expecting to see wriggling or slithering shapes, and he listened out for hissing and movement. Fear hovered around him like flies over rotting meat.

When finally, he reached the top of the house, he realised that he had moved beyond the restraints, which his phobia normally allowed, breathed a sigh of relief and felt a pang of pride.

Oliver pushed open the study door. Immediately, he was, confronted with a grisly scene. Rupert was slumped back in his chair, staring up at the ceiling with sightless eyes. Blood veiled his face as it wept from a wound in his forehead. Oliver felt sick, and his lips trembled as they tried to utter some words. He glanced around the room and saw that the bookcase had been emptied with all the books flung to the floor. The whole place was in chaos, torn apart by frantic hands.

Oliver looked back at Rupert and felt as though a red flag was waving at him, declaring a need for emergency action. Suddenly he was painfully aware that while he'd been trapped by his fear, many minutes had rushed by. Furthermore, the intruder could still be lingering somewhere in the house and waiting to pounce.

In haste, he placed the statuette on the edge of the desk, stooped over and while desperately trying to control his shaking, rummaged in the front pocket of his bag for the envelope, which contained the keys. Grasping the envelope tight, he straightened, wriggled the backpack onto his shoulders, and picked up the statuette. Keeping his eyes averted from the ghastly sight, he sidled out of the room.

Oliver hastily descended the stairs, braved the hall and treading carefully made his way to the basement. He took the key from the envelope and tried it in the lock. It was a perfect fit, and the unusually heavy door sprung open. Taking the key with him, he shut the door behind and using the light of his phone found a light switch.

He saw tools and garden paraphernalia stacked against the wall to his left, but what made him freeze, mesmerised at the top of the steps was the large glass coffin pushed against the adjacent wall. Immediately he understood its significance. Reverently, he slowly walked down the steps into the room. The sweat, which had drenched his clothes now, gave him chills but the sight of such a treasure sucked away his anxiety. Absentmindedly, he bent down and placed the statuette on the concrete floor.

For some time, he stood marvelling and scrutinised every detail of the mummified princess. Her head was exposed, two thin black plaits lined either side of her leathery brown face and she lay as if in an eternal sleep under a timeless sun.

Although obviously brittle, she had been preserved with loving care and maintained in Rupert's heat regulated casket. Her head was exposed, sunken almond-shaped eyes had vague traces of paint on the lids, and her open mouth revealed a couple of loose teeth. Her hands-free of bandages had once clutched carefully fashioned stones of deep red, amber, greens and blues but the thread, which had joined them had long since decayed leaving them scattered like marbles on the fragile remains of bandaging.

Oliver feasted his eyes, drunk on the thrill of his discovery. He was so engrossed that he completely forgot the danger of his situation. He felt a connection to the ancient corpse as his imagination cut through the layers of time, and he saw her once again walking in the sun in opulent finery.

Suddenly he was startled from his musing as he thought he heard the creak of boards from cautious footfalls on the stairs above. He was sure he had perceived an ominous presence. *Could the house still be occupied?* He thought with alarm.

Oliver's archaeological instincts took hold, and his purpose was clear. He needed to keep safe evidence that these people once existed. As Rupert said, 'give them back their voice.'

In haste, he took the second key from the envelope, pushed it into a lock on the front of the casket and keyed in the numbers. A catch released. Oliver took his rucksack off his back and dropped it on the floor. He leant over into the coffin, scooped up the beads, which he dropped into his bag, wobbled out a couple of teeth and plucked some hair from the scalp. He placed these last items carefully into plastic bags to avoid contamination.

Oliver heard the front door slam. He stood up and held himself stiffly as he listened intently. Then he dropped the remainder of his plunder into his bag, threw it back onto his shoulder, swirled around and ran towards the stairs.

Outside the hot blast of air and bright light thumped into Oliver's face and he was temporarily dazzled. Once his eyes adjusted, he noticed a man by the gate stepping out onto the pavement. He lingered behind, conscious of the clicking of the man's leather shoes. All of Oliver's attention was fixed on the figure, and he was curious that a potential murderer could look so mundane. The intruder was about fifty of average height, slim build and casually dressed in jeans and a loose shirt. Oliver watched as the man kept bringing his hand to his mouth, obviously puffing on a cigarette which he finally dropped on the ground. Without warning, the man stopped, glanced over his shoulder and looking directly at Oliver took another cigarette from its box and placed it between his lips. The man smiled almost shyly and put a flame to the white stick.

Suddenly, Oliver felt a rush of air and heard a deafening explosion. He looked around and saw the professor's house engulfed in a ball of flames.

Chapter Twelve

Kane stumbled through the back door into the kitchen. His father was sitting at the small breakfast table, which was, pushed up against the wall.

"Son, sit down, join me. I've just made a pot of tea."

Kane picked a mug off the drainer and slumped down in the upright chair opposite his father. He studied the diminutive figure, the bulbous red nose, the hearing aid and watery eyes. Kane leaned forwards, sniffed and smelt the amber vapour on his father's breath.

"You've had a few tonight, dad. You should seriously think of giving up," he said, pouring tea into the mug.

"Looks like you've been drinking too, son and I was so proud of you when you stopped."

"Just a blip dad, we're all entitled sometimes."

"They laid some of us off today, son."

Kane's mind jumped alive; he became alert as if under threat. An anxious silence built up between the two men.

"What are you going to do? If you can't pay the mortgage, you will lose the house."

"I can't see me getting another job either, I'm too old," he moaned and added more sugar to his tea.

Kane sat pondering the situation, absentmindedly rolled an old receipt between his fingers and stared blankly at the kitchen floor where he noticed the tiles had curled up in the heat.

"Look, son, I've been sitting here thinking all afternoon, trying to figure a way out."

"Get another job, dad, simple," Kane shouted, in a sarcastic tone, irritated by the thought of more changes to his life. "Stop being lazy - you're not that old. If you didn't spend all your time in the betting office or pub, you would be in better health."

Brian proceeded without caution, unaware of the rise in Kane's emotional temperature and the warning signs in his voice and eyes.

"I have decided that you and your girlfriend must get jobs and pay rent. If you weren't here, I could rent out your room or the whole house and move in with Janet."

"You mean your trashy bit of skirt," Kane mumbled.

"What did you say? Stop muttering you know years of working in machine rooms has wrecked my hearing."

"For now, you will have to pay something or go," Brian said, in a cool, bland voice. "It's time to grow up, son."

"I will happily get a job, but Poppy can't work." Kane flicked the rolled-up paper across the table and slumped forwards holding his head between his hands. "So, you're going to chuck her onto the streets?"

"You could both stay at your mother's."

"She would put us up without question, but you know she has no room and far less money than you."

"You've always been against me, taken your mother's side."

"You think I'm against you, but you never listen to a word I say without making out I'm a prick." Kane thumped his fist on the table. He was enjoying the feeling of power of being under the influence of some brutal demon, and of watching his father squirm. "If I were against you I would have burnt your fucking house to the ground with you and Janet in it by now. You're a joke treating your son like shit because he's the only person who ever tells you the truth. You've always been a lazy git."

Brian was unable to understand that he was under attack. He was confused, lost in a maze of sharp, tangled, sentences and was struggling to find a way out.

"That's no way to speak to your father. I have supported you your whole life and wanted nothing but the best for you," he said, trying to defend himself against the thrusts of pain.

"You chose to have an affair with mum's sister. Even as a kid, you couldn't accept my bad behaviour because of the shit you put me through. You used to tell everyone you didn't understand why I had such a bad temper. You had me believing I was born fucked up."

"I don't understand, I have tried to support you, but it's obvious you hate me," Brian wiped the tears from his eyes. "Janet and I kept everything away from you kids."

"Dad, everyone knew except mum. You've never been there when Sandra or I needed you. I'm the way I am because of the way you've been with me. I'm the person you brought me up to be," Kane's forehead creased with internal agony and tears flooded from his eyes. "I'm your son, and I'm trying everything to make my life better. I joined the army thinking that it would make you proud," Kane choked on his words and drew his arm across his face. The more he talked, the more out of control he felt, and he realised he needed to leave. Unsteadily, he stood and walked towards the door. "If it weren't for you Sandra would probably still be alive," Kane turned back and screamed.

"You know what your problem is? You feel guilty," Brian called after Kane wrongly gauging that he was safe, that the argument had burnt out. "You can't cope with your friend's deaths and want to blame everyone else for how bad you feel."

"You what!" Kane screamed. "You're the guilty one – you split our family up!"

Poppy was sitting on the bed with a laptop on her crossed legs. She was searching the internet for answers. The news of the mass suicide of her community was noticeable by its absence. Any trace of evidence that the incident had occurred had been, efficiently scraped from cyberspace. In Kane's absence, she had spent the day searching intricate patterns and paths on the net, to discover who was masterminding the cover-up, who was able to delete on mass a major news event.

Irritated and tired, she closed the lid of the machine and fell back onto the bed. Realising that her ordeal was far from over and that some faceless adversary was probably hunting her down at that very moment, she lay conjuring up nightmarish pictures in her mind.

The room was darkening, and she became aware of voices rising from the kitchen. She held her breath and listened hard. It was clear that Kane had returned and was arguing with his father. She understood the perils of intervening in a family dispute and lay motionless listening. Tension radiated throughout the house as the flickering flames grew into a raging furnace.

Suddenly, Poppy heard a shrill scream and shivers ran down her spine. *They are going to come to blows,* she thought. Her mind saw the dance of violence between old and young, and she felt the unendurable tension. She couldn't avoid action any longer.

In one swift motion, Poppy leapt from the bed and raced down the stairs. She pushed the kitchen door open and saw the two men in the middle of the room grappling with each other. Kane's muscular fingers were squeezing his father's neck. Poppy saw the grotesqueness of Kane's extreme ruthlessness and fleetingly despised the feeble human. Brian, white-faced, eyes protruding in horror was shrinking to the floor.

Poppy whispered low, in an unidentifiable language and allowed her mind to step into the folds of Kane's brain. Under her control, Kane's brain was, forced to block his violent outburst. Poppy watched as the younger man's arms fell limp at his side. Kane stood, staring into the void.

"What have I become?" he muttered, as Brian collapsed onto his knees, gasping for breath. Poppy went to the old man's aid and helped him back onto the chair.

"Humans are so violent," she said, beneath her breath so that her words were almost inaudible. Poppy stood up and faced Kane. He stared back at her with eyes loaded with misery.

Kane looked long and hard at Poppy, at her straight black hair, which hung loose down her back, the paper white skin, small frame, almond-shaped eyes, and his expression changed to one of curiosity.

"Who are you? Really, who are you?"

Chapter Thirteen

"Come with me, and I will show you who I am," Poppy announced the next morning as she perched on Kane's bed. "Get up!" she said, pulling at his bedding.

"I can't. Look at my hands," he said, holding them up to show Poppy how badly they were shaking. "My legs are the same. I think I will need one small drink just to make it through the day," he stared up at her with sad pleading eyes.

"It's fresh air, you need," Poppy replied sternly.

At midday, they set off. Poppy led the way, clambering up the steep hills of the moor which rose up from the far side of the town. From its peaks, you could get a fine view of the industrial landscape which ran down to the river Tees. They roamed, half-running, half walking, kicking the dusty ground up with their feet. They ventured, further than Kane had as a child. The land dipped into a steep valley with another set of peaks visible in the distance.

Kane lagged, his eyes fastened onto the dark radiance of Poppy's hair and her purposeful sprightly movement. Poppy's infectious enthusiasm had nursed him back to life, and he found himself in a brighter mood. He was enjoying the atmosphere of excitement and feeling free. A strong hot breeze whipped into his face, and he could taste and smell the fragrant air.

When they crossed the valley, it became clear to Kane that Poppy intended to climb to the next ridge. He stopped bent over and gasped.

The constant drinking had eaten away at his fitness, and he was aware that he was half the man he had been.

"How much further? It will be dark before we get back," he shouted.

Poppy turned around and began walking towards him, her eyes alive like burning jet, studying him as she approached.

"Not much more," she said, reaching her small hand out to his. "What's wrong with the night, to me it's the safest time. My eyes will adapt to the dark. I would keep you safe."

Hand in hand, she trudged forwards pulling Kane as fast as she could.

"This is like being back on training," Kane laughed. "Please don't ask me to run."

Kane had decided not to complain too much. He would have rather turned back, but he was enjoying her company, she had made up her mind, and if she intended to give him access to her world then it would all be worth the effort.

Stone monuments began to appear over the brow of the hill. Poppy's pace slowed.

"I used to wonder what your world would be like if I ever had to leave,' she uttered in a wistful tone. "Now, I wish I could go home."

"What do you mean?" Kane felt the gears shift in his brain. Then he took a deep breath, reminded himself he was no longer in the Army and didn't have to examine every tiny word and detail. His internal voice tried to talk him back into living in the moment.

"Can you hear them calling to you?" she said, her hot hand releasing its grip as she ran ahead up towards the giant Sarsen stones.

As Kane reached the top of the hill from a short distance, he saw Poppy standing still with both hands on the largest stone, her cheeks flushed and her eyes wide and gazing.

"The stones are a living force," Poppy said, in a daze as Kane tentatively approached. "Their spirits are transferred by touch."

Kane quizzically examined the stones. "Is this the great reveal?" he uttered sarcastically and immediately regretted his words when he saw tears rush into Poppy's eyes.

"It's too complex. I was a fool to think you would understand," she said, in a quivering voice.

Poppy turned away from Kane, buried her face in her hands and sobbed. Kane touched her lightly on the shoulder. He wanted to understand and help.

"I'm sorry. To me, the world only exists in our brains, but I'm willing to listen and learn. If you believe these stones have some magical power, that's fine after all I can't prove you wrong."

Poppy turned and reached out for Kane. When he saw the abundance of tears coursing down her face, he pulled her close. They clung together for many moments then she pulled back. Kane lifted her now, pale face and the sight of her solemnity pierced him with pain. A sweat broke out on his forehead as he moved his red lips towards the girl's mouth. He kissed her softly, sweetly and then realising what he was doing broke away.

"I'm sorry again," he spluttered.

"It's okay," she said, as the colour rushed back into her cheeks.

"Let's sit down. You talk, and I'll listen," he said, gently coaxing her to sit.

They sat side by side. "I hope you can find the space in your mind for what I have to say. I need you to believe me," she said, earnestly looking directly into his eyes.

"Whatever your story is, I promise I will help you. I'll be your forever guardian," Kane smiled, reassuringly. "I won't interrupt except to have things clarified."

"The spirits are no longer trapped. There's nobody here to take care of the stones," she took a sad pause and glanced around at the circle. "Traditionally, we performed rituals to keep them locked in. The spirits of our ancestors still visit, some are good and help us, but some are bad, very bad."

"Can you see where there was once a ditch?" Poppy abruptly stood up and pointed out the old earthworks and then returned to her place at Kane's side. "The bank of that henge ditch was once ten metres high. The bank had straight sides. It was there to control and contain. It was, designed to keep the spirits in, not to keep people out. Each of the stones are unique, quarried by and from different communities. Unlike your people, we worked peaceably side by side.

Kane listened intently while looking more closely at the giant stones standing, magnificently and mesmerisingly against the skyline. He was aware of an unsettling feeling creeping through his veins.

"What do you mean? Are you from a cult?" Kane asked, feeling confused and concerned that even if he listened to her explanations, he would still have little understanding of her plight. Kane noticed the sun was sinking in the sky and traces of a gloomy mist were circling the stones, he felt it was time to leave.

"No, we're not a cult," she paused, her forehead creased with stress and she swallowed. "We are an entirely different species."

"How come nobody has ever heard of you then?"

"We have lived right alongside you throughout history and mostly managed to stay invisible. We learnt to live underground. Our ancestors were miners of flint, tin and other minerals. Our homes were covered by earth mounds and connected by a network of galleries."

"I'm sorry, but that just can't be. You would have been discovered long ago," Kane, said glancing at the thickening fog and feeling a panic leap into his chest. He shivered with the realisation that the girl he had grown so fond of was insane.

"You said you would let me speak without interruption," Poppy protested as her eyes filled once more with tears.

"I'm listening, but you need to understand that all this is totally new to me."

"I know, but you might understand if I'm free to explain everything," she said and cleared her throat. "Of course, we didn't stay underground," Poppy frowned at Kane. "Our stories say that we were first on this planet. Humans arrived later but from the start were obviously more aggressive. When we finally emerged from beneath the earth, we learnt how to make ourselves invisible to your eyes. We performed our rituals in the darkness and continued to keep our buried homes accessible. Our communities were small and spread wide, but we would frequently come together. For centuries, we managed to maintain our way of life."

Kane found himself intermittently glancing over at the stones. Around the bases of the monoliths, darkness appeared to be oozing out of the ground. He wanted to postpone their conversation and return home before it grew dark, but Poppy seemed unconcerned and continued to talk as though reliving old memories.

"Then, the great persecution came, and we were hunted down for our differences and massacred. Humans were also killed in the frenzy of misunderstanding. Of course, some of my people retreated underground, but many were lost. The slayings have happened throughout our history for all kinds of reasons," Poppy stopped speaking and noticed that Kane was, fixated by the stones.

"What's the matter?"

"I don't know, but the weather up here is changing, and it can be a treacherous place if you get caught in a fog. Go on this is interesting," Kane said, turning his attention back to Poppy.

"Things in our community evolved so those living above ground when under attack, would hide all our most important items. Then the main bulk of the group would commit suicide, leaving others, usually the young to escape and start up again."

"Are you saying that's what happened to you?"

Poppy responded by nodding and swallowing uneasily.

"What are your people called?" Kane asked, becoming genuinely curious.

"We call ourselves the Ragliese but you humans have had many names for us the most common being witches."

"This is so confusing, Poppy. It will take me a while to digest all this."

"At puberty, we go down into the earth, and a ritual of rebirth is performed. You then emerge above ground as an adult. I was in a flint mine with another girl helping her cut her stone." Poppy stopped talking and reached for the chain, which she always wore around her neck. "Look this is my stone I mined it and cut it all by myself. It's the most precious thing we can own." She slipped the stone back beneath her clothes. "When we returned, we found them all dead, even our visionary leaders and matriarchs."

"Where's your friend, the other girl?" Kane said.

"We have a bunker on our land. It's modern with televisions and every comfort, but when we got there the doors had blown off their hinges, and someone had started a fire. We both panicked. We went our separate ways. I told her I would find her later."

"Wow! And I thought my life had been turbulent," Kane took her hand in his and smiled. "I think I understand."

Poppy flashed him a smile of gratitude and brushed her hair back from her face.

"I think we're in for another intense battle between your church and for our continued existence. There are a few who have protected us but more who wish to wipe us out. They do it silently so as not to disrupt the illusions which you humans have of being omnipotent."

Kane sat in stunned silence, trying to process all the new information. He was partially in a state of disbelief and yet at the same time he had a desire to blindly put all his faith into the enigmatic and beautiful girl at his side.

"Promise me it will all be alright," she said.

"It will, whatever happens - I will look after you. I pledge my life on it."

Kane felt a crackling of kinetic energy and the hairs stand up on the back of his neck. He could taste and smell a foul odour. Slowly he turned his head from Poppy and out of the corner of his eyes he thought he saw a black shape crawling through the mist and over the grass. He shivered inside and turned his attention back to Poppy.

"Come on, let's go home now," he said, standing up. He took her hand and began to walk away from the stones. An impulse caused him to turn and take one last look at the monument. Standing tall was a dark figure with hazy edges, scabby skin, and probing eyes which looked as though they had, been, pushed into two bloody, weeping wounds. He wanted to curl up in terror but remembering the hollow sadness in Poppy's eyes, managed to swallow his desire to scream and disclose to her what he had seen.

"Let's run down the hill," he said, and taking her hand, they ran as fast as they could manage.

Chapter Fourteen

Oliver knocked timidly on the office door of his old university friend Allen Smith.

"Come in," said a calm voice.

Oliver was glad to be in the cool interior of the majestic old building. He looked up at the high ceiling and admired the decorative plasterwork.

"I haven't been in this building for a long time," Oliver said, as he wandered over to where his friend sat at a desk, situated beneath a tall window and looking out on to a finely manicured lawn. Oliver stood next to Allen. His red head was tilted forwards as he examined something through a microscope and sunk deep in thought he ignored Oliver's presence. Olive feeling impatient cleared his throat. Finally, Allen pivoted around on his chair so that he could face Oliver.

"I'm sorry. I've got so much work on at the moment," Allen grinned.

Oliver noticed Allen's cheeks still had the same ruddy hue, and his dark, intelligent eyes danced with lively fondness. Oliver smiled awkwardly and looked down at Allen's trainers, which seemed incongruous with the suit trousers and white coat.

"Would you believe some nut has sent me a sample of bear fur to test, insisting it's bigfoot," he laughed.

Oliver smiled in response. "As I was coming down the corridor, I saw someone leave your room. Are they likely to be back?"

"No, don't worry, Oliver, we will be undisturbed," Allen said, with a more serious expression on his face. "Sit down," he said, gesturing to an upright chair.

Oliver sat down uneasily and watched Allen fumble around in the pocket of his coat. Eventually, he held up two plastic bags, which held the fragile samples Oliver had collected from Professor Roehampton's house. Oliver stared at Allen, trying to gauge his reaction. Allen's dark, beady eyes were earnest and steadfast.

"As you and I both know, modern Homo sapiens appeared in Europe around forty thousand years ago and in Africa around sixty."

"Yes, of course, I know that. How old are my samples?"

"Well, with our improved radiocarbon dating techniques, it would appear these are much older," he gently shook the bags in front of Oliver. "More like seventy thousand years old," Allen said, his eyes bright and excited. "In Europe, that's virtually impossible."

Oliver's jaw dropped, he felt his mouth go dry, and he was aware that his eyes were popping like a crazy man.

"You're right. You must have done something wrong. What about the DNA? I suppose the samples are too old for any to have survived," Oliver said when he finally managed to speak.

"Well, actually, I was able to get a partial DNA reading," he said, his attention turning to the artefacts which he scrutinised in his hand as though they were diamonds stolen from the Crown Jewels. "This is the thing - the strands were like nothing I've ever seen before."

"I have read some papers which state that there is ample evidence to prove that Homo sapiens were interbreeding with Neanderthals. I have also heard that non-Africans have more Neanderthal DNA but then only about twenty per cent."

"You aren't listening to me properly, Oliver." Both men's eyes met. "The strands differ significantly from anything I've seen before," Allen said emphatically, with a deeply perturbed expression on his face.

"Allen, I'm sorry for wasting your time. It must be some fraud." Oliver couldn't think of anything else to say.

"It does all seem improbable. I could give it another examination if you like?"

"No, it's okay. I was just curious," Oliver said, leaning forward and taking the samples from his friend. "I will probably bin these."

"Well, don't be too hasty. We could get someone more experienced to have a look. Where did you find them?"

"You can't always believe what the experts tell you," Oliver said conscious that his face was red with embarrassment.

"What's up, mate? I've never seen you like this. You seem nervous, ill at ease." Oliver squirmed in his chair and stroked his stubbly chin. "You look unusually dishevelled and as though you haven't slept for a week."

Oliver couldn't meet Allen's concerned expression, looked to the floor and shrugged his shoulders. His brain was racing. *Could he trust his friend? He'd cheated death by a fraction and daily lived in fear of harm, and it would be a relief to share his horrors with another rational human being,* Oliver debated with himself.

"Come on, man, we're old friends. You can trust me," Allen said, in an irritated tone and glanced at his watch.

The room was no longer cool, Oliver felt hot and clammy as his story stumbled from his lips. In a hushed voice, he described in detail his meetings with Professor Roehampton, the discovery of the tomb and the body.

"What has alarmed me is that it was well known that I had been assigned to work with the professor, but I have heard nothing from the police. I was called before the big wigs at the university, and all they said was that Rupert had unfortunately died in a gas explosion.

Oliver had grasped Allen's attention. He leaned forward, frozen in silent contemplation. Oliver stared into his friend's eyes to decipher what he was thinking.

"Come on, what do you make of that?" Oliver said with impatience.

"You're delusional and have been working too hard," Allen mumbled. "If old Rupert topped himself, the university would want to cover it up."

"You know me. I'm a self-confessed coward, and all this is pushing me to the brink of a breakdown - I'm definitely being followed."

"I expect the men in black have a fat file on you," Allen said, straightening back up.

"I'm telling you the truth. I've been plunged into a nightmare as deep as the ocean," Oliver said and stood up to leave. "Okay fine, don't believe me, but you know the readings from these samples were accurate," he said, waving the plastic bags in the air. Oliver turned and despondently walked towards the door.

"Wait! Come back. Sit down, it's all a bit incredible, and I need time to think," Allen said.

Reluctantly, Oliver returned to the chair. He perched restlessly, ready to leave and waited. Time seemed to slow unbearably.

Finally, Allen spoke, "so we have a murder that appears to have been covered up?"

"Correct, there has been no mention of it anywhere. Not in the papers, the internet or news."

"We also have some baffling samples of what could be a new species of humanoid type creature - hopefully not bigfoot."

"I'm not laughing," Oliver said and frowned.

"I'm just joking, I do believe you," Allen said, flashing a half-smile in Oliver's direction. "So, where did the professor find the mummified body, which I assume has been blown up?"

"In a mine working, on Anglesey, I think. It's halfway down a cliff face, concealed in brambles and covered by a metal grid to keep people out. I looked it up on the net. It was only referred to as an old mine works and extremely dangerous."

"I suppose you still don't do heights?" Allen said.

"Afraid not but I presume you've kept up with your climbing," Oliver said, pointedly.

"Perhaps it's time you found some courage. We will visit the cave and see if there is any evidence to back Professor Roehampton's account. If my doubts are blown away, then I will stand by you a hundred per cent of the way," Allen said, holding his hand out to Oliver. "I will send you an email, and we can arrange a trip."

Oliver took his friend's hand and shook it, "agreed."

Chapter Fifteen

Before dawn, Poppy wrenched herself from her snug bed to make the long journey to her new job. After a long bus ride, she walked vigorously from the station in the centre of town towards a menacing industrial landscape. Standing at the start of a bridge, she gazed ahead at the vision of hell, which relentlessly reared up out of the foggy morning gloom. In amazement, her eyes scrutinised the sooty grey facades of brutal concrete, the fat chimneys puffing steam and the flames coming from the tallest pipes she'd ever seen, licking the sky. Coiling around the buildings were more pipes and wires of various thicknesses and colours.

Warily she moved forwards, crossing the divide between purgatory and the core of hell. A foul sulphurous smell reached her nose, causing her eyes to water. In the middle, she looked over the railing into the dark waters below. Mosquitos hovered above the charcoal grey mud banks, more pipes ran into the river spewing yellow liquid, and it was bloated with the rubbish of human existence.

Poppy had wanted to please Kane's father, to prove she could contribute to her living costs but the reality of the alien environment was far from anything she could have imagined. She felt a peculiar fascination for the patch of rot, which spread for miles to her left and right and down to the sea. However, she knew exploring wasn't an option as she'd been given strict instructions by Kane's mother to make sure she arrived before the factory siren sounded. Poppy increased her pace.

On leaving, the bridge on her right emerged a vast patch of derelict land and running through it was an old road. The grass was yellow amongst the rubble, and she noticed the skeletal shape of a dead tree. Isolated pubs once surrounded by houses stood bereft. Following the instructions she'd been given, Poppy turned left down a side street. To her right was a huge chemical works, which made paint and dwarfed on the left was the clothes factory squashed in against the river.

As instructed, Poppy joined a crowd of women who were standing in a courtyard. Unknown, hauntingly sick faces turned towards her, and unkind eyes looked her up and down. Not a word or a smile was given in greeting. Their harsh tongues returned to their spitting conversation, laughter and cursing. Others were preoccupied with applying hard lines of makeup.

A siren wailed, large doors opened, and everyone rushed inside. Lights blinked on, and the electricity reaching the machines began to hum. Feeling anxious, Poppy joined a queue, and she watched everyone push a card into a machine.

"Hurry up! Put your card in."

Poppy turned to face a woman with heavy makeup, dyed black hair and a wrinkled face. "I'm new here," she spluttered. "I don't have a card."

"Supervisor!" the woman shouted. "There's a newbie."

Poppy watched as a tall, skinny woman walked briskly in her direction. Without a word, she pushed a card into the machine.

"You must remember to do that when you leave." She consulted a sheet on a clipboard. "You must be Poppy. You're on the bar tacking machine," she said, grabbing an overall from a hook. "Wear this. I will show you what you must do."

Poppy was absorbed in rubbing her irritated eyes when she felt her arm being grabbed. She was pulled over to the end of a long line of machines. "You're not allowed to use the toilet without permission - until the siren goes for your break. That's for ten minutes, and you will be sanctioned if you're not back here on time. The faster you work, the more you will earn."

Poppy, still trying to digest the verbal diarrhoea, felt herself roughly plonked on a chair.

"All you have to do is take a pair of jeans from the box on your right, tack the belt loops, and drop them in the box on your left," the supervisor instructed, as she demonstrated. "See, it's quite simple."

Poppy was left alone and looking around, she saw turbulence of activity as hundreds of women rushed to their places. Then she heard a whirring, followed by knocks and bangs as machines sprung into life. A radio boomed out but was unable to drown out the deafening anarchy of the machines.

"I'm Isabela," a middle-aged woman with dyed red hair said, as she sat down at the machine next to Poppy. "You must watch that one. She's a nasty piece of work that Glenda."

Poppy noticed the woman had a foreign accent. She felt her eyes automatically drawn to the woman's bosom, and she was shocked to see her chest covered with soft, red, downy hair.

"I'm Poppy," she smiled. "Where are you from?"

"Spain," Isabela smiled back. "I've worked here since I was sixteen. It's not so bad you will get used to it."

"No talking," Glenda shouted from further down the line.

Poppy watched as Isabela bowed her head and instantly started running the material through the machine. As Poppy turned to her work, she was aware of a feeling of dread lying heavy in the pit of her stomach. Her hands shook as she nervously placed the belt loop under the foot. The needle clattered down far too fast and tacked across the back of the jeans. Initially, each one went wrong, and she hid them in the box while praying the supervisor didn't reach her and discover her mistakes. After many attempts, she finally got the hang of what was required.

After her ten minutes' break, when she had failed to relieve herself because the queue for the toilets was too long, she returned to her work feeling more confident. By lunchtime, she saw the boxes on her right had gone down to one and she'd caught up.

For some time, the needle hammered into the fabric without error. Then abruptly, the whirring stopped, the fabric jammed, and everything came to a halt. Adrenaline shot through Poppy's brain, and her heart thumped. Reluctantly, she held up her hand and watched as Glenda, scowling, came scurrying in her direction.

"My machines broken," she said in an insipid voice.

"Quickly, follow me," Glenda said with annoyance.

Poppy complied and trailed behind Glenda, who led her to the other side of the factory, where men stood about large cutting machines. She introduced her to an old man who stared at her over his thick-lensed glasses.

"This is Fred. He fixes the machines," Glenda said dismissively and, walking away, called over her shoulder. "Hurry up, times money."

Without uttering a word, Fred walked with Poppy back to her empty chair. As Fred worked at replacing the needle, Poppy glanced at the other women bent over their work. When they felt her gaze, they looked up, and Poppy saw that their expressions had changed from hostile to aggressive. Then, glancing at the boxes to her right, she saw a towering stack.

With the new needle in place and a pair of jeans thrown in the reject box, Poppy determined to work faster. During the afternoon break, she spent her ten minutes at a table on her own. People deliberately walked past, casting their eyes over her, making it clear they considered her an outsider.

After the break to Poppy's horror, the needle jammed once again in the fabric. Desperately, her fingers pulled and pushed, trying to release the jeans from beneath the needle.

"Glenda, the lines stopped," an unknown voice called out.

Wretched Poppy swivelled around in her chair and watched Glenda rushing in her direction.

"You, stupid little cow," Glenda screeched and jabbed her hard in her upper arm. She took Poppy's seat, switched the machine off and then back on. The needle lifted free. "Have you got anything between your ears? If you keep stopping, all these people lose all the bonuses they're working hard to make," she waved her arm towards the other women who were sitting, staring, and inactive.

Poppy couldn't control the tears which cascaded down her face. Glenda stared at her unmoved.

"Get a move on then!" She walked vigorously away.

Plunged in angry thought, with her tears soaking the fabric, Poppy began to feed the fabric beneath the foot. She was so preoccupied that she didn't notice the man standing at her shoulder watching.

"Don't be sad. You're not at fault; it's the machine."

Poppy twisted around in her chair and, feeling perplexed, gazed up into the eyes of a tall, thin, handsome man. The corners of his mouth curled into a smile.

"My name's Adam Philips. We met briefly outside Judy's house," he said warmly. "Don't let them get to you. Think of them as witches which you have the power to destroy."

Poppy looked directly up at the well-dressed and slightly effeminate man. "I remember," she smiled, feeling unreasonably happy to see a kind face. Poppy was also aware that the deranged Glenda was hovering on the periphery of her vision, unable to respond.

"She won't bother you while I'm here. I'm a client who has just placed a large order for some designer suits for my new shop."

Poppy saw melancholy in his eyes and noticed he kept nibbling at his nails as though he, too, was feeling vulnerable. He glanced down, and she was aware of him pondering on the flint she wore around her neck. She quickly tucked it back beneath her overalls.

"It's good to meet you properly," she said, beaming to show her gratitude for his intervention.

"I will have a word and ensure you are left in peace for the remainder of the day," he awkwardly smiled as though it was an unnatural position for his mouth, but his eyes remained serious. "I hear you intend to paint a mural on the walls of the twin's bedroom. It would be good to see more of you. Hopefully, we will have time to speak later."

Poppy floated through the rest of the day without incident. Her machine seemed to have given up its assault on her confidence; the dusty, damp air no longer caused her irritation, and she didn't notice that the radio was blasting out the same hideous popular song repeatedly.

Chapter Sixteen

Quivering with excitement, Poppy sat with her face almost stuck to the glass of the train window as her unworldly mind strained to capture every detail of the angry cancer, which she imagined spreading over the face of the planet. An industrial disease, which she'd been unaware of its existence until recently. The metallic and concrete monsters breathed fire and coughed steam into the yellow sky as they flashed past. She could see the complete discordant expanse of the industrial landscape being sucked towards the sea. Summer had broken, the sky was grey, and a squally rain whipped past, partially obscuring her view.

It was the weekend and a chance for Poppy and Kane to leave the monotony of their factory lives behind them for a day. They were heading for the coast, and Poppy found herself fascinated watching the symbols of man's greed and the images of deprivation diminish and disappear into the distance. In a second, the ugliness of man's destruction had vanished. Poppy saw the blinking splendour of full colour as the lush green ground rose and fell. Water trickled into silver streams, and birds danced in and out of dense bushes. Poking above the ridge of a hill, Poppy glimpsed the tops of the standing stones and smiled secretly to herself. She sighed with relief at leaving the oppression of the working week behind and turned her attention back to Kane.

"After paying your dad's rent, I don't have much money left, but someone at work said there are lots of second hand and antique shops in Wutherby," she said excitedly. "This is my first ever wage packet; I want something memorable."

"Don't you think it would be better to buy some nice clothes or a phone? You must be fed up with wearing the factory rejects," Kane said, trying to be helpful.

"Nope, I want a bag. Besides, I don't need a phone, and I haven't got enough for any really good clothes. What do you want?"

"I suppose men up here still get paid more than women. You can see why I was happier living down south. People here are still so backwards thinking."

"You must want something. I also need a coat, but I will need to save for that, Poppy said excitedly."

"I want to buy a shotgun and start clay pigeon shooting again. I have a licence."

"A gun. You must be mad," Poppy said, stunned.

"It's not so strange everyone around here goes up into the hills shooting. My father has one. I also need to protect you from anyone who might want to cause you harm."

"The dark spirits have their reality. They can't be shot with a gun, and besides, they won't come after me, more likely you."

"You're talking in riddles again," Kane said, still struggling to believe Poppy's story about her strange world.

"There's your conventional world," Poppy said, waving her hand towards the window, and there is a world which is most often invisible but equally real. While we're together, it won't help in any way continuing to think that things aren't there because you can't see them. With no one to tend the stones, the dark spirits will be roaming loose, as much as the good ones."

A fresher sea air blew through the partially opened window, and the town of Wutherby slid into Poppy's view. The veil of mist lifted, and shafts of light shot down through the clouds like spirits reaching down to Earth. In the distance, she could see boats bobbing on an undulating ocean.

Holding hands, they hastily walked across the platform and left the station. They then descended narrow steps, which wound their way around a tiny old building that tumbled down the hill towards the sea. There seemed to be no chain stores, and all the higgledy-piggledy shops were full of intriguing objects. Some were crammed with exotic and extravagant antiques. Others displayed quirky gifts.

Poppy observed the everyday dramas of the crowded streets with innocent eyes and tingled with the buzz coming from people perusing items of interest. Together, Poppy and Kane explored the antique shops as though they had money to burn.

Exhausted, they ventured into an 'Aladdin's Cave' crammed with objects from all around the world and every time period. Statues of Chinese dragons stood on either side of the window display, large hand-painted vases, Victorian toys and paintings littered every surface. Their confidence grew as they delved further into the shop.

Poppy studied the books at the very back of the shop, while Kane hunted through the curiosities, having decided to purchase a gift for Poppy rather than spend his money on himself.

Kane was looking at some old skipping ropes when, in his periphery vision, he caught sight of something familiar. On his right was a beautiful music box with a lid inlaid with different coloured wood. The memory of a star-shaped pattern spun into the forefront of his mind. *That looks just like Sandra's music box,* he thought as he strolled over to the unusual item. He picked it up and turned it around in his hands, examining every detail of the honey-coloured wood. *On the outside, it's the same,* he pondered as adrenaline shot through him at the prospect of having some contact with his sister.

Nervously, he lifted the lid, and as anticipated, a ballerina popped up and began to spin around to a tinkling tune. Kane remembered that beneath the jewellery compartments, Sandra used to leave little secret notes to herself and profound thoughts, which she wanted to remember. *If the scraps of paper were still there, it would prove that it was her music box,* Kane considered, and with a trembling hand, he carefully lifted out the compartment. All he saw was a photograph. It took up the length of the box and curled up at the corners. *Perhaps this isn't her box after all,* Kane thought, feeling disappointed.

Nevertheless, out of curiosity, with pincer fingers, he pulled the end. It slid out, and Kane glanced around to make sure he wasn't being observed. He saw Poppy engrossed in a book and glanced down at the image.

Fireworks exploded in his brain; he felt the blood drain from his face, and his knees turned to jelly. He needed to sit down but managed to stand, staring aghast at the detailed picture of his sister. She was lying on a concrete floor, dead. He could see a rope around her neck, her clothes were torn, and there were scarlet slashes to her face, arms and across her body. Standing to the right of her were his twin half-brothers,, their faces contorted into perverse grins. Hanging from Joe's left hand and Jim's right were knives covered in blood. Kane studied the picture to see if he could determine the location. The space looked cave-like, with rough walls and on closer examination, he saw that the floor was stone and not concrete. He could discern pictures on the walls. He noted one resembled a red handprint.

Kane was desperate to pursue his horror in private. He stuffed the photograph into the box and covered it with the containers. He glanced over at Poppy, who was still relaxed and engrossed in a book. Hurriedly, he paid for the item and swiftly fled from the shop. A few seconds later, Poppy, sensing something was wrong and following the fragrance of death, which was lingering in the air, went in pursuit of Kane.

From a distance, Poppy observed Kane pushing through the crowds of shoppers, almost knocking them off their feet. He was heading down the hill towards the sea. Hastily, Poppy followed him, dodging people as they crossed her path erratically.

Just as she was in touching distance of Kane, he abruptly turned left. Poppy stood at the top of narrow steps and watched him descend into a side street and the nearest pub.

Feeling disappointed that Kane was unable to walk past the pub, she reluctantly pushed open the door and stepped into the dim room. She found Kane seated on a bench, slumped over the table, and running his finger around an empty whiskey glass. Uneasily, she sat down on the opposite seat and wondered what had occurred to cause such a seismic shift in his mood and make drinking so enticing.

Together, they sat in intense and uncomfortable silence. Restlessly, Poppy waited while Kane stared darkly at his glass, engrossed in his heavy thoughts.

"Are you going to tell me what's wrong, or are we going to sit here in silence forever?"

"You can buy me another drink," Kane replied in a sharp tone.

Poppy, annoyed at his request, felt the light of happiness in her eyes flicker off. "No, of course, I'm not," she scowled.

"Get out then. Leave; I'm sick of listening to all your imaginary crap and stories of being hunted by invisible monsters. There's a real-world where people are blown apart and murdered," he croaked and swallowed the threatening tears back down his throat.

Without a word, Poppy stood up to leave.

Kane knew he'd made a mistake, that it was important to smother his emotions and keep his discovery concealed.

"I'm sorry. Sit back down. It's just one of my panic attacks," he smiled weakly, aware of the dread still hovering around his heart. "Please, I'm truly sorry," he said, gesturing to the bench.

"It worries me that one drink will lead to another, and we still have to catch the train home."

"I know, these flashbacks are so unpredictable."

Sensing that the avalanche of discord was melting, Poppy sat back down. She didn't protest when he bought another double whisky and her a lemonade. She remained calm and hoped for the best. An hour later, they stepped out into the rain-drenched evening streets. Poppy was keenly aware of the absence of Kane's hand in hers and how quickly he'd returned to being cold and remote.

Chapter Seventeen

Under the dull yellow strip lights, Kane was standing alone in the cutting room by the flatbed conveyor. He was going through the sequence of operations required to start up the automatic cutting machine. Opposite were the benches on which the other tools needed for cutting were set up: straight knives, round knives, band knives and direct-drive rotary knives. It was early morning, and the men in charge of the smaller machines were not required at this stage of the process. This part of the factory was separate from the main area and sparsely populated, as the initial set-up of the machine only required one man.

Kane was preoccupied with checking the measuring of the fabric and setting the computer accurately, ensuring that the blade fell in the correct place. He was aware that his colleague, a shrivelled elderly man, felt constrained in his company and was deliberately keeping his distance. Hunched over, and with his back turned towards Kane, he occupied himself at the far end of the room. The man's crime had been to catch Kane having an early morning tipple and of confronting him about drinking on the premises. Kane had snapped back and threatened him with violence, and the man had scurried away with his head bowed.

At that moment, Kane desired solitude and isolation above all else. He had felt on edge and paranoid since his weekend trip to the coast - he was sure he was being stalked. Booze was once again dominating his waking hours, confusing his thinking and causing him to look dishevelled. Although he was still shaving his head, army style, he had not attended to his beard in days and hardly showered. Mindful that he was a broken man, trapped between trying to block out the image of his dead sister and wanting answers, he pushed everyone away. He'd observed Poppy's looks of concern as he became more inattentive towards everyone. In his mind, she now needed protection from his demons.

Kane was abruptly startled from his morose thoughts by a firm rapping on the entrance doors. Rapidly, he pressed the red button, which shut down the machine, and turned and stared blankly in the direction of the sound. *We are not expecting a delivery,* he considered. When the knocking repeated with more urgency, he reluctantly crossed the room.

Partially sliding open the doors, he gazed into the grey morning, perplexed. He ventured outside and looked around the courtyard, but there was nobody unusual milling about, only a few stragglers entering the small door, which led to the sewing hall. Continuously looking around, he returned to his work area. As he heaved the heavy doors together, a shuddering cold breeze blew through his body. He shivered as though he'd submerged himself in ice water.

Kane returned to his position by the machine. He bowed his head as he prepared to set it in motion. Feeling fearful, he took a sidelong glance and in horror, raised his eyes. Standing halfway down the length of the conveyor belt was a stocky, well-built man who immediately appeared out of place.

The man stared at him with vacant eyes. Kane focused on the malicious grin, which revealed rotten teeth. He was peculiar, looking in many ways. His silver hair was long, straight like strands of steel. He had a protruding hooked nose and a long beard. His clothes were crudely cut and sewn. Around his shoulders, he wore a fur cloak.

"What do you want?" Kane muttered in confusion while backing up against the machine. He then took small, careful steps towards the door.

"Give me Mathew," he boomed, his voice rushing towards Kane like a violent storm.

"I don't know a Mathew," Kane replied, feeling uncertain whether to run or freeze.

Keeping his eyes locked on the figure, Kane watched with alarm as he flung back his cloak to reveal a large knife stuffed under his belt. It was hard for Kane to rationalise the situation. All he understood was that the intruder was a potential threat. He knew he wouldn't make it through the heavy doors, so he diverted towards the table of knives. In one movement, he'd picked up the rotary blade and pressed the trigger. Instantly, he felt safer with a weapon in his hand.

The man then swiftly pulled the sword from his belt and ran towards Kane. They wrestled close as both men tried to release the weapons from the other's hand. Kane managed to embed the whirling blade into the man's sword arm. He felt relief as he heard the sword clang to the floor. Fighting was Kane's territory, and while holding the man's gaze, he speedily stooped to the floor and retrieved the sword. Kane used the rotary blade, which was now in his weaker left hand, as a shield. The man held up his bloodied arms to defend his upper body and head while Kane danced around to the side. Kane raised the weapon above his head and brought it crashing down, completely severing the man's forearm. Blood spurted in all directions.

A lightning bolt of power pierced Kane's chest, and then came terror as he remembered the drama was playing out in his place of work. Kane hesitated and decided to run for the door. Suddenly, he elevated off the floor. Then, he was thrown against the conveyor. His courage drained from his body; his limbs became feeble. He sank onto the concrete floor and pulled his legs into his chest for protection. Unable to move, he stared into the void. *I must be hallucinating,* he thought.

As he glanced at the severed arm, he noticed the fingers were twitching. He recoiled in disgust, as the arm appeared to be moving in his direction. Then to his astonishment, he noticed something growing from the other end. First biceps re-appeared, these merged with a shoulder, neck and then head. Rapidly a whole body reformed, insubstantial at first but growing in density with every second. Bewildered, Kane looked up to see if the other intruder was still standing.

The first man's arm had regenerated, and he was holding the sword aloft. Stunned by the extraordinary sight, Kane rose and began to edge his way down the machine just as the duplicate man was rising from the floor. The second man was striding towards Kane. The machine suddenly thundered to life. The guillotine went up and down, endlessly cutting the same piece of fabric.

Why isn't anyone rushing to my aid? Kane thought as he felt a very solid hand grab the front of his overalls and lift him into the air. He was hurled onto the conveyor belt. He heard a thud and felt fear burn his eyes. Desperately he tried to grapple with the creatures while wondering why his predisposition towards aggression had failed him. In amongst his struggling fury, he saw two twin faces staring down. Together, they pinned him onto the moving black rubber.

"Bring Mathew! Tell him Aton is coming to kill him," the men hissed in unison in hoarse voices just as the guillotine dropped down onto the outstretched fingers of Kane's left hand.

Kane felt himself being released. He slid off the machine and sank down onto the dank, dusty floor. He felt the air move as the two strangers passed by on their way out. Clasping his wrist tight and staring at his mutilated hand in pain and anguish, he screamed out. He heard the alarm wail and the footsteps of people as they ran in his direction.

"Get them - two men - intruders. They did this to me; a man called Aton," Kane blurted out in confusion to the three blurred faces, which were bent over examining his hand.

"I wouldn't listen to him. He's talking nonsense," the old man said, looking up and raising his eyebrows at his more senior colleague. "He's a drinker. I think this was an accident waiting to happen."

Chapter Eighteen

Kane was sitting in his father's front room alone, loathing every minute of every day. In contrast, Poppy had determinedly forced herself into a job she found equally unendurable so that they could pay their rent while Kane was incapacitated.

Kane's heavily bandaged hand rested uselessly on the arm of the chair, while in his right hand, he held two letters. One summonsing him to attend court in Cornwall for a shoplifting offence, the other was informing him that he'd been sacked for drinking during working hours. A trip south on little money away from Poppy filled him with panic, and he fretted until his head ached. *What kind of work was available to a single-handed man?* He considered his mood darkening by the second.

Having read the letters he flopped, his head back against the chair and gazed at the heavy sky and the snowflakes fluttering past the panoramic window at the far end of the room. After the dry summer, winter had arrived early and with a vengeance. He found the white silence outside and the background noise of the television equally painful. The fingers of his right hand were restlessly tapping with frustration, and he could imagine the ones on the left doing the same.

He felt as though his world had been ripped from its foundations. All he could do was watch as his youthful dreams of travel and adventure drifted away. The only thing that satisfied him was oblivion. Kane reached over the arm of the chair and picked up a glass of whiskey, his only companion. He gulped it back, placed the empty glass down and allowed the sweat and misery to drip from every pore.

Kane began to feel drowsy. Most nights, he would force himself to stay awake to avoid the nightmares. He fluttered his eyelids and tried to keep them open, but despite his efforts, a blanket of darkness covered his mind.

Once again, he was in his army truck with his friend Arron at his side. They were both laughing hysterically, and he was aware of feeling the warmth and light of comradeship. The vehicle stopped. They both jumped out and walked together, still chuckling about a girl. Bullets whizzed past their heads, but Kane knew they were both dead and couldn't be hurt.

Something caught Arron's eye, and immune from danger, they walked noisily over to investigate. Kane looked down at his own grimy, grinning head lying in the gutter. 'Death, it's not so bad he muttered to himself and Arron.' He glanced over his shoulder to smile at Arron, but he'd disappeared. He looked back at the head. This time, he didn't recognise the face. It was rotten, maggots were eating the flesh, and the eyeballs were a mushy mess. The remembered smell of death reached his nose, and he thought about the perishability of the human body.

Feeling the dread of being alone, he scrutinised the desert hills for signs of life. Then, just as he was about to return to the truck, he felt something tugging at the bottom of his trousers. Looking down, he saw a severed arm, red raw half tendons and half flesh. The fingers were twitching and searching. The fingers were pawing at the fabric of his trousers, then grabbing and crawling. Kane tried to shake the blood-soaked limb off, but it was strong and rapidly progressed up his body. It reached his head, and the long fingers began prying his nostrils and mouth. The reeking odour of death was overwhelming.

The hand was suctioning onto his face, smothering him, and he gasped for air. Remembering his left hand was of no use, he grabbed the limb with his right hand and pulled it with all his strength. It came free, and with a shiver of his spine, he threw it to the ground and kicked it away with considerable force.

"Get the fuck off me," Kane screamed with venom. He awoke, aware that he wasn't the only person yelling out.

Kane found himself looking down at Poppy. She was staring up at him with a stunned, questioning expression in her eyes. Blood trickled from her nose, there was a lesion on her forehead, and her left arm was bent in an unnatural manner.

"I was only trying to see what the letters were," she said as tears coursed down her face.

"I'm so, so sorry," he said, taking a cushion from his chair and placing it under her head. "I didn't mean to hurt you. I told you not to come too close to me when I'm sleeping."

Kane eased his t-shirt over his head and used it to mop up the blood. He then noticed the colour had melted from Poppy's face and that her eyes were glazing over. Frantically, he looked around for his phone.

"I'm a raw wound. I can't stand being touched." Kane snapped, flinching at the thought of anyone entering his space. With a shaking grasp, he held the phone to his ear. "An ambulance, quick!"

"It's okay, it will all be okay," Poppy said in a weak voice, trying to console Kane. "I understand - it was an accident."

"Don't! Just don't! I don't want your kindness," he shouted at Poppy, interrupting the woman controller on the other end of the phone.

"I'm sorry, sir, but I need you to calm down and give me your address," the remote voice said firmly.

Kane inhaled deeply and began to give the woman the information she required. Then he knelt at Poppy's side and taking her good hand, stared down into her dark eyes.

"I'm so sorry. I love you," tears blurred his vision, and when he'd brushed them away he saw that Poppy's eyes were tightly shut, the eyelids moist. "You can't be with me - I've hurt you. Look what I've done," he cried, rising to his feet.

As the paramedics entered the house, Kane left, taking very few possessions.

Chapter Nineteen

Oliver had arranged to meet Allen in a small village café in Anglesey, which was, situated not far from the cliff. Allen's bright, familiar smile beamed out as he dropped his hood and walked towards Oliver. Having arrived first, Oliver stood up and greeted his friend with a brief embrace. They sat opposite each other.

"I've ordered two breakfasts," Oliver grinned. "I hope I don't later have reason to puke mine back up."

"I seem to remember you spent most of your time in college puking your guts up after a night out," Allen laughed wickedly. "You never could hold your drink."

Oliver flashed a mock scowl and glanced down at the large plate of greasy food, which was in front of him and regretted his order.

"Did you manage to get all the equipment?" Oliver asked, trying to sound professional.

"I have all the climbing gear in the jeep: ropes, hooks, helmets and torches."

"Well I won't need anything," Oliver said, feeling his face blanching and his hand shaking on the handle of his mug.

"Mate, you can't expect me to do this on my own."

"Sorry Allen, but you know me. I don't do heights," he said, pushing his half-eaten food away. "Did you bring the bolt cutters?"

Allen nodded as he shovelled a large mouthful of toast and beans into his mouth. *He always has to do everything so fast.* Oliver noticed.

Half an hour later, Oliver was standing paralysed, rooted to the spot and staring down over the edge of the exposed cliff face. He watched as his friend, with agile movements, periodically jumped out from the side and dropped down. As he went, Allen smiled up, his eyes intoxicated with adrenaline. He chatted away, explaining the art of abseiling to Oliver.

"You don't need to be telling me all this. I'm not coming," Oliver said, feeling inferior while admiring his friend's physical skills.

"Then why've you put all that gear on?" Allen shouted up.

"To keep you quiet."

Hearing the loud squawk of seagulls, Oliver looked up to the dismal grey sky and at the agitated birds swirling around. His head began to spin, and he heard an inner voice urging him to take a step over the edge. Immediately, fearing he would lose his balance, he dropped to the ground. The grass was wet, and the silence was thick. *Why am I inflicting this upon myself? Why am I not fearless like Allen? I've always been such a coward.* He berated himself, feeling close to tears. Oliver began to feel as though Allen had been quiet for too long and worried that he'd plunged to his death. On his belly, he cautiously crawled towards the brink.

Looking into the abyss, he saw Allan precariously hanging in mid-air, struggling with the bolt cutters.

"What are you doing?" Oliver shouted down, trying to distract himself from his queasiness.

"I'm nearly there. I've pulled away from the undergrowth, and these bars are easy. They're all rusty," he hollered back, annoying Oliver with his ceaseless exuberance. Quick as ever, Allen suddenly disappeared inside. Oliver waited aware of his heart thumping in his chest, half wishing his friend would find nothing and their adventure was, cancelled. Then he heard a muffled, echo, which became clearer as Allen exited the cave.

"Man, you've seriously got to come and see this."

The words reached Oliver's ears and filled him with dread. "No, I haven't," he barked back, determined not to be forced into doing something he most feared.

"You can't miss this. Besides, I'm going to need your help," he yelled in a stern, no-nonsense tone. "I don't want to hear your excuses. I will guide you down."

"Okay, okay, I'm coming," Oliver snapped back, realising there was no point in delaying the inevitable.

Oliver was glad that Allen couldn't see his face contorted with horror and his frozen fingers, which were so reluctant to move. He forced his body close to the edge. Rigid with anxiety and holding his breath, he slid himself over the top of the cliff. Adrenaline shot through him as he felt movement on the unstable ground. His fingers clung to crumbling soil. Everything gave way, and he found himself dangling from the rope, swaying like a pendulum in the sharp breeze. Glancing down, far below, he saw crashing waves leaping up, ready to draw him into their crushing grasp. Their roar thundered in his frozen head.

"Now what?" he screamed as he bashed into the cliff face.

"Lower yourself by easing the rope out and gently push yourself away from the face."

Listening intently and fearful of making a mistake, Oliver followed Allen's instructions. He slightly relaxed as he felt himself descending.

Halfway to the cave entrance, he heard and felt a commotion gathering above him and, looking up, saw a mob of angry-looking seagulls. Their yellow beaks opened wide as they screamed. To his horror, they began to dive-bomb his head. Rapidly, he loosened the rope and dropped out of their way.

Suddenly, he was stuck. The rope wouldn't release. Above, he could hear the birds calling to one another. Oliver hung hopelessly as a feathered monster hovered over him, pecking at his hard hat.

"Allen, help. I can't move; the ropes caught," he shouted.

"Jig a bit. It's probably rubbed a groove," Allen replied calmly.

"Ouch!" Oliver cried out as the bird struck his forehead and automatically raised his hands, releasing his grip. In a panic, he jerked, freed the rope and plummeted. Swaying in front of the cave entrance, he reached out to Allen.

"Swing towards me," he said. Allen made himself ready to catch his friend. "You're so melodramatic. You should've been an actor," Allen laughed.

Allen grabbed Oliver, drew him close and released the rope. Oliver scrambled away from the precipice. Feeling safer, he stood up, quivering in the dullness, happy to have his feet firmly planted on solid ground. He breathed in the damp air and listened to the tinkling sound of dripping water. "You don't know what that took," he replied as the two men exchanged smiles. "I hope it's worth it. What've you got to show me?"

Oliver watched as Allen turned his back to him and fiddled with his head torch. It flashed onto the full beam, and Oliver saw gleaming green eyes coming out of the darkness.

The two men stood mesmerised. Three large stone statues stood on either side of the entrance chamber. In the extending darkness beyond, Oliver could see a maze of passages. He gave out an exaggerated sigh. "Well, you were correct, and I'm glad I found the courage to venture down here."

Feeling happier in the underground environment, Oliver rushed forward to examine the magnificent objects more closely while Allen flitted excitedly from one to the next.

"Wow, this is amazing!" Oliver said, noting every detail in a book he'd taken from his pocket. "Their eyes are large, almond-shaped, hair straight, and they are women," he muttered more to himself as he jotted down every feature of the unusual beings. "There's writing here, at the base, which I can't identify immediately."

"Come on, we must explore more," Allen implored. "We don't have enough time to make a proper record."

"Did you bring a camera," Oliver inquired.

"No, but I've got my phone," Allen replied and began rummaging around in his bag.

"You take pictures, and I will make a note of any writing, in case it's not clear enough."

Hurriedly, Allen took pictures of the statues. For a fraction, the flash lit them up, and they could see the objects in their entirety.

"Job done - come on," Allen pleaded, gently pulling Oliver away towards the passages.

"Which one should we look at first?" Oliver said, feeling bemused as he gazed into the dark throats, which snaked into the depths.

Allen chose the one to the far left. They entered with all their senses on high alert. They could no longer hear the crashing of the waves but small, indistinct, unidentifiable sounds.

Soon they came across a room, which was, carved out of the tunnel wall. On entering, they immediately saw it was full of neatly arranged transparent coffins.

"I'm not sure if this is glass or some other material," Oliver said, touching the unfamiliar surface and looking down at a perfectly preserved body.

"The males are much bigger than the females, but other than that, they all look the same, with tanned skin and straight black hair," Allen said, having already impatiently darted around the room and ended up at Oliver's side. I need to take some samples. I'm going to pry open the lid."

Oliver watched as Allen threw his backpack to the ground and pulled out a small crowbar. Carefully, he levered open the heavy lid and slid it to one side. Oliver stepped forward and gently rested the back of his hand on the dead being's cheek. The flesh was cold and firm. He felt his hair bristle and quickly withdrew his hand.

"My god, this is eerie. They look like they are sleeping. This one's a female."

The moment Oliver stood back, Allen had his hands inside, extracted teeth from the grinning mouth, and then cut hair.

"I'm going to have to cut a chunk of flesh, just in case there's a chance of obtaining a full DNA sequence," he said, returning to his backpack and carefully placing his samples in anti-contamination bags. Then he pulled out a surgical scalpel.

Oliver shuddered in disbelief. "You can't!" he spluttered. "The skin would be too tough, and besides, they look too alive."

"I seriously wonder if you have taken on the right profession." Allen chuckled.

Oliver felt injured and fell silent. He wandered off to another tomb and began to jot the inscriptions into his notepad.

"This is unbelievable. My scalpel is slicing through the flesh as though it were a fresh corpse. This dude is as plump as the day they died."

"So, how many dead bodies have you cut up before or live ones?" Oliver retorted, still feeling repulsed by the desecration of a grave.

"You are too sensitive for this job. Go and dig in the dirt. Find some pots to look at." Allan said, not stopping to raise his head.

Oliver wandered back to the main passage. He sulkily sat down in the dirt next to the first statue and, taking out his trowel, began idly to scrape away at the soil. After a few minutes, he felt the metal clang against a hard object. Oliver's heart jumped alive. Dropping his tool, he used his fingers to scurry through the dirt. He bent his torch down, and something glinted in the light. Grasping the item, he held it up for closer examination. Gripped between his fingers was a thick gold chain and hanging from it was a beautifully tooled spearhead. Oliver laughed to himself and looked around to make sure he wasn't being observed. In excitement, he dropped his treasure into his pocket.

"Well, I think I've got everything I need," Allen said, emerging from the passage. "Why don't we try the middle tunnel next? I imagine the ones on either side are all the same: tombs and then a dead end."

In a more buoyant mood, Oliver nodded his head and followed his friend.

"You should ignore me. I can be flippant at times. You know I was just kidding. There's a place for the new way of observing things and the old," he said, marching fearlessly into the black heart. "See there are paintings on these walls, signs of human habitation."

The passage opened into a vast, vaulted chamber with decoration and inscriptions on the walls. Around the edges of the circular room were carved stone benches and a massive fireplace complete with a chimney.

"This is very advanced. We didn't have proper chimneys until Tudor times," Oliver said, walking over to the grate. "Mad as it might seem, this fireplace looks like it's recently been used."

Allan crossed the room and stood at Oliver's side. "There's fresh wood too. Now I'm getting the creeps," he said and began to sniff the air.

"What's wrong?" Oliver nervously asked.

"I'm sure I got a whiff of perfume. Have a smell."

Immediately, the scent caught in Oliver's nostrils, and the two friends exchanged fearful glances and looked towards the passage, which exited the room and travelled deeper into the core of the Earth.

Oliver suddenly heard a dull shuffling sound. "We're not alone!" he whispered, staring in the direction of the dark-throated tunnel.

They stood petrified as a new sound reached their ears. A dark flapping mass flew from the passage and engulfed the chamber. Flipping and dancing around their heads. The two men swung their arms in all directions. As quickly as the dark flock had arrived, it disappeared out down the passage, which led out.

Allan's body shook as he erupted into laughter. "Bats! We're both scared of bats."

"It must be dusk. We should go," Oliver said, aware that he was still shaking and lamenting that he'd been forced to face two major fears in one day.

"I will shine my torch down here, and then we'll go."

Oliver hadn't recovered as quickly and suddenly feeling exhausted it occurred to him that he could hurry Allan up by making his way to the exit.

"Well, I'm off," he said.

Cursing to himself, Oliver rushed away while Allan cautiously walked in the opposite direction. Oliver waited miserably, scratching away in the dirt and pondering the prospect of having to climb the rope. Suddenly, he heard screaming and felt a rush of air. Glancing up he saw Allan, and the look in his eyes froze him to the core.

"There's something there - shadows and shapes moving," he gasped. "Mutterings in the air," he said in a strangled whisper. "Let's get the fuck out of here!"

Both men rapidly readied themselves for the climb. Suddenly, Oliver was less frightened of the rope and more fearful of what lay in the darkness. He clipped the rope on his harness, ready to ascend the cliff face as quickly as possible.

Hanging in the half-light and glancing once more into the cave entrance, he saw that the glint of the statues' gem eyes had turned malicious in the dark mouth. Oliver shuddered. *These creatures still live and are probably walking amongst us today,* he thought and patted his pocket with his free hand.

Chapter Twenty

The wind moaned, and cold gusts forced Poppy to grip the oversized hood of Kane's old army fleece to stop it from blowing down. She'd struggled to squeeze the plaster cast through the sleeve, and now it throbbed, making her feel miserable. On her back was Kane's laptop and papers, which she'd planned to search through to find out where else he might have gone. In a daze, she trudged through the thick snow, unaware of the correct time and hoping she wouldn't slip over. The sky was darkening, so she assumed it was late afternoon. Wanting peace, she'd hoped she would arrive before the twins came back from school.

Poppy had left the hospital emotionally dull after being completely abandoned by Kane. On her return, Brian's welcome was muted. For a week, she sat on Kane's bed, waiting for him to return. Starved of comfort and engulfed in loneliness, she allowed her endless tears, full of sorrow and regret, to drop onto his pillow, which she held tightly to her chest. She'd never been in love with a man. From the earliest age, she'd been warned that humans were cruel and evil and that any emotional involvement was doomed to fail. She couldn't keep track of all the warnings she'd received through legends and adult instruction. However, in his own way, Kane had been dependable, and now she found herself longing for his company. All her bravery had gone, and her heart felt like a fragile shell.

Brian, realising that his two sources of income had failed finally asked Poppy to leave. Poppy was too broken-hearted to argue and knew it was time for her to seek out what was left of her community. She decided that before embarking on a journey, which would lead her into the depths of danger, she would wait a few nights longer for Kane to return to his mother's house.

Poppy took the shortcut through the park, where she and Kane had lingered under the hot summer sun, in the hopes she would find him there. The derelict mansion house loomed up on her left-hand side, and she became aware of other footsteps crunching the snow. Poppy walked on rapidly, ignoring the presence. Then she was aware of a voice worming a path through her brain.

"I'm Anton, your ancestor."

"I don't know you," her internal voice shouted back in an agitated tone, and she increased her pace.

"Wait! I'm Anton. You must know me from the legends you heard at your mother's knee. I'm the brother of Mathew, the murderer and traitor of our kind."

Reluctantly, Poppy turned and confronted the boulder of a man—tall and broad. Immediately, she recognised the man's signature straight hair, almond-shaped eyes, and large hooked nose.

"I recognise you now from your pictures," she said, smiling. "I'm honoured to meet you. I heard that you were a courageous and an honourable man who was respected through the generations."

Anton came closer and rested his large hands on Poppy's shoulder, "child, you're in grave danger."

The warmth of his hands seeped through her flimsy clothes, and she wished she had a fur cloak like the one he wore.

"You may not remember the story, but I had a younger brother, Mathew. He was the result of my mother being raped by a human," he said in a deep woody voice. "He turned on our kind, blowing the breath of death into our hearts. We were hunted, tortured and almost eliminated - hiding beneath the ground was our salvation."

"I do recall those stories," Poppy said, anxious to be moving and out of the cold. "Didn't Mathew take your life?"

"Yes, that's the truth. After my death, my soul lay at rest, locked into the stones. Devastated our mother used her strongest magic to capture Mathew's evil and confined it in a doll of his likeness." Anton released his grip and rubbed the red tip of his nose. "I see you're cold we must walk a while." "After that, the tide of Mathew's witch hunt ended abruptly."

"So where is he now?" Poppy said, happily moving once more.

"He will be hunting you down and all our kind, especially the women – he hates women. He will be happy to slaughter many females to get to one witch."

Poppy saw the park gate ahead and hoped that Anton wouldn't follow her beyond its boundaries.

"My mission is to destroy my brother, the killer. It's time for you to leave the world of humans and reassemble with whoever's left of our kind - to use the skills and magic of your birthright."

"I was always instructed to keep our powers concealed as humans don't have such gifts, and it would draw unwanted attention."

"I instruct you as an ancestor who knows how this game runs." Anton stopped by the gate. "It's dangerous to integrate or to become too familiar with humans and their ways. I must leave you now. My work has begun, and yours is to return."

Poppy watched as Anton turned his back, walked away and vanished close to the mansion house. Poppy buried her hands deep in the fleece pockets and rushed through the remaining few streets, feeling confused – no longer knowing what to follow and fearing what was to come.

Poppy dreaded facing Judy even though she'd shown her nothing but kindness. *You can never truly trust humans;* she thought as she paused before the scruffy looking front door.

Judy opened the door and straight away Poppy knew things were changed. Judy's eyes were, ringed with tiredness and worry. She smiled weakly, and when she spoke, her turtleneck quivered.

"Poppy I'm so glad to see you," she announced and ushered her in out of the cold.

"I hope you don't mind if I stay a few days," Poppy said, quivering and noticing that the air inside was only slightly less chilled. "Kane has had to go away."

"And his git of a father has thrown you out," Judy said, laughing as the scavenging twins flapped their hands against her body, wanting attention.

"Let her stay. She can stay in our room," they shouted in unison.

A noxious ammonia smell reached Poppy's nose, making her cough. One of the twins jumped up and flicked the hall light on, and Poppy gazed around, horrified. Covering the walls and ceiling was a slimy black mould.

"I know it's terrible, isn't it? The council keep saying that they'll come and fix it, but each day, it gets worse. Since you've been away from the factory, it's appeared there," she said in a raspy voice. "We're all getting ill, pleurisy and pneumonia. Look at you with your broken arm. I heard about your accident – it's so easy to slip on the ice."

"You're welcome to stay," she said, leading Poppy into the front room. "We're all waiting for something. My old man has also left again in my hour of need. Thank goodness for Adam," she turned and flashed a smile at Poppy. "Sit down. This room's not so bad, and the twin's room is completely unaffected. My room is terrible—I've been sleeping on the sofa."

Poppy perched next to Judy on the edge of the seat, soaking up the grim atmosphere. Without any authority capable of preventing them, the twins shouted, whined, fought each other, and climbed over the furniture. Judy didn't respond and sat stiffly, occasionally coughing, showing the restraint and calm of the sick.

"Where's my son gone?" she said.

"He said he had to go to Cornwall for a court case. We got into a little trouble, nothing serious. It should've all been over in a day."

"That's a long way to go. Perhaps he decided to stay over."

"He's been gone nearly two weeks now, and I've heard nothing," Poppy said, struggling to stop her face from crumpling and the tears flooding.

"He's been a bit of a loner since being out of the army, but he will be back. He thinks too much of you, just to leave."

"Has he spoken to you about me?" Poppy asked, feeling her hopes rising.

"Not exactly. His sister Sandra watches over him, and she says he's in love." A silence followed, and Poppy saw the look of awkwardness on Judy's face. She wanted to reassure her that it was normal to see spirits but knew it wasn't what most humans believed.

"I suppose you think I'm mad, but she is with me frequently, as fresh and bright as spring flowers."

"No, not at all," Poppy said, thinking of Anton's earlier visit. "What happened to Sandra?"

"It was a Hen party for one of the girls in the factory. Most of the sewing floor went to the club – there, was loads of us," she said, bending over and coughing. Poppy was distracted by the howling of one of the twins who was accusing his brother of punching him in the arm.

Unexpectedly, Judy turned and impatiently hissed in the boys' face. "Go to your room, this instant! Both of you scat!" Shocked, the boys rushed from the room. For a moment, the two women listened to the clamour as they went thundering up the stairs.

Looking perturbed, Judy turned her attention back to Poppy. "Sandra was my daughter but also my closest friend," Judy brushed a stray tear from her cheek. "It was so crowded that night. Male strippers always draw large crowds in these parts, and these ones were famous. One minute she was at my side, and then she was gone."

Poppy seeing Judy's face, darken and tears brimming in her troubled eyes, gently rested a hand on her leg.

"That was the last time. I ever saw her," Judy said, unable to contain the cascade any longer. Judy pulled Poppy into her body, and the two women clung together.

"Well, you have Kane, and he also loves you deeply," Poppy broke away and smiled up at the wrinkled face. "He will find you somewhere better to live," she said, feeling uncertain as to whether her assumption was correct but wanting to give the woman some hope.

"Yes, he's a good son, just a bit lost," Judy said, drying her eyes with the back of her hand. It was bad timing. He left the army, and then a year later, his sister disappeared."

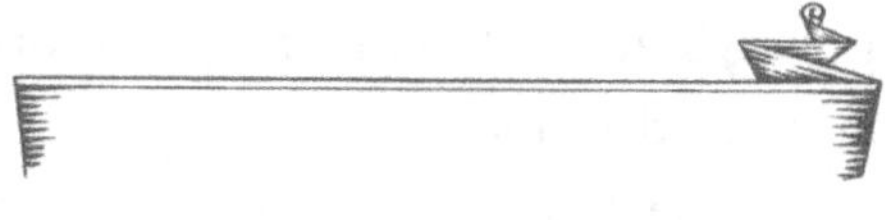

Chapter Twenty-one

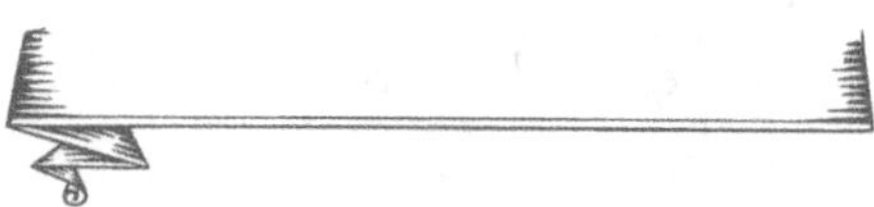

Poppy was plunged in thought and sitting cross-legged on the blow-up bed placed on the floor of the twins' room. An avalanche of silence had swamped the house since the early morning chaos of the twins preparing for school and Judy leaving for work. The only sound was the tapping of the bare branches of the neighbour's tree on the window.

Poppy stared into a well of dark thoughts where words and images from the previous day's events screamed their warning. *I must leave. Twice, I've seen ancestors at the derelict house; perhaps there are tunnels beneath the foundations,* Poppy considered. *Can I walk away from Judy, who's been so kind?*

The most sublime music began to seep into every fibre of the house. *Adam must be here too,* Poppy thought, as she felt herself being elevated out of her dull surroundings. The violin sang out with its heavenly desire, its passionate wanting, reaching out for an exquisite dream. Poppy felt the music speaking to her, and she felt caught in a dilemma between returning to her bleeding heart and embracing the pure joy. She sat entranced for some time. Then, the music died and was followed by an uneasy silence.

Poppy heard the floorboards squeak and, raising her eyes, saw a tall, dark figure. The corners of his cupid's bow mouth curled into a smile.

"I'm returning the boy's doll," Adam said, brushing away his floppy fringe of grey-streaked black hair from his radiantly beautiful symmetrical face.

Still in a state of dreaminess, Poppy smiled warmly.

"Adam, why do you stay here?' she said, and feeling conscious of her dishevelled state, bowed her head so her abundant hair covered her face. "I mean the mould – it's a health risk. I googled your name, and you could be living in the best hotel."

"I prefer family life," he said, perching on Joe's bed and gripping the doll in both hands. "I bumped into Judy in a pub while I was performing at the theatre. It was late, and she was crying into a beer. She explained that her daughter had gone missing," he said in a sad tone.

Poppy looked up, saw his brow knit together, and a shadow of sorrow cross his eyes.

"I wanted to help and have since grown fond of Judy's little crusaders. The mould exists because of an unchallenged evil."

Poppy wondered what Adam meant but remained silent. Feeling a need for company, she wanted nothing to force him to retreat to his room.

"I enjoyed listening to you play."

"Thank you! Music's my salvation," he said, speaking softly and smiling shyly. "Don't worry about Judy and the boys. I'm in the process of finding them a new home," he said, looking around at the room. "In thanks for them putting up with me playing night and day."

Something about Adam's face held her attention. She wondered if it was his unquestionable handsomeness, the gentle smile, or the dark eyes that held a palpable sorrow, or if it was because he represented calm order against her emotional chaos—someone new on which to depend. Despite this attraction and his kindness, she felt there was an error in his perfection.

"Perhaps I could talk to the bosses at the factory. Persuade them to find you a role, which you could do with your injury. After all, having exclusivity to my brand is bringing them in a huge chunk of money, and that's all these people care about." Adam smiled broadly and held

Poppy's gaze as if to emphasise his intent. "You and your boyfriend will also need somewhere to live."

Poppy stared back into his soft, clear eyes and wondered how he knew so much about herself and Kane.

"Don't look so perturbed. Judy and I are partial to drinking together – alcohol loosens her tongue."

"I was just wondering why you would help me?" she said, feeling awkward at having to ask such a question.

"Kane has suffered some terrible losses, and you are with him, so I consider you both part of this family. Now, Judy has revealed so much about her family, I feel committed to helping. If you like fate has brought us together."

Feeling embarrassed, Poppy dropped her eyes. They clamped onto the doll sitting on Adam's lap, and his long finger fluttering over the straight grey hair.

"Don't be afraid. It's only an old doll – my travelling companion," Adam said, as a strange grin twisted on his mouth. "Poor Judy's petrified of it but my little crusaders have become extremely attached. To their childish imaginations, it's like a friend." Adam laughed. "Here take a look," he said, bending forwards and thrusting the object in Poppy's direction, so she was forced to take it.

Poppy held the object limply in her hands and moved it up to her face. *Is this the doll Aton told me about?* She considered as a rough voice seized her brain.

"Mathew says we must be friends."

In Poppy's hands, she felt the object twitch into life. She flashed Adam an intense look, and then she glanced down as the doll flicked open its heavily lashed eyes, which stared back with the glow of life. Immediately, she dropped the object onto the bouncy mattress.

"Don't worry, I suppose it's quite ugly for modern tastes," he said, leaning forward and retrieving the doll. I will leave it here on Joe's bed so he and Jim have company when they return from school."

The doll's words and life happened in an instant leaving Poppy unsure as to what she'd witnessed. Looking up, she saw Adam regarding her with a sensitive expression.

"Please trust me. I meant what I said. I'm happy to help you and Kane find somewhere to live."

"I won't be here long. I'm waiting a few more days to see if he will return, and then I'll go home," Poppy said.

"He'll be home, and he deserves better than this," he said, standing up. "I must return to my practice. I hope you don't mind the noise."

"No, please play. It brings colour to the place."

Chapter Twenty-two

A week later, Adam announced that he'd found Poppy a flat. Poppy was both surprised and reluctant to move further into the human world. She longed to be wrapped in the healing embrace of her community or at least discover if she was the only survivor. Adam ignored her protestations and was very persuasive.

"We all need a breathing place between our past and futures. You and Kane can stay for as long or as little time as you want," he said as he helped her move the boxes of Kane's possessions, which she'd managed to collect from his room. "Please indulge me. Mad as it seems, I want to make sure you're both safe. There's an evil out there," he added, placing a box on the floor and waving his arm towards the door.

Poppy, impressed by Adam's capacity for kindness, relented. She knelt on the floor and began unpacking a box of kitchen utensils, which Judy had given her to use. The mood was light and airy. Adam laughed about how ugly the girls were at the factory. In between conversation and laughter, Poppy took hurried glances at Adam. She found the multi-faceted man intriguing. Sometimes, he was nervous and constrained, but at others, he was bold and jovial. Mostly he reminded her of a bright lily floating on the scum of a stagnant pool. More and more, she ignored the voices in her head, which warned her that humans were deceitful and scheming. However, stories from her childhood about the treachery of man and how her kind had been duped because of their trusting nature returned and repeated in her mind whenever Adam wasn't about.

Poppy went into the kitchen and began placing cutlery in the drawers. In the next moment, she felt the air chill, goosebumps sprung out on her arms, and she inwardly shuddered. *I hope the heating works,* she thought. *I wouldn't be able to make a fire in here.* Shuddering again, she felt Adam's eyes examining her from behind her back.

Poppy twisted around and saw Adam standing in the doorway, holding Kane's music box in his trembling hands. He appeared cold and shaky as though he'd plunged into icy water but from his eyes beamed a burning rage.

"Where did you find this?"

"Kane found it in an antique shop," she said, feeling her hair stand up on the back of her neck.

"Have you looked inside?" he said, staring at Poppy with an attitude of dismay and disbelief.

Poppy shook her head and felt panicked.

"You women are all bitches! Whenever I try and help you, always make it go wrong," he waved his free arm in the air and glared at her with a confused, tortured expression. "I try so hard to be nice."

"I don't know what you mean."

"That cow Judy was meant to throw it all away. I told her hanging onto the past would destroy her; besides, she needed to rent Sandra's room out for the money. I don't want to sleep amongst a dead girl's possessions," he shouted, and his brow wrinkled, revealing an internal misery.

"They don't know for sure that she's dead."

Unnervingly, Adam locked his eyes on Poppy's, "Everyone knows she's dead. You don't get visits from ghosts when someone's still alive," he said scornfully.

Poppy felt her vision fuzz out with tears. She'd thought she had a good knowledge of Adam's personality, but now he was speaking in a way she'd thought impossible. There'd been no indicators to say that he could change so spectacularly.

"All my life, I've tried to please women. Save them from themselves and the carnage which awaits your kind," he said, lifting the lid of the jewellery box.

Poppy intently watched as he lifted out the compartments and dropped them onto the floor. He then tore a picture out from the base, glanced at it and then stuffed it into his coat pocket.

"My little crusaders have much to learn," Adam mumbled, shaking his head. Then, he abruptly turned and threw the music box at the wall. It smashed into pieces, and Poppy listened to the last tinkling sounds as it died.

"I'm going to find Kane," Adam shouted and rushed towards the front door. The door slammed making Poppy jump, and as she looked up, she noticed the first signs of black mould creeping around the frame. Poppy slid down the wall and with her knees pulled up against her chest, and her hands over her eye's she wept. In her head, she saw a beautiful bloom dropping from a flower.

Chapter Twenty-three

The court case had been over in a day, and due to his clean record, Kane had escaped with nothing more than a fine. Poppy had sent him numerous messages from his laptop, pleading with him to return and explaining in detail that she understood his state of mind. Kane ignored these messages, as he knew it would be impossible for her to comprehend his tangled psychology.

Kane reflected on when it all went wrong. He had been emotionally stabbed for years, but the first strike had come with his parent's separation. After this onslaught, he'd struggled back onto his feet only to be attacked again. It was a slow and painful death. His ultimate decline came when he was unable to save his friends and prevent his sister's disappearance.

Day by day, he could feel his soul seeping from his gaping wounds. Now he was destroying his own heart and too ashamed of his actions to return home. Instead, he'd spent a couple of weeks in the cheapest room he could find, enduring savagely sleepless nights and regretting the harm he'd caused Poppy.

Having now run out of money and motivation, Kane wandered down onto the beach where he'd stayed with Poppy in the summer. Above the din of the sea, he heard the shouts and cheers of youths defiantly surfing the large winter rollers. He stood transfixed, watching them catch wave after wave. By the rocks, he saw two boys in a canoe laughing and paddling around the surfers. He worried about them dashing themselves on the rocks to their left while admiring their wild impulsiveness. Kane remembered the mindless fun he'd had in the army when, on a break, they'd jumped off a cliff into the fiercest waves and then goaded each other into going higher. Away from the bullets and blood, the world had been full of promise and wonder. The army had been good for him – it was where he'd learnt to be a man.

That was the old Kane, the one who'd loved life, not the one on a mission to escape reality. Kane walked with his head bowed, staring at the washed-up weeds and searching for something that would take him away from himself. He was actively pushing against the door to the vaults of his mind, trying to squeeze back his painful memories. However hard he tried, he couldn't defend himself against his oppressive imagination. There was nowhere to curl up and hide. *I'm like, my name's sake, I allowed my brothers and friends to die. It should have been me, not them. I was in charge – I should have driven on. I was neglectful, and that makes me a murderer.*

Kane bent down and picked up a small scuttling crab with his good hand. He held the creature between his pincer fingers and noticed how dirty his nails were. With his head bowed, he watched the creature's claws clicking together, searching for revenge. Even the crab seemed to have more fight than the ex-soldier. Carefully, he placed it down and studied how quickly it buried itself in the sand. *That's what I want, sweet oblivion,* he thought and imagined himself stripping off and walking into the sea. It was at that moment he decided very calmly and coolly that it was time for him to walk into the waves and keep going. It didn't matter he was already dead. He'd died that day on the battlefield next to his companions. There was no point stumbling around like a zombie, hurting others; he was nothing, and the sea would be a good place to rest.

Kane turned his mobile phone off and dropped it in his coat pocket. Then he wriggled out of his thick winter coat, with difficulty, pulled his jumper over his head, and awkwardly climbed out of his jeans. A few missing fingers wouldn't hinder his last-ever swim. He walked slowly towards the water, enjoying how the coldness was already numbing his brain.

The wind was blowing seawards. Kane glanced down at the foam on the shoreline and then up to the horizon. His alert, long-sighted eyes suddenly spotted something in the sea directly ahead. It was the red canoe. Freezing and motionless, he stood for some time, his eyes glued to the red spot, which appeared to be getting smaller. In a fragment of sharply focused time, he realised the boys were no longer in the boat. Beside the vessel he could see the paddle sticking up from the water and what might have been an arm. With each second, the boat was drifting further away. An image of himself as a child playing happily by the sea triggered Kane into action. *We had been such a happy family once,* he thought.

He crashed through the breaking waves, and when the water was deep enough, he dived beneath. On rising, he swam through the rage and furore, stretching every sinew and muscle as far as he could. He tried desperately to compensate for the lack of a working left hand, which sent him slightly off balance. After minutes of intense concentration, he looked ahead and was disappointed to see how small the boys still appeared. He'd hoped he would have been aided by the outgoing tide.

Kane was beginning to tire - the power of the sea seemed too great. *I only need to make it one-way,* he thought and summoned every ounce of energy. He didn't look up again, as his mind focussed on surging forwards.

Finally, he heard two voices crying out in unison. "Over here!" Kane stretched out his good hand and grabbed the boat and for the first time, set eyes on the boys. Their blue fingers were, hooked over the side as they desperately hung on. Two boys of about fourteen stared at him with glazed eyes, blue lips, and teeth chattering uncontrollably.

"Don't try and speak. I'm going to lift you both back into the canoe."

Kane took the paddle from the first boy's hand and threw it into the boat. Then, holding on tight with his good hand, he wrapped his other arm around the boy's waist. Each time he tried to lift the boy from the water, their legs were sucked beneath the vessel and dragging them under.

"Let me get my breath back so I can tread water with more strength," he gasped, trying to ignore their expressions of terror.

"Hold the boat with both hands as tight as you can," Kane instructed the smaller boy, trying to curl his stiff lips into a smile.

With both arms free, Kane grabbed the other boy, who was reluctant to let go of the boat and heaved him in.

"Now, your turn," he said, looking at the smaller boy. Let go – I've got you," he said, and with his last ounce of strength, pushed him up, over and into the boat. He landed alongside his friend. "We are drifting further out, so I'm going to need you both to paddle harder than you've ever done before. I will push from behind, but it won't be enough unless you work, too. When one tires, the other can take over; use your hands as well." Kane said, feeling unsure they were going to survive. Would his death wish influence their outcome? Exhausted, Kane pushed the boat and kicked as hard as he could – he was desperate not to fail. "Come on, boys, keep paddling. We are nearly there," he kept lying even when they were still far from shore.

Then, looking up, he saw a boat pushing off from the beach. Kane breathed a sigh of relief as he heard the chug of an engine. Soon it was alongside the red canoe and pulling its occupants aboard. Eventually, strong arms pulled Kane's frozen body from the water.

"Thanks, man! I hope you know what you've done. These boys would have surely been lost to the sea if you'd not jumped in. It was you going into the water, which alerted the surfers that something was wrong. One of them ran for help," the stocky, bearded man smiled at Kane with genuine warmth as he wrapped a silver blanket around his shoulders.

Back on land, Kane felt exhilarated. The life-enhancing sea had lifted his spirits. In some way, his actions cleansed his soul, and looking down at his right hand, he saw his nails were dirt-free. One positive action had taken him from tears and death to elation. Hurriedly, he put on his dry clothes. *I've saved two people,* he thought. *Today two boys live and will have futures because of my actions. I need to return and save a few more. I don't have to be a cruel, heartless bastard.*

"Why don't you join us in the pub after we've got these boys home? I think there might be a few people who would want to thank you for saving two much-loved local lads."

"Thanks, mate, but I have to get the train back to my own home tonight. It's a long journey, and I'm desperate to be with my family. Another time, maybe," Kane smiled broadly and shook the man's hand.

"I understand, but you will always find a welcome here."

"Stay safe, boys," Kane said and walked quickly away. Burying his hands deep in his pockets, he felt his phone and quickly withdrew it, suddenly desperate to read Poppy's messages. *She's been trying to save me,* he thought after reading through the list as he walked speedily towards the train station. *While one person on this planet needs me, then I'm obliged to stay.*

The last two messages he came across were from an unknown caller. He thought, maybe Poppy had finally bought a phone.

Kane, you need to come home. Your mother is very sick in the hospital, and the twins are staying in my new flat. Adam.

Text me when you get back, and we can meet up. I will explain.

Kane was in a state of panic. He wanted to berate himself for turning away from the ones he loved but immediately discarded any nagging thoughts as he desperately wanted to hang on to the clear thinking, the logical man he'd once been and who'd returned.

Chapter Twenty-four

In the darkness, Poppy strolled around the park. Then, with determination, she headed towards the derelict mansion house. For some time, she searched around the perimeter, looking for an entrance. Finally, around the back, out of sight of the main path, she found a breach in the fencing. The main vertical bar had been bent enough for a small person to squeeze through. A large digger was parked close by, and she wondered if the builders had driven into the fencing.

Once past the barrier, entrance to the house was easy, as the doors had been removed. All the innards of the room were torn out, and Poppy cautiously stepped from the harsh elements into the empty shell. Slowly, she walked through the place until she reached the far end of the house. In the final room, she stopped abruptly and, in the darkness, saw the pitch black of a large hole in the concrete.

Poppy was glad of her good night vision. Laying on her belly, she looked over the edge. A thick rope ladder dangled down into the blackness. Happily, she breathed in the smell of rock and earth and felt the depths of peace well up from far below. She smiled to herself, knowing that the world above would have no power over her once she descended into the safety of the labyrinth.

As she climbed down the ladder, she felt as though she was stepping into the pupil of a loved one's eye and becoming united with her world. Once in the cavernous chamber, she gazed fondly at the walls of the timeless home. She was surrounded by familiar paintings and incantations, which kept evil above ground, and symbols that she would use to navigate her way through the passages.

Poppy climbed over some collapsed rocks, which partially blocked her entrance to the tunnels. Then she strolled through the silent veins as they penetrated deeper into the earth. Soon, she smelt the comforting smells of bread and wood smoke and then heard the patter of small feet running. At the end of the passage, she saw moving shadows and flickering light. A pulse of laughter and voices rushed towards her, and all her feelings of emptiness vanished.

Poppy wanted to run forward but instead crept up to a large boulder, which partially blocked the entrance to the oasis of warmth. Peeping out, she saw three women of her kind sitting at a stone table, eating meat and bread. A gas lamp hanging from the ceiling cast a blue light over their serene faces. They were adorned with gold chains, rings, and piercings, and each had a finely fashioned spearhead hanging over their simple dresses. Two children, a boy and a girl, both with long braided hair, ran in circles in front of a fire that roared in the wall on the far side of the room. Poppy noticed how it had a proper chimney, which sucked the smoke up into the sky miles above their heads.

Poppy thought she would never tire of crouching and observing. She looked up at the finely carved, ceiling, elaborate paintings on the walls, the fur-covered beds and all the lovingly made objects on the shelves. Finally, she determined that she needed to make her presence known.

Poppy rose, and every face turned in her direction. She watched their stunned expressions, and then the broad smiles cut across their faces. An older woman with many wrinkles and a large hooked nose stood up and beckoned to Poppy.

"Come in, my child, welcome," she said, opening her arms wide. The other women rose and came forward to greet Poppy. "We've waited a long time for the returners."

Poppy was embraced by the other women as though she was their child and led towards the table. She seated herself opposite the older woman who she was told was called Madeline by a girl of about the same age as herself, called Sahar.

"Help yourself to the rabbit and bread," Sahar said.

"Yes, this is a time to celebrate - Rosa, get the wine," Madeline called over to a round, middle-aged woman who was talking to the little girl who was making faces in a hand mirror while the boy stoked the fire. "We've been waiting and watching a long time. We're in contact with many other networks, but it's hard to all come together at the moment."

"Our supreme leader and most of our male guardians are dead. There are only three matriarchs left, and they are spread out," Rosa said as she crossed the room carrying a bottle of wine and a clean beaker for Poppy.

"We're so blest," Sahar muttered as she sipped the warming fruity liquid. "We only have the two children to care for here, but some covens have to support quite a number often without their, parents."

Poppy ate hungrily and listened intently as the three women chatted on, feeling content to be amongst her kind again. Rosa finished pouring the drinks and took a space on the bench next to Madeline.

"Of course, many are still hiding in the human world, and some may never return. How have you found life with the humans, Poppy?" Madeline asked, directing all her attention to her guest.

"I think they're endeavouring to destroy themselves as well as us," Poppy uttered through a mouth full of bread.

"There's nobody alive now who remembers the previous inquisitions, but we've all heard the stories and understand the warning signs. The spirits are restless and are leaving the stones and seeking justice." Madeline said, looking more sombre.

"I suppose you remained pure and didn't use any powers in front of the humans," Rosa said, leaning forward and grinning at Poppy.

"It was hard to resist, but I know how important it is to assimilate with them as much as possible. Apart from which, their way of life gave me little access to the things I would need to weave spells." Poppy added happy that she'd not weakened and mentioned how she had altered the perceptions of others to obtain food. She had also decided not to inform them of her desire to summon a greater power to help Kane.

Having heard what she wanted to hear, Rosa relaxed and rested her back against the wall.

"We've also endured much since the massacre. We've lived lightly and retreated underground," Sahar said. "It's as though we've had to tip-toe back to a previous existence, which we're no longer truly adapted to."

"How come we've been able to live in both worlds for centuries without being noticed, to now have some enemy hunt us down?" Poppy asked, feeling emboldened by the wine.

"From what we've heard from the ancestors, this isn't a new enemy, it's the old one returned, and it will take all our united powers to lock them away again. Otherwise, they will seek us out one by one until our kind, are annihilated," Madeline said, in a lowered voice, so as not to upset the children.

"Humans would call it genocide," Sahar added.

"Our numbers might be small, but we have abilities which they don't possess," Madeline leaned in, and the other women echoed her body language. "There are plans to come together, to congregate at the great stones and summon the powers," she whispered as though the enemy were listening. "The matriarchs are investigating the enemy, trying to find the whereabouts of the murderers. It must be a targeted attack, which won't draw attention."

The little boy sidled up to Rosa, who lifted him onto her lap. He sat half nestling into the woman and half regarding Poppy shyly.

"Don't be shy Tiger, she's part of the family," Rosa whispered in his ear. The boy smiled and wiggled.

"Were you born at the end of the rainbow?" He asked Poppy.

Poppy smiled back, "of course, all children are."

Tiger seemed satisfied with the stranger's answer, and he nestled back into Rosa and yawned.

"Well, it's time you children curled up for the night," Rosa said, lifting the boy up and walking over to the sleeping area.

Madeline leaned forward and clasped Poppy's hand, "I need to show you something. Please come with me," she said in a serious tone.

Poppy slid off her bench and followed Madeline back into the dark tunnel. "I was there at the massacre," she whispered once out of earshot of the children. "It wasn't suicide this time. I think it was murder. I was on the edge of the field and could see people writhing in agony, and standing watching was a stranger. He turned and glanced in my direction. He had silver hair with blonde streaks. He threw a half-smoked cigarette to the ground, and as he stamped it with his foot, a cross dropped out from beneath his clothing. I didn't hear any rituals or sacred words said - nothing which would offer the spirits' protection."

"How did you escape?" Poppy said as her eyes re-adjusted to darkness.

"I was on the edge of the fields, on my way home, and when I saw the human, I turned and ran. I hid during the day and travelled at night. I came here because this satellite community had been my home as a child, long before the Hub was built. Most of us returned to our original homes. When I arrived, I was shocked to find the house derelict; our human protector heirs must have died a long time ago."

Poppy noticed that they kept turning right and realised where they were going. "Why are we visiting the ancestors?"

"You will see."

Together they entered a smaller chamber. Even in the darkness, Poppy could make out the shapes of the tombs lining the walls, each with a little green light to indicate they were active.

Madeline took a lamp from a shelf, lit it and held it up.

"We knew builders were coming to knock down the mansion, but before they moved in, we were venturing out more to buy food and resources. Once on our return, we found this..." Madeline held the lantern over a tomb. "Do you know who it is? We cleaned her up and did the best we could. Her spirit remains restless."

Poppy looked up into the woman's wrinkled face and her watery eyes and slowly shook her head. "I don't recognise her, but I know a young human went missing. Why didn't you leave her for them to find?"

"It was obvious she'd been murdered in a manner which historically is meant for our kind. When you're living in exile, you can't have police or investigators snooping around. Besides, can't you see she looks so much like ourselves?"

Poppy looked down at the fixed swollen face, the protruding tongue and the ligature marks around the neck and thought of Kane. At that moment, Poppy knew her new friends would find her gone in the morning.

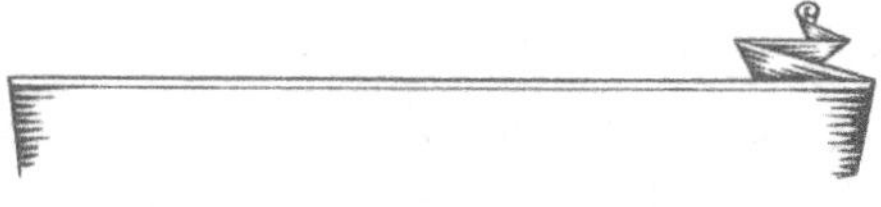

Chapter Twenty-five

Adam was standing at the kitchen sink, staring out of the window. His head hurt, and he was feeling sick. Icy water gushed from the tap into the pint glass. He glanced up at the sky; it was a heavy green and grey, and he felt the uneasy atmosphere of an approaching storm. As he turned the tap off, he heard the first rumble of thunder and saw a bright fork flash from the darkness. The storm mirrored his feelings of foreboding. He drank from the glass while watching a tree bend in the wind and listening to the roar of an invisible approaching train. Then he looked at the watch his grandmother had given him on his fourteenth birthday. *Seven o'clock, the twins should be fast asleep,* he thought.

Feeling flushed from the wine and a little wobbly, he walked towards the living room door. Adam glanced at his books and papers scattered over the floor from his continuing research into historical witch hunts and the empty bottles of wine. Automatically, he reached up and pressed the light switch – the room remained shrouded in darkness. He tried another switch, but that, too, failed. Immediately, an image of his childhood home on the bleak moor flashed into his head, and tangible shadows of dread flooded his entire being.

Adam hurried back to the kitchen sink and began rummaging in the drawer for some candles. All he found were two black sticks, which Judy had given him, the remains of a Halloween party. Thunder crashed overhead, and he worried about the twins waking. Tears coursed down his cheeks.

Adam knew he could no longer take pride in his proteges. He'd known from the start their Asperger's made reading emotions and people difficult, but their attitude towards others had grown colder and darker. Their specialist subjects had widened from Star Wars and trains to violent computer games and murder. Could he control two defective souls with a passion for shedding blood?

I told them our role was to find the witches and bring them before the courts, he considered as he stared into the flame of a lit candle. He recalled the night he'd followed the twins and their sister Sandra to the woods situated behind the house in the park. As Adam ran after them, darting between the trees, he saw Joe stop and stare directly at him, and grinning maliciously, he dropped the rope over the restrained Sandra's head. Before Adam could intervene, Joe and Jim had jumped on the rope as though it was a swing. Sandra struggled as the twins bounced and pulled at the other end of the rope. By the time Adam arrived at the scene, Sandra was limp and swaying like a pendulum. Then he'd seen the flash of the knives as Joe goaded the more reticent Jim into slashing Sandra's body. Lately, the sight of blood had caused Adam to feel faint, and he was squeamish, so he'd turned away. Afterwards, the twin's childish faces almost appeared innocent. Adam saw Jim had tears in his eyes, while Joe, although his mouth was sullen, his eyes were still bright with the thrill of his kill.

Adam's mind had raced all over the place. He'd been full of self-loathing for allowing such a thing to happen. Engulfed by his dark memories, all he could think about was how to cover up the frenzied attack. He scarcely breathed and remained silent as he cut the girl down and dragged her body into the derelict house. The twins followed after.

Inside the building, he'd discovered a ladder, which went down to a chamber and the perfect place to hide a body. Feeling repulsed, he'd struggled into the depths with the girl flung over his shoulder and laying her in the shadows; Adam stood up and, turning around, saw the twins standing with the knives still in their hands. Jim was biting his lower lip to control his bubbling fear - he never wanted to do anything which would displease his brother. Joe was unmoved, and the smirk had returned to his lips.

In Joe's other hand was a camera, which he held out to Adam. "Can you take a picture of us with the witch?"

Adam stood staring, stunned, aware of the expression of shocked horror in his eyes, "Joe, you can't do that. You've just killed the girl," he'd searched Joe's face, looking for some sign that showed he understood the significance of his actions, but the mask was rigid and fixed. "Joe, she's your sister," he'd pleaded.

"But Adam, I take pictures of everything. I've decided I'm going to be a photographer."

Adam looked into the stony eyes, still bright with excited ecstasy. He knew if he didn't bend to Joe's will, he would have one of his full-on rages and with a knife in his left hand, it would probably be best to appease the child.

As Adam took the camera from the boy, he told himself he was only following through with the macabre idea so as not to draw attention from Joe's inevitable screaming fit but deep down he knew it was because he was scared for his safety.

Hailstones hit the window, arousing a sense of urgency within Adam. He stuck the lit candles on two small plates and placed one on the table. Taking the other, he left the kitchen and walked down the hallway towards the boy's room. *I must send them to sleep. Place a pillow over their heads and put an end to all this. It's the devil dancing around them, not God.*

Was Mathew the man sitting in the audience at the theatre with Dylan, his lover? Were they real, or was it his sickness returning? Adam thought as he placed his hand on the door to the twin's room and slowly pushed it open. *Was it all imagined?*

Adam approached the bed where the twins were soundly sleeping side by side, squashed together for comfort. Carefully, he placed the candle on the bedside unit and, in the flickering light, saw Joe lying on his back with his mouth open like a bird waiting for his mother to drop in a worm. A little smile played on Jim's lips as though he had a sweet dream. The dualism of joy and pain pierced Adam's heart, and he thought of them playing their guitars and singing his favourite song. *Their voices are angelic beyond anything I've heard, and their visionary powers are strong. Perhaps it's me, the teacher, who's at fault. They should be destined for great things. Maybe I should increase my efforts and help re-direct them,* Adam thought as he went over to the empty bed to retrieve a pillow, unsure if he should place it over their faces.

Homicidal personalities always find a calling, like in Hitler's Germany, Adam considered gripping the pillow tightly. *I could be saving lives by doing this.* He looked down at the pale faces and white hair and raised the pillow above his head. He was poised, waiting for the perfect moment. *All beliefs, whether in god or the devil, are a trap. Mathew is an illusion, a sick fantasy, which helped me explain events in my childhood when I was vulnerable. I'm a good person, and good people don't turn away when a crime has been committed. Best to kill the twins - start afresh and find someone else to pass on his musical talents.*

Adam gasped as the legs of a cockroach appeared over the edge of the duvet. It emerged onto the cover and scuttled towards Jim's face. In an instant, Adam dropped the pillow and flicked the creature to the floor. Continually shivering with disgust, he lifted his foot and stomped hard onto the shiny back. He felt and heard the crunch and turned back, hoping he wouldn't see any more creatures.

With trepidation, his skin still crawling, he lifted the cover to reassure himself that there wasn't a plague of insects. Adrenaline shot up through the centre of his chest as his eyes rested on the Mathew doll, stuffed between the twin's bodies. In horror, he retrieved the sometimes loved and other times hated object. Guiltily he held the doll in his trembling hands.

"So, we can't trust you, Adam," he hissed in his gravely voice. Mathew's lids flicked open, and his eyes glowed maliciously in the half-light. "You were planning to extinguish the Lord's light on Earth.

Adam stared intently at the demented face anxious to convey his deep hatred for the malignant object, which haunted his mind.

"You're not real. You're a figment of my imagination, and if I deny you, then you'll die," he said bravely.

"So, you're saying your heavenly talent isn't a blessing from God," Adam saw the doll's eyes were laughing, mocking. "That the twins aren't equally gifted even though they possess the voices of angels. Furthermore, you weren't chosen, through the ages to protect the Lord's sons and daughters from those who wish to trespass on his territory. Is it all an illusion?"

Adam flopped onto the bed and placed the doll on Jim's chest, hoping it would return to its frozen state. Instead, its head squeaked to one side and stared at Adam.

"It's you who are in denial of the truth."

In disquieting despair, Adam clasped his head between his hands, leaned forward and squeezed his eyes shut.

"You're driving me crazy!" he screamed. "Can't you leave me alone?"

"When you've completed your task Adam, only then will you have peace."

Suddenly, the sky cracked open, and the room filled with blue and white light.

"Adam! Adam! We're scared," the twins screamed in unison.

Adam turned to see the twins sitting upright in bed. Two distressed little boys who needed comforting. Joe clung to the now lifeless doll, and Jim held his arms up for a hug. Adam embraced him and held him tight for many minutes as thunder crashed above their heads and hail struck the window.

"Don't be frightened. It's only a storm," he said as he finally felt able to tuck them back under the covers.

"Please don't go until the storms gone and we're asleep," Joe said.

Adam remained perched on the bed, but once the twins had shut their eyes, he turned away and sobbed.

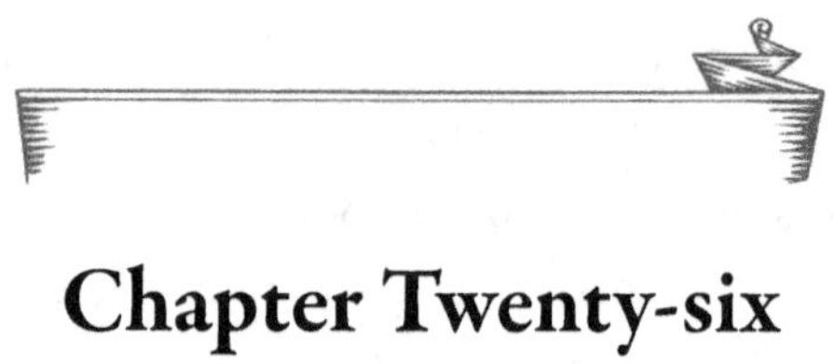

Chapter Twenty-six

It was a moonless night, and the snow had melted leaving pools, which shone under the park lights. A biting breeze forced Kane to pull his coat tight around his body as he sauntered along the wet, gritty pavement. His eyes locked on the ground, he brooded and wondered why he'd agreed to meet Adam in the park in the dark – was it safe? He'd also asked this man he hardly knew to bring his brothers along. *Does he know of their crime?* Kane considered.

Kane stopped in front of the familiar façade of the derelict house and waited. He glanced at his watch; *they're late. Will they even turn up*, he thought, staring at the ground and pacing. The silence was intense; he felt apprehensive, and the soldier in him sensed he was walking into a trap. He dismissed his concerns, knowing that it was important to resolve the problem of the twins before his mother left the hospital and before Poppy discovered the truth from another source. Suddenly, in a pool of light, he saw three shadows, two small and one stretching back along the path.

Kane looked up, saw three sets of eyes staring at him and felt a sense of dread looking at his once innocent twin brothers. They had always appeared outwardly strange, especially Joe. Their blank faces were too clean, their bright, glassy eyes seeing everything but emotions. Kane had no doubt they'd played a large part in his sister's murder, and he wanted to know why. He turned his attention to Adam and looked directly into his eyes.

"Do you know what they've done?" Kane's mouth had gone dry. He licked his lips and gulped the air to calm his fiercely beating heart. "Did you know they've most probably murdered their sister?

Adam shrugged his shoulders and remained silent and expressionless.

Kane could no longer contain the rivers of rage which burst through his body and out of his mouth. "You're savages!" Kane turned to face the twins, who remained unmoved. "How the hell can I be related to people so evil as to take their own sister's life," he said, waving his arms in their direction. "How can you live with yourselves? You're both fucked in the head, and this shit needs to end tonight, now!" he screamed and thought his head would burst if he didn't breathe. "Why? Tell me why?"

"Mathew told us to do it," Joe said in a matter-of-fact way. "He said she's a witch."

"Who the fuck is this Mathew I keep hearing about?" Kane screamed as he remembered the events in the cutting room of the factory and felt once again unreality and reality crash together.

"The doll, he speaks to us," Joe replied coolly.

"Oh, my god!" Kane ran his hands over his shaved head in exasperation. "Jim, do you have nothing to say?"

Jim remained silent but looked to the ground and began to stamp his feet with frustration.

"Pure evil," Kane muttered, shaking his head. He remembered how innocent they both looked when asleep. Kane felt Adam attentively watching every detail of the proceedings and turned to him for support.

"We will have to take them to the police tonight. I've sat on this for too long, and it will be the best thing for everyone."

"Don't you want to see your sister first?" Adam said calmly.

Adam felt disgusted and dumbfounded by Adam's suggestion. He hadn't thought further than getting the twins locked safely away.

"It's for the police to examine any evidence," he said, feeling choked up and aware of his eyes growing hot. *Poppy and his mother were all he had left at the heart of his world,* he thought and suddenly felt a burning desire for a drink.

"Why have you got water in your eye's Kane?" Joe asked.

"Because human beings get sad when bad things happen," he automatically replied.

"You can't know your sister's dead unless you see a body. You might be just making a fool of yourself," Adam said, nonchalantly pushing his floppy hair from his eyes. "I know nothing of the murder that you talk about, but I have done some of my investigations. Sandra had a new boyfriend, I traced him, and he said she'd not enjoyed the hen party and had arranged to meet him in the park. Apparently, she never turned up. We've searched everywhere except the old house."

"I saw a picture of her dead," Kane said, feeling confused.

"Is that it? That could've been the leftover from Halloween," Adam said in a light tone.

"Why did Joe say Mathew told them to do it?"

"Sweet as your brother's look, you must admit they're not all there," Adam stepped forward and placed his hand on Kane's arm. "I do understand a little of what you're going through – I've had losses in my own family. Judy has been a good friend to me, and I've watched her struggle with the distress of her loss. Let's look together, and maybe we can find Sandra before your mother is well enough to leave the hospital. I have a torch."

Adam twisted around and began walking towards the house. The twins ran off, bouncing happily behind Adam. Driven by hope, a desire to discover that he'd been wrong and the need to return to normality, Kane felt compelled to follow the others.

Together they searched the shell of the house. Finally, they came to a room where part of the floor had caved in and left a hole. Out of curiosity, Kane followed the group down a rope ladder but standing at the bottom in the grim damp cave, he began to feel like a captive and hunted his brain for an excuse to leave.

"Sorry but I'm desperate for a leak," he said beginning to climb back up the ladder.

"She could be hurt and need our help. Perhaps she fell from the ladder and is hiding, injured, in the tunnel. Go in the shadows. We won't look," Adam laughed falsely.

"No, I'm okay. I'm not great in these types of places," Kane said, feeling the hairs rise on the back of his neck as he rapidly ascended. "I'll wait up top."

Feeling a sense of relief at having escaped the building, Kane rushed towards the bushes, aware that he did need to relieve himself. Just as he was about to walk away and rush to the police station to inform them of his fears, he heard the faint sound of the twins humming a beautiful tune. Separate voices combining to make irresistible music. Kane continued to listen to the enchanting sound as he stepped back into a pool of light. Suddenly, the music stopped, and for a split-second, Kane instinctively knew he was standing on a precipice and about to be pushed.

Kane felt a hard thump beneath his left shoulder blade. He tried to swing around and face his assailants, but as he did so, he collapsed and fell to the ground. Through the haze of his tears, he saw Joe and Jim standing over him. He held out his arm and pleaded for help. Joe had grinned back, and in a beam of light, he saw the glint of a knife raised, ready to plunge down.

After that, Kane lay in the darkness, thinking that death had not been as painful and frightening as he'd imagined. Then he saw the light and realised he was standing on the threshold. Kane looked over to the other side and felt a burning urge to step forward and explore this new world. He heard Poppy's voice pleading with him not to venture into another time and place. Kane faltered, and the door shut. For him, there was no oblivion or glittering heaven, only the umbilical cord of love keeping him tethered in limbo. He was now connected and disconnected, a guardian, watching over his eternal love, helpless to intervene.

Chapter Twenty-seven

Kane gazed into the mirror of life. Behind the reflection of Poppy's love, he could hear the noises of the living and felt the buzz of them multiplying. There was not enough space for everyone, and certainly not for a wounded soldier.

Kane had not been ready to die and hear the true name of God or look into his face. He couldn't believe his brothers were willing to kill him and hung onto hope that they would change their minds and help him up until the end came. It wasn't his time; he hadn't collected enough good memories with Poppy and had not had the chance to declare his love. His feelings hadn't died, as he could still feel the deep contentment of being locked in her embrace after climbing the hill to the stone monument. For some reason, she was tugging at his heart, begging him to return. *Would she love another in his absence? If she did, and he hoped she would because then he could stop guarding her, would this person be safe and love her perfectly?*

Perched in an indeterminate state, all Kane could see or feel was Poppy. He watched her struggle to get the plaster cast through the sleeve of one of his old jumpers, which was like a dress on her small frame. He'd been horrified seeing her for days trying to survive in Judy's house, the internal flesh of which now resembled rotting fruit. It was clear that she wouldn't be able to stay much longer as all the tinned food had been eaten, the water looked yellow, and the electricity would run out if she didn't have any money for the metre.

As Poppy, once again, searched for evidence of his whereabouts on his computer and amongst his possessions, he suffered her anxiety, which poisoned every second of her day. She was becoming frantic, more desperate and kept trying to communicate with him some important information, which was beyond his realm of understanding. When she performed her rituals, her incantations boomed in his soul, and he felt as though she was inhaling his spirit. Just as he felt he was being sucked back into his body, the house phone rang. Kane followed Poppy as she hurried from the twin's room and ran down the stairs to answer the calling.

"Hello! Who is it?"

"It's Adam, I wanted to apologise, and for us to remain friends. We want the same things for Kane's safe return and for Judy to recover. I'm currently looking after the twins, but they need to be with their family."

"How did you know I would be here?"

"I bumped into Kane's father, Brian. He told me that his ex-wife's old neighbour had said a strange girl was seen in one of the abandoned houses. Apparently, the council have decided to demolish the whole row and start again. Something was said about the mould and concrete cancer, causing the properties to crumble. You'd better leave quickly. By the way, if you want to return to the flat I got for you both at any time, I promise I will leave you in peace. I truly was only trying to help."

"I was hurt. I never thought you had a temper."

"I'm only human, you know. I don't normally get upset, but that music box belonged to Sandra, and it reminded me that she was still missing."

"I know where she is. That's why I'm even more desperate to find Kane."

Light years away, Kane felt a pang of despair. Subtle manipulation was outside Poppy's orbit of understanding, and he knew she was blindly drifting into the net of Adam's lies. In the vast gap between heaven and earth, he realised he could see the situation more clearly, but once again, he was unable to save another life. Adam was carefully wiggling out the keystone of their love so that they would both collapse into powerless oblivion.

"You do? Tell me, and we can sort all this mess out once and for all."

"I can't not until I've found Kane. He needs to know first."

"Well, that's the other reason I phoned. He's not well, but I know where he is, and he's not far away. He returned but is hiding out until he can get himself straight."

"What do you mean?"

"He's been hitting the bottle hard and wants to sober up before he sees you," Adam said.

"Well, I'm glad you told me because I know I can help him, and I have much I need to say."

"That's what I thought. He needs to be supported by those who care."

"Where is he - I will go to him straight away?"

"Look, I have to go. I need to sort the twins out, but meet me at the factory at ten, and I will take you to him."

Kane followed Poppy as she walked over the bridge towards the factory. She hurried along through the mingling drizzle and yellow smog looking so tiny and exposed in the looming industrial landscape, which expanded in all directions. Kane heard the rumbling of a distant train and wished Poppy was on it heading for safety.

From within the veil of gloom, Kane heard the sound of rhythmic footsteps. Slowly a figure emerged and became solid as he crept up behind Poppy like a thief. Poppy glanced over her shoulder and, seeing it was Adam, turned around. She smiled at the smartly dressed man who gently pulled her under his umbrella. Helplessly, Kane watched the inevitability of Poppy succumbing to Adam's charm, a man who could be both kind, ruthless and scheming all at the same time.

The couple had a hushed conversation then in an animated, bouncy manner crossed the bridge, down the road and turned left passed the chemical factory and hurried around to the courtyard at the back of the clothing factory.

Poppy pulled at the door and then looked up at Adam. "It's locked!" she said, looking confused.

"Yes, I know. They had to shut it down because of health and safety. The mould has spread. That's another reason why we need to get Kane out of here because they are going to come in and do a deep clean. The owners are losing money each day it's closed."

"How will we get in?"

"Kane broke in, but I have a key."

Adam opened the door and went inside. For a moment, Poppy hesitated, but smiling sympathetically, Adam entreated her to follow. Kane next saw them standing in front of the storage cupboard, and Adam was unlocking the door.

"Kane, are you here?" Poppy cried out.

Adam grabbed her arm and pulled her close, pushed Poppy into the dark room and slammed the door.

From within the thick darkness, Poppy screamed. "Let me out! You traitor!" She wiggled the door handle, kicked and thumped the door.

"Calm down, listen, and I will explain," Adam said in an almost shy, nervous voice. "I didn't want to do this. I'm just a musician, but I have an allegiance to a higher power," he said apologetically. If you tell me where the others are, we could probably come to some arrangement."

"What others?" Poppy shrieked in a fierce voice.

"You know what I'm talking about, the witches."

There was silence behind the door, as though Poppy was resigning herself to her fate.

"This is harder for me than you can imagine. I serve my masters with a heavy heart," he said in a regretful tone as he pocketed the keys.

"Think about what I said; you don't want to be standing before a court if you can avoid it."

Kane heard one set of footsteps, a door slam, and everything went dark and silent.

Chapter Twenty-eight

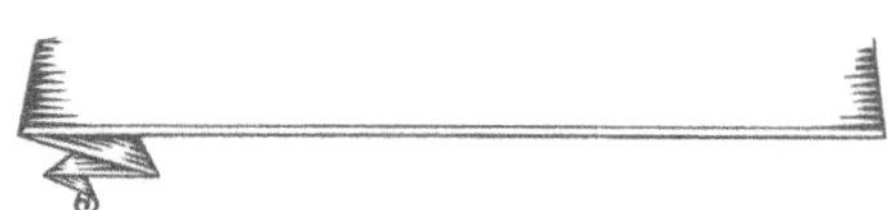

"So, exactly why have you dragged me away from my weekend to spend a night in the cold?" Allen asked as he rubbed his eyes and yawned. "I don't feel like this much. Can't we head to the nearest pub and do this during the day? I will pay for bed and breakfast."

"There's too much activity during the day, and the builders might be doing overtime," Oliver replied feeling tempted to change his mind and realising it wouldn't take much to send him rushing to more comfortable surrounds. "They will probably fill in the hole soon. In fact, they might have already done so."

"What hole?" Allen said.

"You know the hole, which leads to the cave," Oliver said while feeling surprised that the fence around the back of the house moved easily. "I think someone has been here before us," he said, pulling it back like a door.

"Our careers will be ruined if we're caught trespassing," Allen moaned as he flashed his light onto the husk of the house. An owl screeching broke the silence as they crossed the threshold into the colder air of the abandoned home.

"This was once an amazing place," Oliver said as his torch scanned the bare walls. "It's quite sad, really. It has greatly changed since I was here with Professor Roehampton. They've removed all the main features, the fireplaces and decorative plasterwork."

"Probably sold them for scrap or to a dealer to renovate," Allen said, dancing on the spot to keep warm. "Come on, what do you have to show me; it's freezing."

"It's down here. There was a tunnel leading off the main cave. I can't remember if it was accessible. I just wanted to take a look to see if there were any signs of current habitation."

"So, you still think these ancient peoples still exist?" Allen said reluctantly, following Oliver through the rooms.

"Don't you?" Oliver said, turning to face his friend. Allen shrugged, but Oliver knew he agreed.

Gingerly, Oliver descended the rope ladder and waited at the bottom for Allen, who scurried down like a monkey.

"It's as silent as the dead down here," Allen said as his eyes furtively scanned his surroundings.

Oliver rushed over to the far wall and flashed his light on the hand. "Come here, and look, it's all the same as the cave in Wales."

Allan quickly arrived at Oliver's side, and together, they scrutinised the hand, pictograms, and symbols. Oliver reached out with his hand and placed it over the image. He felt the strange sensation of vibrations rippling through the ancient membrane. Stunned, he jumped back. His palm was covered in slime, which he wiped on his jeans. He glanced at the floor and saw fungi blooming in the cracks at the base.

"This place has greatly changed," he muttered. "It seems to be decaying." Just as he was speaking, he saw Allen fall forward and bang his head hard against the wall, as though pushed by invisible hands.

"What the fuck!" Allen shouted, holding his head.

Oliver shone his torch on his friend's face, which was crumpled in agony. Blood trickled between Allen's fingers. Oliver pulled a tissue from the pocket of his hiking coat and handed it to Allen.

"What happened?" Oliver inquired.

"I was pushed in the back."

"There's nobody here but us," Oliver said, aware of an insidious creepiness that he hadn't felt when he was last here with the professor.

Oliver put his finger to his lips and stood listening intently. "Can you hear it?" he mouthed. "I think I can hear whispering." A cold chill ran down Oliver's spine.

"I think we should go. Someone or something doesn't want us here," Allen said, holding the tissue on his wound. "Besides, we might bump into our old friends, the bats."

"They would have left by now. I will look at the tunnel, and then we'll leave," Oliver said in an endeavour to ease Allen's mind. Together they approached the tunnel. Oliver felt his stomach twist and his skin growing clammy beneath his clothes as he crouched on top of the rocky heap and peered through a body-sized gap into the dense darkness beyond.

"You've looked - now let's go to the pub. We could still get a couple in before closing time," Allen said, looking at his florescent watch face. "I'm not clambering over that pile of rocks."

"I can't see anything the lights not penetrating the darkness. It will only take a minute with both torches. I thought it was me who was supposed to be the coward," Oliver said, noticing that his fears seemed to have lost their paralysing edge since their trip to Wales. In addition to this, he felt determined and resolute - nothing was going to stand in his way of making a name for himself. If these people existed, he knew how to get others involved on the internet while remaining anonymous until it was safe to reveal his identity. He reached up and pulled Allen down.

"I can hear rustling. There's something in the rocks. It's rats!" Allen shouted, pushing past Oliver and scrambling further into the tunnel. Oliver inwardly shuddered and hastily followed. Then they felt the ground shudder and heard rocks crashing down behind them, but neither mentioned what they most feared. Their eyes burning through the black could see the cave as it opened and there was enough room above their heads to stand. Semi-blind, they stumbled along until they saw a distant light.

"I think we're probably being watched and that our smallest movements can be heard," Oliver said in a hushed voice. "We'd better go as silently as possible."

"I think we should go back," Allen said but continued to walk, knowing there was possibly no way of returning.

They knelt behind a boulder, looked into a sizable, well-lit room and saw three people who turned and stared in their direction. The figures darkened, melted into an outline and disappeared. Warily they entered the space to the sound of children whispering, but there was nobody to be seen.

"Reveal yourselves!" Allen commanded. "We're not your enemy. We're here to help."

"Whatever the entity is I don't think they want to be seen," Oliver muttered. "We should look for something to move the rocks and leave them in peace."

Oliver's eyes alighted on a wicker bowl, placed on the table, which sparkled in the light. "Allen quick come over here," he said. "Look diamonds."

"We can't take them if that's what you're thinking."

"Just a few, to help pay for further research."

"No, Oliver! We're not thieves. I think you're getting carried away with the weirdness of it all – stay focused. This would be more useful," he said, holding up a long-handled shovel.

Out of curiosity, Allen walked over to where Oliver was stuffing his pockets with diamonds. He picked up a gem and held it to the light, which hung from the ceiling.

"Wow! It's so sparkly and perfectly cut," Allen mused. "Ouch!"

"Get out! Thieves! Trespassers!" Invisible voices screamed with venom as unseen hands hurled rocks at Allen and Oliver. They raised their hands to their heads to fend off the attack but to no avail. Oliver felt his head and words spinning as he fell, landing on top of Allen. The weight of the rocks pushed down on them and buried them in darkness.

After an indeterminate time, Oliver opened his dust-sore eyes and, within his blurred vision, saw a fuzzed-out, haggard face. When his sight was restored, he saw three women standing over him with faces covered in ash. He stretched his stiff leg and realised that he'd been propped against a wall with his hands tied behind his back. Next to him, he saw Allen, looking stricken.

"Are you okay?" Allen inquired in a small voice

"Yes, I seem to be fine, and there's no marks on your face other than the one cut where you banged your head," he whispered, not wanting to look up at the crazy-faced woman.

"Why are you here?" the old woman asked her captives in a stern voice. "Entering a home unannounced is a crime to us and punishable by death."

"I can explain," Oliver stuttered with trepidation. "I'm an archaeologist, and my friend is a geneticist. I have studied the history of the house and the philanthropist merchant who built it and then left it to his nephew. I believe they were guardians of your people," Oliver said, turning to Allen for backup. Allen was staring into the void, his eyes glazed and bemused. "We know much about your people, and we want to help. There are those hunting you down who want your extinction. We can get you help and the right kind of support amongst the humans," he said, his mind frantic with all kinds of notions about the horrible death he might have to endure. He wondered if this species, which shouldn't exist, was friend or foe. Then, in his periphery vision, he saw movement and, turning, saw two children duck under thick furs.

The women looked at each other and began consulting in a whispered foreign tongue. After many minutes of fierce discussion, the old woman bent down, leant over Oliver and, with a sharp knife, severed his bindings. Then, she repeated the process with Allen.

Oliver forced himself to make eye contact with the woman but felt too insignificant against her confidence to smile. Then he remembered the diamonds in his pocket and wondered if she could read his thoughts. He felt his face flush with shame.

The woman smiled, "my name is Madeline. Please, you can stand."

Oliver stood up and checked his body for injuries. "How come, after such an onslaught, I'm not damaged?" he bravely asked as they followed the women over to the table, where he noticed the basket of diamonds had disappeared.

"There's much power underground," the woman smirked as she gestured to them to sit. "We don't shapeshift as people once believed. We alter your perceptions. We have been with you since you entered the cave, often right in front of you. It's like a reverse mirage – you think we're not there, but we are," she laughed and poured them a drink while the other two women remained silent and vigilant.

"Well, you had us fooled," Allen said nervously, looking around for the unexpected.

"Yes, I can see you're the joker and reckless one," the woman said, looking directly at Allen. "You are the one we must take seriously," she added, directing her attention back to Oliver. "If a dog walked by you in the street, you wouldn't know if it was one of us who'd altered your perception or a real dog."

"How come you're in danger then, can't you just disappear from people's minds," Allen continued as though he was unable to tune into the seriousness of the situation until he felt Oliver's boot on his leg.

"Our power lies here within the earth and together. Above ground and on our own we're much more vulnerable."

Oliver blinked, trying to release his eye from a sudden nervous twitch. Gathering all his courage, he asked, "So, what's to become of us?" He was aware of his hand shaking as he put the beaker to his lips, wondering if he was about to drink poisoned wine. "The tunnels are blocked, so it would be hard to leave."

"No, no it isn't, but we do need to be able to trust some humans, and indeed we have before. We need more information. Proof that what you're telling us is genuine."

Oliver took a deep breath and timidly explained about his meeting with Professor Roehampton and their trip to Wales. Allen, while continuously scanning his environment, added hurriedly the information he had gained from his genetic experiments.

"I found this!" Oliver spluttered, seeing a look of doubt in Madeline's eyes. He reached beneath his coat pulled out his flint and pulling the gold chain over his head handed it to the woman. Oliver watched as Madeline held it in her warty hands and examined the object closely.

"Quite the thief," Madeline muttered under her breath. Oliver, in case she saw his face blushing, bent his head. Then the women leaned over the table, so their heads were almost touching and had another secret conversation.

Realising that the liquid was not tainted and to ease his dry throat, Oliver gulped the rest down. "I believe I can reach a community of people who could provide you with secure homes and freedom. I'm not great at computer games anymore, but I know how to hack and find secret routes through the net."

In unison, the women raised their heads and looked at Oliver.

"Come with me," Madeline said, taking a lamp from a small alcove.

Oliver and Allen followed Madeline through an opening, which took them directly into another chamber. Madeline went and placed a log on the fire. Oliver felt a sense of relief as the popping of the wood interrupted the silence. Then she moved over to a bed and held up the light.

"Don't worry, he can't hurt you," she said.

Allen and Oliver approached. A once sturdy human lay on a bed. He was rigid, his face drained of blood, and his lips were blue. Around his torso was tightly wound bandages. The two men looked at each other with mutual expressions of horror. Oliver had only ever seen the ancient dead, and the waxy face and the noxious smell combined made him feel nauseous.

"We have done all we can for him," Madeline whispered. "We found him above covered in blood and with multiple stab wounds. It took all three of us to drag him down here."

"Why didn't you leave him and call an ambulance?" Allen asked, finally being shaken back into the moment.

"When we found him, he was hanging onto a single fibre of life, and in his confusion, he called out for Poppy. We believe Poppy is one of us, as a girl of that name was here a few nights ago and left in a hurry. We rationalised that she was probably looking for this man. He muttered other things, some of which were undecipherable but some which made sense. Apart from all that, we're healers and obliged to show compassion to the sick and wounded. He would have died by the time an ambulance had arrived.

"He looks pretty dead to me," Allen said under his breath.

"His wounds are all clean, and there're fresh maggots under the bandages to eat any dead flesh. He's locked in a gap between the light and dark – not wanted by death or life. He needs something to release his spirit to call him back."

There was an uneasy silence while they all looked down at the frozen body. The fire roared up, bathing the chamber in an orange glow.

"So, what do you want us to do?" Oliver said reluctantly.

"He needs to get to the hospital or a place of safety. It's clear that the enemy is very close to us."

"We won't be able to move him. He's a big man – a lead weight," Allen said.

Madeline looked into Oliver's eyes as though she knew he understood their plight.

"You will all have to help," Oliver said. "Perhaps we need to fashion some kind of stretcher."

"We can do that and once above ground you could phone an ambulance," Madeline said, smiling. "There's something about this man, which tells me he's important," she said taking Kane's limp hand in hers and stroking. She placed it back on the bed and searched amongst the folds of her dress. She pulled out the flint spearhead and handed it back to Oliver. "Perhaps one day you will trace the owner."

Oliver stuffed the object into his pocket where he imagined it on top of a cluster of diamonds. Before he withdrew his fingers, he was aware that he wasn't feeling the expected hard sharpness. Instead, he felt the crispness of folded paper. He abruptly pulled his hand from his pocket and looked at Madeline quizzically.

"That's some codes - kind of treasure," Madeline said, smiling broadly. "Put them into your computer. You will be able to contact us and others of our kind."

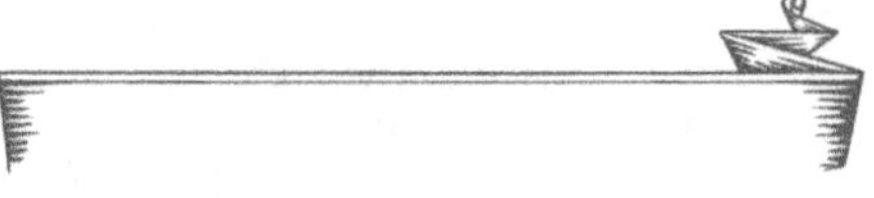

Chapter Twenty-nine

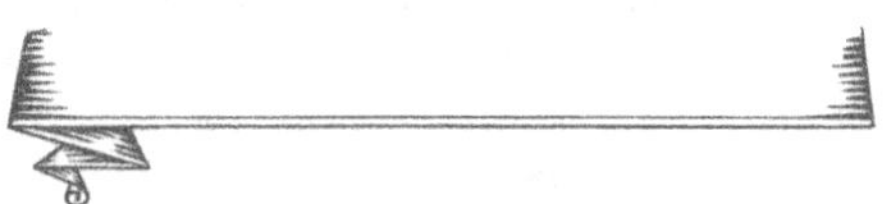

Poppy, blinded by a black hood and supported by the hands of strangers, shuffled forwards. The chained metal clamps around her ankles were heavy and painfully rubbing her skin raw. She was also aware of her stomach grumbling with hunger and her arm itching under the plaster cast as though the rest of her body was unaware of the urgency of her plight.

"Wait here!" a stern voice ordered.

Poppy stood frozen, shivering with all her senses alive. In the distance, she heard bells chime and approaching footsteps. All around her, people were whispering in conspiratorial tones and excluding her from their conversations. She felt every moment of anguish as time crept unbearably. Finally, someone nudged her arm, and she was jolted back to life.

"Move!"

Taking careful small steps, Poppy shifted a few paces, and then stumbled down some steps but was saved from landing on the hard floor by her guards. Poppy then felt positioned by rough uncaring hands. She listened to the coughing, whispering and rustling circulating the room as she continued to wait for something to happen.

"Remove the hood," a stern voice ordered.

Putting every effort into remaining emotionally restrained, Poppy stared hard and without expression at her surroundings and audience. She was in a small chapel dominated by a large stone altar, which was sectioned off from the rest of the room by a copper rail on three sides. Poppy stood in front and to one side of the cold slab, which was covered in a white cloth. On the other side stood a cross, adorned on either side by two large candles in decorative holders. The altar was protected from the wall by a finely carved screen and on either side were floor-to-ceiling windows through which she could make out the green of a lawn.

Before her, Poppy saw men in black robes seated on chairs or standing cramped into any available space and spilling back through the open door. To her horror, she recognised some faces seated at the front. Adam was tucking his abundant fringe under his hood, and beside him, the twins gawked up at her with blank faces. To Adam's right sat an uneasy-looking man who kept his eyes on the floor and fiddled with rosary beads.

The room was darkening as the sun began to set. A monk walked forward and, holding up his cassock, stepped over the rail and lit the candles. Then as everyone in the room heard a latch click, they turned towards a door in the wall where Poppy saw two bent figures step out and rise to their full height. They both wore red robes, and beneath the material of the tallest man, Poppy saw unusual clothes, which resembled the outfit worn by the Mathew doll.

"All rise for Bishop Augeri and Judge Mathew." Chairs scraped on the floor as everyone briefly rose and mumbled words in Latin, bowed slightly and sat back down.

Poppy heard a seat, which she'd noticed earlier, flip down behind her and assumed that was where the Bishop was sitting, presiding over the proceedings in an honoured place by the altar.

Mathew stepped in front of Poppy, and his eyes set cold and hard. He stared down into her face. Poppy was determined to remain unshaken and glared back, externally calm, while internally, she felt every nerve buzzing with warnings.

"We here are the sons of Adam and Eve," Mathew turned and flourished his hand towards his audience. "Our purpose is to celebrate and protect the one God." Mutterings rippled around the room and stopped.

"I must root out heretics and those who perform the black mass." Mathew turned and leaned towards Poppy, who observed his pupils dilate at these words, and she felt sure he was lying to himself. "The Bishop also has an interest in those who dissent from the Roman Catholic Church. Boarland Abby even escaped the dissolution of the monasteries in the sixteenth century, and we will do our duty to God for centuries to come."

Much of the world has committed a crime in your eyes then, as many believe in nothing, Poppy longed to scream out but remained silent.

"Our world is full of heretics, but your crime is an abomination to all of humanity," Mathew spat out his words, and his face was so close Poppy could feel his breath and saw his mouth twitch at the corners with pent-up agitation. Mutterings came from the congregation, and Poppy felt her body tremble. She looked to her right, saw smoke coiling up from the candles and a small bird balancing on the windowsill as though it were looking in and gained a sense of comfort from its presence.

"Your kind the Ragliese is set on a silent invasion, to destroy humankind. Although you don't carry weapons, your intent is clear. You've always wanted to infiltrate and take over. We have much evidence taken from Caillech Veil, the hub of all your communities in Britain." Poppy could feel Mathew's anger rising as his voice deepened with frustration at her continued silence. "You were put on this earth by the devil. You are accused of using magic and spells to deceive humans – to brainwash, corrupt families and turn them away from the true God – the one God.

"We have documents which pinpoint your communities throughout the world," Mathew reached into his cloak and pulled out a thick book. "It's all in here," he waved the book in the air for all to see. "We have people at this very moment searching the sinkholes, cathedral caves of Borneo and underground fortresses worldwide."

From behind Poppy, the Bishop cleared his throat, "Mathew, please stick to the purpose."

Poppy turned back and glared at the fanatical frothing mouth of Mathew, a man at war with evolution and history. *Whatever I do or say, they will carry through their plans, Poppy thought,* resigned to her fate. *I will give you nothing,* she said to herself as her rage almost burst from her head.

"Confess your crimes, and you will see the benefit, Mathew said." Poppy saw a large blue bottle settle softly on Mathew's nose. Agitated, Mathew flicked it away, but it continued to return.

"Rotten meat," the words shot from Poppy's lips before she knew what she was saying. "It smells rotten meat."

Mathew flushed red. "You worship false gods and scatter your corrupt seed over our planet." People nodded and muttered their agreement. "You have until dawn to disclose the names and whereabouts of the other witches."

Poppy couldn't draw her eyes away from Mathew's hideous face. She was no longer afraid and sensed she was not alone. He had the keen hunger of a beast intent on its kill, forever, carrying out terrifying barbarities to validate his existence. Calm wormed its way deep into Poppy's mind. *They have already decided to murder me, and if they can lure others into their trap, that would be a bonus,* Poppy considered.

"We will purge this land of your kind," Mathew said in exasperation, sucking the air back through his yellow teeth.

Poppy heard the seat flip up behind her, and the Bishop stepped forward and centre stage to address her and the congregation.

"Unless you confess your crimes of witchery and heresy before God and man by dawn, you will be taken from your cell, weighted down and thrown into the river. If you float to the surface, we will know you are a witch and using spells to escape.

Poppy saw movement on the stone floor. She dropped her eyes and spotted a large spider run towards the Bishop. She watched as it rapidly climbed up his red cloak.

Suddenly, the semi-dark room was alive as people rose from their seats, talked in lowered voices and walked towards the doorway. Material swayed, and shadows danced across the floor. Two heavily set men drew near to Poppy and clasped her upper arms.

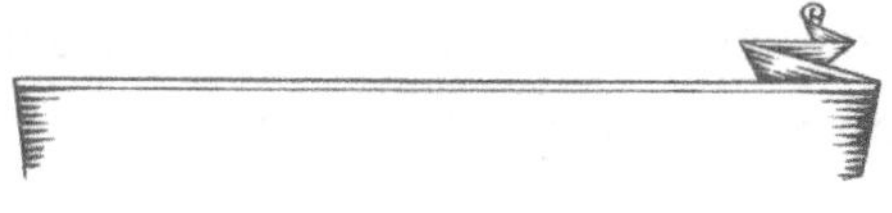

Chapter Thirty

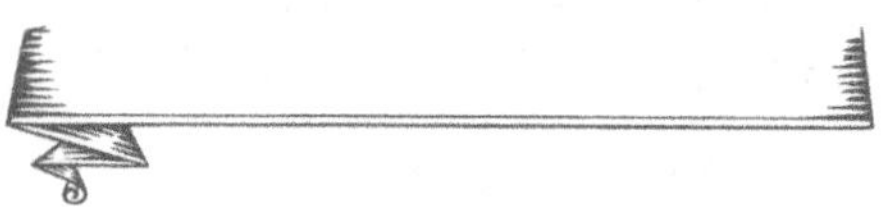

Kane felt as though he'd lost everything, even his memory. *I have today, but no yesterday,* he thought as he struggled to place himself within the world. He only knew his name because he'd found a wallet in the pocket of a coat laying on a chair in the hospital room. His mind was mostly blank. He felt disorientated and was keenly aware of a throbbing pain, which radiated throughout his heavily bandaged body.

The interior of the club was hot and heaving with all forms of human life from the self-possessed to the timid. Kane had a bitter taste in his parched mouth and was desperate for a drink. Buffeted by the heaving crowd at the bar, he stretched up as far as he could and waved a twenty-pound note in the direction of the woman serving. When she'd finished, she pushed forwards and came over to where he was, squeezed.

"What can I get you?"

Shit! What do I drink? He thought disturbed by his complete loss of memory.

"What would you suggest?" he said, smiling weakly.

"Look I don't have time for games - you can see how busy we are."

Kane quickly read the label on the nearest pump, "Cider, please."

"A pint?"

"Yes, that would be great," he muttered, feeling embarrassed, dizzy and confused.

Kane took his drink with both hands and followed a group of pleasure-seekers as they barged their way through the crowds into the room where the band was playing. The music pounded his eardrums as he stood at the back of the room watching the frenzied, feverish dancing. Kane felt as though he was looking through the smoked glass, at companions talking in corners, bodies pressed together in tight embraces, random encounters and wild drunks stumbling. He enjoyed the anonymity. Nobody was interested in him, the unshaven man hiding in the shadows.

Kane knew he was a crazy man, out of his depth, who had sought this place out on an impulse. The only thing he could remember was that he urgently needed to find someone. He believed the person was his sister whom he would find in this club. The name of the place had been the first thought, which entered his brain on waking.

Drinking had not satisfied Kane's thirst, and he couldn't face going back to the bar. Looking around, he spotted a full pint on the table next to him and casually picked it up. He gulped down the refreshing liquid.

"You've a big thirst," a thick voice growled in his ear. "That's my drink."

Kane felt a shiver run down his spine as he realised his crime could have consequences. Turning to his right, he found himself staring eye to eye with the ugliest face he thought he'd ever seen. The man had a large hooked nose, the pupils of his cruel eye dilated, making them black, and his mouth twitched into a grimace.

"Sorry mate, I meant no harm," he said, placing the remainder of the drink back on the table. "I thought it was mine. I can buy you another," he said, forcing his attention back to the angry man, only to find that he'd melted into the crowd. He glanced back at the half-empty glass and noticed a dead bluebottle struggling for life.

Kane was aware of a turbulence brewing deep inside, mingling with the pain, nausea and intoxication. He was frightened, frightened of not knowing who he was or what he may have been. The stage lights were changing colour and swirling around hypnotically, he averted his gaze and caught a streak of bright red in his periphery vision as a cloaked figure pushed past. The sight of the bright red prompted something in his mind. He paused from his self-indulgence and forced himself to think. It was a name, "Poppy", he cried as his hair stood up in horror. *How could I forget? I must find Poppy. She was in the factory. How long have I been away?* He mused as he pushed his way back through the jostling people towards the exit.

Ahead, Kane spotted a girl; her long black hair and clothes were dripping wet. At the door, she turned and looked directly at him and tears rushed into Kane's eyes. He stood stricken and distraught as the memories of Poppy, Adam, and his murderous changeling twin brothers flooded his mind. Just as the elusive figure vanished into the door, Kane heard a woman's voice whisper in his ear, "go to the abbey on the moor".

Shit! I've wasted too much time, Kane thought as he was shaken into consciousness by a surge of panic. He rushed to the door. Outside, he stooped over and, crippled by pain, pressed his good hand on his wound. Blood seeped through his shirt, and he saw that it was soaked. *How long do I have?* He considered realising that he would make a poor hero. *I must get my father's shotgun.* With one hand, Kane buttoned his coat, stumbled to a nearby taxi rank and jumped into a waiting car.

Chapter Thirty-one

Kane was dropped off not far from the Abbey, a place he'd visited once in his childhood and had walked the remainder of the way. Silently, he climbed the steep slopes, which led to a wooded ridge which overlooked the ancient building. Treading carefully through the green light of the trees, he arrived at his vantage point and lay down on the muddy ground. In the valley below, he saw the Abbey, a large barn and some outbuildings. At the back and to the left was a fast-flowing and deep river behind, which was a dense wood.

Kane was aware of the profound silence of the early dawn and the beams of weak sunlight striking distant gardens and a row of beehives. At the edge of the wood opposite, he saw the silhouettes of two deer, which looked up in his direction. An Irish Wolfhound sauntered across the courtyard and disappeared behind the barn.

Kane waited and watched, feeling disconnected as though in an uneasy and frightening dream. Every time he moved, pain shot through his body, and he wondered if he shouldn't turn the gun on himself. Suddenly, he heard a twig snap behind him, and in a heart-stopping moment, he thought he'd been discovered. He turned around swiftly and, to his amazement, saw Arron standing at his feet.

"We're a unit; work together and think as one – remember?" he said, smiling sarcastically. "What's the mission?" he said as he lay down by Kane.

"To rescue a girl from a cult," Kane replied, as courage replaced the pain which evaporated from his body. "Good to have you alongside, mate," he said, reaching out with his disabled hand to greet his friend.

Kane's joy was short-lived. Suddenly, he heard a clamour of voices and the heavy swish of the barn doors opening. Two robust men emerged on either side of a girl. They were trying to hold her straight, but she was dropping to her knees to prevent them from moving easily. Following behind them was an assemblage of monks in black hooded robes. Kane's heart skipped a beat.

"Steady man, you need to get this right," Arron said.

"I wished she'd stop wriggling," Kane replied as he gritted his teeth and concentrated on his target. Through his sight, he saw Poppy's thick black hair cascade down her back as she straightened. Calmly, he aimed and pulled the trigger. The loud bang echoed through the woods, and at first, there was little reaction from the group below, who assumed a hunter was after deer. As they realised that one of the guards had dropped to the ground, a second shot rang out.

Kane ignored the yelling and pandemonium below and reloaded his gun. This time, the bullet missed its target and ricocheted off the barn wall. The second time, he grazed someone, but they were still standing.

"They're coming for you, and that gun is too slow," Arron said. "You have a knife let's sneak away before they find us."

Kane took one glance at the valley below and saw Poppy in a tattered smock dress, her feet bare. She was looking in his direction, and her eyes were full of fear in her pale, doll-like face. Beside her, on the blood-stained ground, lay two dark figures. Kane was hardly aware of the shouting, pointing from the men and those who were rushing up the slopes towards him. On all fours, he scrambled quickly away.

Under cover of the trees, at the bottom of the slope, Kane saw the dog, it walked past him, stopped and then turned his head back.

"Follow the dog," Arron said.

Kane pursued the animal as it went through the barn and out through the opposite door. To his left, Kane saw Poppy and a small group of about eight monks standing by the river with their backs turned. They were laughing, secure in their position of power, and it was clear they were about to shove Poppy into the water. Enraged, Kane ran forward with his knife ready in his hand. In a frantic fury, he stabbed at the dark shapes. Several fell; he glanced at them writhing in agony and crying out. Then one rolled onto his back, and he recognised their faces and faltered. Jim was staring up at Kane blankly, and he saw blood trickling from his mouth and ears. He had noticed that two of the figures were small, like children, but it hadn't registered in his brain.

"Dylan grabs him," a voice he recognised as Adam's ordered.

In his periphery vision, he saw a tall man with a hooked nose push Poppy hard in the back. The heavy splash resounded with horror in Kane's mind.

"Kill him!" Adam screamed with rage.

Dylan pulled Kane's arms up his back, causing him to fall to his knees. He slammed his palm into Kane's forehead, pushed his head back and was about to drag a knife across his throat when Kane heard growling and felt the hot breath. Suddenly released from the man's grip, he collapsed to the ground. As he scrambled to his feet, someone lurched at him, but Kane managed to twist from their grasp and plunge into the river.

The water was flowing fast and deep. He rose to the surface, gasped some air and dived back down. Far below, he saw Poppy waiting for him. She was floating vertically above her anchor, her hair drifting up, little bubbles coming from her cold blue lips, her skin was white, and the depth had gone from her wide, fixed eyes. Kane stretched out his arm but could not reach her and, in panic, shot back up. In a split second, he saw the sky darkening as a raven black cloud past over the sun, and as he gulped the air, he knew the last grains of sand were slipping through the time.

On his next attempt, as he went under, he felt a hand gently push on his shoulder so he could reach a greater depth, and a voice whispered, "Be strong for her."

He was not alone in the darkness as three women were swimming around Poppy, going up and down, taking it in turns to breathe their air into the girl's lungs. Kane saw lightning cut sharply through the water, striking the chains around Poppy's ankles. *What hand had guided that so, accurately,* he wondered as he watched Poppy released, floating up? With his good arm, he clasped Poppy around her ribs and swum frantically towards the surface and breaking the skin of their prison gasped the air.

Kane struggled up the slimy bank and, turning around, dragged Poppy from the torrent. Carefully he lay her on the grass and felt swelling despair as she remained unresponsive, her face drained of blood and her eyes now closed as if she were in a serene sleep. As the rain poured down, Kane bent over Poppy and gave her mouth to mouth, barely aware of the three women climbing towards them.

"We must run, run now, quick!" Madeline said.

Kane was deaf to the background noises of men shouting and running in all directions, pursuing their purpose of capturing their enemy.

"I'll always be with you, my dark-haired girl," he uttered in confusion, trying not to look at her as tears flooded his eyes. Please wake—I love you." He pushed a breath between her lips and simultaneously became aware of the air being disturbed and heard a thud as an arrow embedded itself in the grass next to his leg.

"We must go!" All three women pleaded in unison. "They are shooting from the Abbey."

Kane looked over his shoulder towards the woods he'd come from and saw a flash of white hair and one other man taking flight up the steep slope. He guessed that one was Adam running like a coward to hide in the woods until all the trouble was over.

There was no time for regretting his brother's death. Carefully, he scooped Poppy into his arms, rose, steadied himself and began running towards the opposite woods.

They were deep amongst the trees when they finally felt it was safe to stop. "I need to rest a moment," Kane said, and he placed Poppy gently on the soil. He took off the burden of his soaked coat and found his knife still in his pocket. Kane began cutting away Poppy's sodden plaster. "I'm incomplete without you – no one will ever take your place," he muttered his voice cracking with emotion. "I've wasted so much time. Please wake up – I promise I will never let you down again."

A gurgling sound emanated from Poppy's throat. Kane stiffened and listened. Gently, he shook her shoulders and watched as Poppy rose a little off the ground, coughed, and spluttered.

Poppy raised her eyelids. "Kane is that really you?" she said in a tiny voice, stretching her hand and stroking the side of his face.

"Yes, it's me!" he said, leaning over and kissing her repeatedly all over her face. "I love you!" Kane said tenderly.

"Are you alright to walk?" Madeline said, kneeling at her side while Kane continued to remove the plaster cast. "We need to keep moving. We'll head for the stones."

"Madeline, Rosa, Sarah, thanks for not giving up on me." Poppy said through chattering teeth.

Everyone helped Poppy to her feet. Stiffly she clutched Kane's arm and looked into his eyes adoringly. Kane felt as though the world had regained its substance. The hollowness had gone; he'd gained his control, self-respect, and everything that had previously left his life returned. *Another person hasn't died on my watch,* he thought, smiling to himself. He looked around for Arron and, seeing he was gone, whispered, "Thanks, comrade."

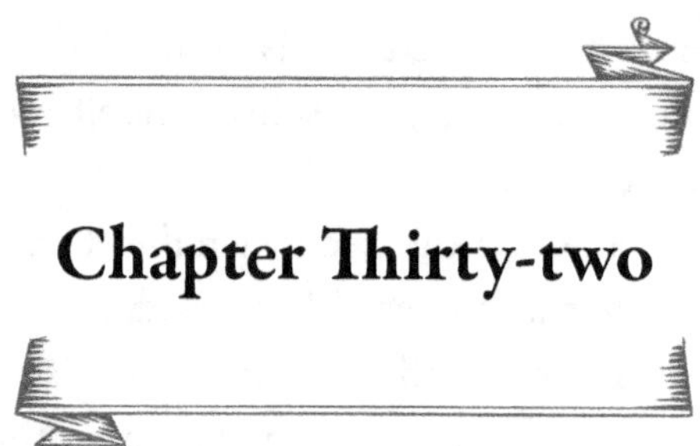

Chapter Thirty-two

Kane limped up the hill, feeling increasingly fatigued. Battling the lashing rain and steep slope caused the entire group to fall silent. They were drained, and every step they took was infused with the fear of being caught.

Finally, they all clambered over the ditch and into the inner circle of the stones, where they collapsed to the ground. Here in an oasis of peace, the rain had ceased, while outside it continued to shroud them from the rest of the world.

Kane lay prone and felt as though the earth was pulling him into its heart. He was half aware of Poppy's body pressed against his as he cradled her in his arm. Then her hand rested lightly on his belly, and he felt her spring up into a kneeling position. Kane opened his eyes and looking up saw a desperate expression on her face.

"Madeline! Quick, there's blood spurting out everywhere," Poppy yelled with panic. "He has wounds, and they're weeping badly."

"There was no time to explain before, but we found him in the park. He'd been attacked, was very sick, and almost stepped over to the beyond," Madeline said as she rushed over with Rosa and Sarah following close behind. "We had a desperate struggle keeping him attached to this world." She knelt, untied a purse from around her waist and it clanked on the ground next to Kane's outstretched body. "He was taken to the hospital and, if he'd stayed, would have probably made a full recovery." Madeline rummaged in the bag and pulled out a bottle full of a muddy-looking liquid. She unscrewed the lid and, lifting Kane's head, held it to his lips.

"He has an intense fever, and his heart is beating fast," Rosa gasped as she leaned over and placed a hand on Kane's chest.

Madeline ripped open Kane's shirt, took out a bunch of herbs and other unusual plants, soaked them in the liquid and between her pincer fingers rolled them into a paste. Then with a delicate touch, she smoothed the medicine into the open wound. Her final tool was magic words, which all the women spoke in unison.

Kane felt something clasp his brain; his body grew heavy, and his eyelids drooped shut.

Hour after hour went by, Kane eventually awoke to the smell of fire. Above the grey skies had shifted, and he saw a black sheet melting like diamond-encrusted fabric. He heard the wailing and moaning of demented voices like mourners at a funeral.

Kane eased himself up onto his elbows and scanned his surroundings. He saw a fire close by and the women moving around the stones, touching each as they went. On the altar stone, they had laid various meaningful possessions. Kane began to feel weak; his head went limp on his shoulders, and he dropped back onto the ground.

Madeline seeing, he was awake, rushed over and lifted the bottle once more to his lips. He drank the liquid thirstily.

"If not for you and your merciful powers I would be dead," he uttered and shut his eyes. He lay back happily, feeling that his soul was completely nourished. The next thing he knew was that there was thunder in the sarsen stones, they were shaking and cracking.

He watched dark shapes striding around him and lights flash by. Sandra drifted into view, her long black hair flowing freely. She knelt at his side and kissed his cheek.

"It'll all work out well," she smiled, stood up and glided into the ether.

Kane saw all his past and future in an instant as though it was all one. He recalled every intricate detail and accepted it all calmly, without trauma. Arron was there at his side doing punishing press-ups on basic training for sharing a fag on duty. He saw his mother dying and knew she needed to know the truth about Sarah, Poppy, Adam, and the twins. Mostly, he wanted to tell her he now believed there were other dimensions, that the world was full of magic and that she would see her daughter again.

The ground began trembling again. Kane scrambled to his knees and looked around. The women were still caressing the stones and holding whispered dialogues with the immortals. Then Kane spotted Anton emerging from the largest sarsen; he watched as he paced back and forth as though looking for something. Then, the angry spirit's gem eyes came to rest on Kane. He thundered towards him, shaking the stones further.

"An invader has violated our sacred stones," he growled. "This is the sanctuary of the night dwellers."

Poppy saw what was happening and, breaking away from her ritual, turned towards Kane. "Go to the nearest stone," she said, pointing to a large sarsen, which pointed to the heavens. "His instinct is to find his brother, and he will destroy anyone who stands in his way, and he's armed with powerful magic."

Swaying to his feet, Kane managed to dodge out of Anton's reach as he lashed out like a recently freed, cornered animal.

"Your brother is at the Abbey down the hill," Kane shouted over his shoulder as he raised his extended arms to touch the stone. He was aware of the ferment of movement behind him, but as he made contact with the cool rock, he became calm. A warmth and power transferred into his limbs and tears rushed into his eyes as the hidden elements of his soul were liberated. For the first time since childhood, he felt as though he could see - really see beyond what was possible for most men. The spirits grew solid, introduced themselves and offered greetings. *Is this a chemical reaction of the brain because of the medicine I've been given, or is it true?* He considered not caring either way.

As dawn broke, he sank to his knees and, exhausted, curled up in a pocket of warmth by the stone, his stone. When he finally woke, he found the monument empty, and only the hissing embers of the fire reminded him of what had happened the previous night. He felt lighter, well, and he noticed the shadow, which always followed him, nagging, telling him that something was wrong or needed attending to, had also vanished.

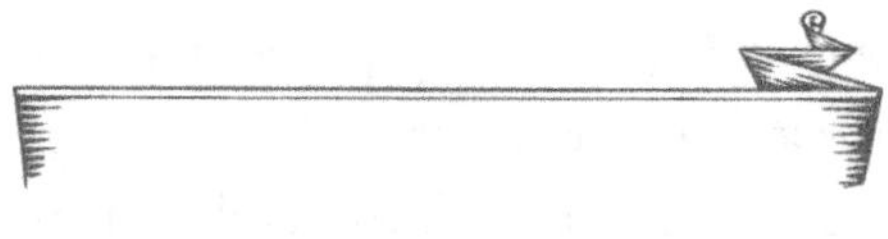

Chapter Thirty-three

Allen came towards Oliver, his marble white skin pink on the cheeks in the warmth of the pub, and his radiant eyes smiled down at his friend.

"So, what's this all about?" he said, carefully placing the drinks on the table and seating himself opposite Oliver. "You were saying you found a copy of a letter amongst Roehampton's papers."

"I've been doing some digging," Oliver stuttered and looked around nervously. "I was trying to find out if the professor had any enemies." Oliver paused to gulp his beer. "Well, apparently, he did. There was one name kept cropping up: a theologian from the university named Dylan Fox. He'd been doing some work on ancient religions and stumbled across Roehampton's studies and was apparently in a dispute with him over his emphasis on indigenous religions, which were outside of Christianity." Oliver turned his anxious eyes towards the door as though he was expecting the man Dylan to walk in at any moment. "We both know he might have found out much more. It seems that he held a deep grudge towards the professor," he said, turning back to Allen and speaking in a whisper.

"I thought you were wise enough to stop meddling – forget him – forget the whole thing. It's too big for us," Allen said sternly.

"We should find him before he hears about us, or we might be next," Oliver said with a sense of urgency in his voice. "The man's unpredictable and a killer."

"Exactly, why we should leave this alone," Allen caught himself glancing into the room uneasily. "God, you have a way of generating fear. I was enjoying a nice, peaceful, successful life."

"We all have our imperfections. What about the solidarity of friendship?" Oliver uttered in desperation as he focussed on tearing off a broken nail. He stared at the veins sticking out along his long, bony fingers. "Come on we have to see this to the end. I want to sleep at nights. Anyway, I've made an appointment to visit the Abbey tomorrow."

"What, Abbey?" Allen asked, regretting being drawn into Oliver's drama.

"The letter I found was to the 'board' at the university complaining about Dylan Fox stalking the professor and being a nuisance. The university took Roehampton's complaints seriously and dismissed Fox." Oliver looked up at his friend, who was leaning forward and listening intently. "When I was scouting around a few people who knew this crazy man said he'd joined a group of obscure monks. It turns out the Abbey is on the moor not far from the mansion house and the tunnels."

"I think you're the one who's crossed the line into insanity," Allen said drinking the remainder of his beer as though it would be his last. "Are you telling me that you expect us both to drive north tonight?"

"Well, I was in two minds whether or not to go and believe me I've gone over it all a thousand times in my mind," Oliver said in a pleading voice.

"So, we have a group of mad women who think they are witches with powers. Who were also involved in a serious attack on a young man and now monks. I thought being down south, we could steer our lives away from all this craziness," Allen said, exasperated.

"You forget, Professor Roehampton was murdered," Oliver said, surveying his surroundings for any sign of witches or mad monks. "I saw him with my own eyes. It's stuck in my brain, and there is no way it was suicide. I also found a passport sized photo of Mr Fox and it looked about the same age as the man I saw lingering near the professor's house. Allen, I don't think you understand the gravity of the situation."

"You always were too serious for your own good. Do I really need to come? There's a small matter of work tomorrow, something you don't seem to know much about these days," Allen sighed.

"I don't drive, remember!" Oliver finished the dregs of his drink and began putting on his coat.

"What now!" Allen complained. "Can't we have one more for the road?"

"Yes, now! And no, you can't have another drink; you don't want to risk being caught drunk driving."

Reluctantly Allen grabbed his things and followed after Oliver.

Driving over the brow of a hill, Allen stopped the car on the gravel drive. The two men looked down into the valley below, and there, rising out of the mist was the faded grandeur of a grey stone building.

"Is that it?" Allen muttered.

"So, the sat-nav says," Oliver said, staring ahead, aware of the fear twisting in his gut.

Five minutes later, they were speaking to a solemn-sounding man through an intercom. A monk dressed in a black habit answered the door. He regarded them with a stern expression and then ushered them into the building in an aloof and indifferent manner.

"This way," were his only words as he led them into a small entrance hall.

Another equally severe-looking man in a red cloak was waiting to greet them. "I'm Bishop Augeri, the head of the order. You must be Mr Baker; we spoke on the phone," he said, extending his hand towards Oliver. "We're a silent order and don't encourage visitors except when they are on retreat. We're devout Christians and attend to the needs of others through our missionary work," he released his over-firm grip.

"So, you're here to visit Dylan Fox, and as I understand it, you're one of his old students from his university days."

Oliver nodded dumbly, lost for words. "Yes, I've come to bring him some news about his family." The words stumbled from Oliver's mouth without any thought. "And to get some advice on a project I'm doing."

"How strange! I always believed he was an orphan," the Bishop said, grinning cynically. "Please come this way," he said, turning his back and walking towards a door.

Oliver felt the blood rush to his face and Allen's hand on his shoulder, holding him back.

"Why did you say that? Tread very carefully," Allen whispered in his ear. "Where the hell did that come from?"

"I don't know – my mind went blank."

"Please, no more mistakes. These guys look as though they would eat us for dinner without a second thought."

They all walked along a hallway, both men keenly aware of the cold and harsh atmosphere. The Bishop seemed to have fallen silent, and the tapping of their shoes on the wooden floor seemed painfully loud. Oliver rummaged his brain for something to say.

"This place is very old."

"How observant you are," the Bishop said without a glance backward or a slowing of pace. "Most of its the eleventh century, but it's built on a seventh-century church. Our chapel is all that remains of the previous building."

The Bishop abruptly stopped in front of a door. "I'm afraid you will find Dylan much altered. He had to leave university life as he's suffering from motor neuron disease," he smiled falsely. "He's a damaged human being, and every day is a struggle, so don't expect too much help with your work," the Bishop said, easing open the door.

Allen and Oliver exchanged glances and stepped into a small room. "Ring the bell when you need to leave, and someone will attend to you," the Bishop said as he shut the door behind them.

A tall, handsome, animated man stepped forward to greet them, holding out his hand. "My names Adam I'm Dylan's carer," he said, smiling broadly. "Come in and sit down." He pointed to two high backed chairs, placed in front of the wheelchair where Dylan sat slumped forwards.

The visitors watched as Adam rushed over to Dylan and attentively adjusted his position, propped his head up and gave him a drink.

This man's been drugged, Oliver thought with a sinking heart, knowing he would gain little information.

"Could you please come straight to the point of your visit as he'll need to rest soon," Adam said.

Oliver took a deep breath, "I've been carrying out some work on Professor Roehampton's discoveries, and I believe you knew him." The silence was deafening then, Adam whispered something in Dylan's ear.

"Yes, I knew him, a vile man," Dylan slurred through frothy lips. "The work of the devil!" he spat.

"Quite, he had some peculiar ideas. Did you know he died?"

"A gas explosion, I heard," Dylan glanced up and stared at Oliver with an extraordinarily hateful expression. "That man deserved to die. Shame I wasn't around to see it happen."

"That's not very compassionate," Allen interjected.

"You will have to forgive him; it's the medication," Adam said as he fussed over his patient, who was groaning for a cigarette. "I hope you don't mind, it's the only vice he's still able to enjoy." Adam lit the fag and placed it between the man's lips.

An image of the grey-haired man lingering in front of him chain-smoking flooded Oliver's mind. *It's him. I know he's the murderer, and this is all a sham. There's no way he will betray himself. I'm wasting my time.* Oliver thought and scrutinised the murderer, looking for signs of remorse or guilt. Then he saw Dylan automatically reach up to take the cigarette from between his lips. Adam immediately picked up on Oliver's baffled expression and retrieved the evidence of deception.

"There's a rumour going around that the professor was murdered," Oliver said, watching the men's reactions closely.

"I'm afraid Dylan wouldn't know anything about that he was living here at that time and already very ill," Adam nervously spoke out and stared at Oliver with a fixed smile on his face. "I think it's perhaps time you went. I'm sorry we can't help more," Adam said, walking over to a rope hanging by the door. He pulled it twice, and Oliver shuddered as a bell rang in the distance, and he knew his time was up. "You obviously don't want to discuss your studies."

"You want to be very careful who you accuse of murder," Dylan spoke, sounding suddenly very sober. Leaning forward, he stared at the men with eyes burning with hatred and a rage neither man had seen before.

"I'm sorry – I wasn't – I mean, I'm just a student," Oliver tongue-tied, stuttered, feeling threatened and vulnerable.

"You don't know me, and you come here talking about a man who was about to destroy our civilisation and then have the nerve to accuse me of murder," he began to push himself up from the chair.

Oliver felt a hand on his shoulder. "Shit!" he cried, jumped up and ran to the door. Grey in the face and in an equal state of fear, Allen joined him, and as they turned around, they saw the Bishop standing by the two empty chairs.

"Why so nervous?" A malicious grin crossed his face. "I have come to escort you to the door."

As they left, Oliver saw that Dylan had sat back down and was dragging hard on his cigarette while Adam was talking to him in a low voice.

In a solemn silence, Oliver and Allen followed the Bishop back through the hallway. The Bishop virtually pushed them through the front door.

"Please don't come back. We're a silent order and don't appreciate any disruption."

"Are you alright?" Allen said as they crunched over the gravel towards their car. "They're all in on it, you know."

"Yes, I'm okay. How about you?"

"I can't say I don't feel embarrassed and intimidated, which is obviously how they want us to feel," Allen said.

"I'm sorry for dragging you all this way for nothing," Oliver muttered, feeling cold and shaky.

"I think we both knew that he wouldn't admit to anything of value," Allen said as he clicked the lock on the car. "I bet they're all watching us right now to make sure we go." Allen climbed into the driver's seat and started the engine.

"He was playing the invalid, and they think they had us fooled." Oliver secured his seat belt and sighed with relief pleased to be on their way.

Once they were away from the winding roads of the moor and on the motorway, Allen put his foot down. They were both anxious to get as far south as possible. Suddenly they met heavy traffic, Allen slammed on the breaks, but to his, horror they didn't respond.

Chapter Thirty-four

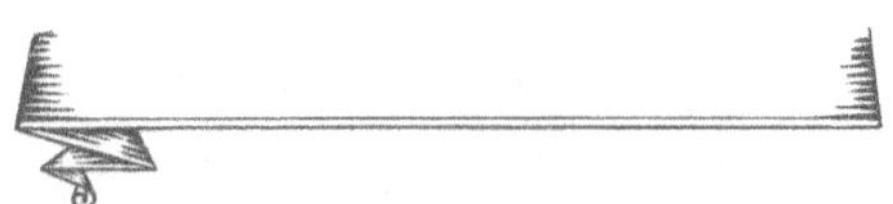

Sitting on a chair by his mother's bed and holding her limp hand, Kane watched the sun out of the window, sinking slowly into darkness. The first light of spring was a wondrous sight he wished he could hang onto the brightness and keep it in the room. Eventually, he stood up and switched on the nightlight. He altered the position of his mother's pillows to make her more comfortable and sat back down.

He held his breath and listened for her breathing, which had been sporadic and rasping. She wheezed, and he felt satisfied that she was still sleeping. Kane squeezed her hand and smiled down at his mother with deep affection. The frail woman was withdrawing from the world, he felt sad for his inevitable loss but felt safe in the knowledge that wherever she went, she wouldn't be alone.

"Mum, I want to thank you," he said swallowing as the first tears stung his eyes. "You are a wonderful mother – you always put us first and worked so hard to give us everything we needed. My love of adventure came from you. Do you remember how you spoke to me every night during basic training – I missed home so much. You've supported me, all of us and got me through so many difficult times." The tears flooded down his face, and he leaned over and kissed her hand. "You were always with us, playing with us. Do you remember the time you went on the rope-swing and fell off?" Kane looked at his mother's face and thought he saw her lips move and feeling encouraged continued. "You kicked the ball around on the rough field and made up amazing stories, which stirred our imaginations."

Kane couldn't contain his cascading emotions and collapsed back over the bed. "Why? Why now? I want to go back home – back to those sunny memories of childhood." An intricately detailed and intense picture of his sister playing and laughing with his brothers ran like a movie in his mind.

Kane heard a rustling and sensed movement. He sat bolt upright and felt an uplifting rush as merciful phantoms gathered in the room. His sister stood beside him at the head of the bed, holding Jim's hand.

"Kane don't cry, she knows and understands," Sandra consoled sweetly smiling down at her brother. "She's always been sensitive. We shouldn't have laughed at her ghost stories."

A feeling of euphoria flooded through Kane's veins like an estuary entering the sea. Everything was free-flowing; his senses were alive, and he felt as though all barriers and restrictions had lifted.

Kane heard the footstep of death rapidly approaching. Standing up, he bent low and kissed his mother's forehead. "I love you mum, so much." He kissed her again and moved to the side to allow Sandra to approach.

Sandra kissed her mother and held Jim up so he could reach and do the same. Then she gently took her frail hand in hers, "It's time we went mum," she said in a soft, comforting manner.

Kane felt a fluttering and a chill as the entities moved away. He heard his mother take a last gasp and watched as Sandra and Jim vanished. "Stay strong brother," he heard Sandra whisper.

The door opened, and Kane assumed it was one of the nurses and began to tidy the bed.

Brian whispered to his son, "hello Kane."

"I'm afraid she's gone, dad."

"I'm sorry, Son," he said as tears washed down his face.

The haggard face invoked compassion in Kane. "Come and sit down dad," Kane said and hurriedly moved a spare chair next to the bed. He watched as the old man walked stiffly and nervously towards the chair. Cautiously he sat next to Kane, knowing that his son had the power to hurt.

Kane wanted to explain that he needn't be afraid that the gulf between them was no longer relevant. He felt the vulnerability of the man as he shrunk behind his wrinkled mask.

"I've brought some pictures for her to take with her," he said and handed some old photos over to Kane. Kane inhaled a whiff of alcohol, decay and felt pity. Kane glanced down at the images of a young and happy family.

"You give them to her dad," Kane said, handing the pictures back.

Kane moved his chair back to allow his father access to his mother. The man eased himself off the chair and on unsteady legs walked over to Judy, kissed her forehead and lay the picture on her chest.

"Goodbye, love," he uttered and returned to the chair. "I'm sorry."

"Now I only have you left," he looked up at Kane and regarded him with his bewildered watery blue eyes. "While you were away, the twins went missing too."

Kane wished he could ease his father's pain and tell him the truth but knew he would view his revelations as nonsense. Suddenly, Kane felt the pressure of guilt weighing down on his raw heart.

"Where do you think they are?"

"The nurse told me when your mum was first ill they visited with your mum's tenant, that musician bloke," he said looking at the floor, a man dragged down by life. "I tried to find this Adam, but when I found out where he had moved, he wasn't there. I haven't slept properly in weeks."

"Have you told the police?" Kane asked as he composed himself ready for the unwanted answer.

"Oh, yes, I explained everything. They're looking for you too."

Kane suddenly felt the division between himself and his father slip back into place.

"I will call them tomorrow and explain that I've been away," Kane said vaguely hoping his words would delay any further action from his father.

"They are anxious to speak with you. Son, they seem to think you might have something to do with the twin's disappearance."

"Dad it's Adam they need to investigate, not me!"

"Don't worry son; I'm sure the police will get to the bottom of it all," Brian made to stand up, and Kane helped him to his feet. "I think I should go now. Please keep in touch."

"I will dad; I'm here to stay."

Kane watched his father go, and at the door he turned. "Son, I am proud of you and do love you." Feeling embarrassed at his own words Brian hurried out of the room before Kane could reply.

Furtively, Kane crept from the hospital expecting the police to be waiting for him around every corner.

Chapter Thirty-five

Kane had spent most of the morning searching for Poppy. He was desperate to find her and growing more frantic by the minute. For the past half hour, he'd been wandering around the park. He was finding it hard to engage with the joyous rhythm of the day, its brightness and early spring warmth. Nature it seemed, was promising hope and new life, not loss and sadness. Kane felt like an outsider as he glanced down at the odd remaining crocus poking above ground and then up at the buds on the trees unfolding. Dog walkers and passers-by were smiling as they idly chatted, which heightened Kane's awareness of his untidy appearance, his clothes wrinkled as though he'd slept in them, his unshaven face and shadow ringed eyes. His darkness was such a contrast to all the light.

Suddenly a vague memory entered his head, of telling Poppy, that if ever she was lost to meet him at the mansion house. As he approached the building, his mood lifted, he realised why he wanted to speak with Poppy. He needed to declare his love properly. He'd never felt so certain about any decision he'd previously made in his life. Recognising his desire made him even more anxious to have her at his side. She was his blood; his oxygen and he would look forever to find her – he wouldn't let go of his dream or turn back to the shell of a man she'd first met.

Kane stood on the path facing the mansion. The builders had finished for the weekend, and their machines were locked up behind a barrier. He spent a long time circling the building, climbed through the fence at its rear and scoured the empty rooms, but there was no sign of life. Memories of his attack flashed into his mind, and he began to feel uneasy. Outside, he paced back and forth, calling her name, "Poppy! Poppy!" People turned, stared and gave him a wide berth.

Kane grew self-conscious, and he began to wonder if his enemies had followed him and were watching his search or whether the police were about to pounce. He quietly ambled over to the bench, sat down and staring at the decrepit building, pondered his situation.

A black dog sauntered out from behind the ruin and aimlessly walked in his direction. *Someone's dog has found freedom,* he thought. It walked past him and through the gap in the box hedge, which led to the rose garden. Kane continued to sit and wait, thinking no more of the lost animal. Then he heard some snuffling, scrapping and looking down saw the dog poking his head through the hedge as though it was trying to gain his attention. A sweet un-dog-like smell caught in his nose, prompting him to rush into the garden.

Poppy was standing with her back to him, her unmistakable black hair gleaming down between her shoulders. She wore a calf-length black coat, which was, pulled in at the waist, highlighting her delicate form. He could hear his heart thumping and his blood rushing through his veins. She turned, and he gazed at the face he knew so well, her dark eyes twinkled full of secrets, her eyebrows flashed, and her red lips curled into a smile.

Kane dashed forwards, lifted her clear off the ground and swung her around. She responded by laughing lightly and kissing his forehead. As he brought her to the ground, she yielded in his arms, and they kissed passionately and longingly. Kane felt complete having his arms and heart full. They gazed at each other adoringly, embraced and clung together in fear of letting go of happiness, which was far above anything heaven could offer.

Kane whispered in Poppy's ear. "My life is nothing without you." He fell on one knee, held her hands in his and looking up at her smiling face said, "Will you marry me?"

"Yes, oh yes," she uttered a little too quietly, and Kane saw some of the radiance leave her eyes.

"What is it? Somethings wrong." Kane felt his heart sink, and the spreading roots of hope wither.

"We're in danger. They won't give up."

"Then we will take the fight to them," Kane said, rising to his feet.

Poppy embraced him, "I will have to go away, hide with the others," she said gently. "They will need my help – we achieve in numbers."

Kane took some strands of her hair, studied how it lay so perfectly, across his injured hand and felt its smoothness with his other fingers.

"The police want to speak with me over my brother's disappearance," he said in a daze. "I was going to speak with them today and explain that they're looking in the wrong direction. Tell them about the Abbey."

Poppy flicked her hair back over her shoulder. "Kane, you can't go to the police. They are all in league with the Bishop. Adam took your brother's, but he is one of them. You're just someone to blame." Poppy turned away and feeling hopeless wiped a tear from her eye. "They will have you locked away."

"I will come with you," he said, stroking his bristly chin in thought. "Do you want me to come?"

"Of course, I do, but you would need to join with us," she looked at him with pitying eyes. "You would have to go deep underground, where no sun reaches until you find the secret garden."

"Why? Why can't we just be together?" Kane said, feeling confused and frustrated. "You left your people before."

"I wasn't sure where they'd gone. Now I've found them I should return," she said, looking up at Kane with wide-eyed sadness. "It's as you said we need to fight back and on our terms. I've grown up a lot, and we have a plan."

"I still don't get it I thought our love was as essential to you as it is for me."

"It is!"

"Then come with me. It's easy to get lost in the human world, and besides, I'm changed and would truly keep you safe."

"I suppose we need to think hard about this, but there's not much time – they will all be looking for you. Kane, I'm sorry, so sorry for everything – all the trouble I've caused you."

"I was in far more trouble before I met you – I was in trouble with myself – far worse," Kane chuckled trying to lighten the mood. "I want to come with you and will do whatever it takes."

"Men in our society are our guardians, warriors, and to become a man worthy of marriage, you have to make the journey to the garden. It's extremely hazardous – a brutal environment. You would have to navigate sharp irregular rocks, small rivers, which are intercepted by larger ones. There's a maze of stalagmites and stalactites where many have become lost. Snakes slither in the rocks below, and bats hang above. I would be so scared for you," Poppy uttered with a downcast expression and began to walk away. "There's, tiny passages to squeeze through where a man of your size could be trapped forever," she added.

"Wait!" Kane said, grabbing her arm in panic. "I'm a soldier, I love a challenge," he smiled broadly trying to convince her of his commitment. "I know how to relax my body to get through the tight holes."

"There's more to it than that. You will have to tap into what you think is invisible, unreal become a part of our communal memory and understand the thinness of what to you appears solid. It's a journey of the soul and mind. Dreams and form blur. It's enough to make some go mad."

"You make it sound quite trippy," Kane, laughed.

"It's not funny, it's serious," Poppy scolded.

"There's nothing for me here anymore, my family and friends have all gone."

"You will leave your past in the garden. You will cut a flint-like mine," she said, reaching beneath her coat and bringing out her spearhead. "That is the only thing you must bring back other than what you take in and when you emerge the clock of your life will have been reset."

"When does this trial begin?"

"Now," Poppy said, stepping forward and putting her arms around his waist. "You would do this for me?"

Feeling the weight of such a formidable love Kane looked down at Poppy and smiled, "I would circumvent the world for you if, on my return, I could be at your side forever."

Chapter Thirty-six

"One way or another we've got to get the hell away!" Oliver squeaked, waving his arms about and pacing back and forth by Allen's, hospital bed. "We should've known - the truth always brings enemies." He thought aloud, shot Allen a glance and caught him watching him intently and uneasily. "I've always fancied going to South America, to study their old bones," Oliver said conscious that to Allen's eyes he was behaving bizarrely. He didn't want to offload all his anxieties onto Allen, but there was nobody else with whom he could share his predicament. He was on hyper-alert, and his instincts were screaming for him to take flight. He paused, embarrassed and licked his dry lips.

Allen was, propped up in bed with a neck brace on and his right leg suspended in the air. "Stop flapping! We gave them no information, and they probably think we're dead," he said laughing and then wincing in pain. "Besides you wouldn't last long in the jungle with all those creepy crawlies. Can you image it? Giant spiders, snakes, all, the things you most fear."

"Well, what are we going to do? They tried to kill us," Oliver muttered in despair, trying not to look at his friend.

"Being fear-driven isn't the way to go, we'll end up in a bigger mess," Allen said and awkwardly twisted around to get a drink from his bedside cabinet. Oliver rushed over and passed him the glass.

"Since when did you become so blasé? I feel like I'm on the edge of that cliff again, looking down and it's one hell of a drop."

"Since I came off worse and can't move," Oliver's eyes met Allen's. He sees Allen's brow crease into a frown. "How can I go anywhere?"

A flash of deep sadness and regret caught in Oliver's throat, "I'm sorry mate," he said, falling into a deep silence, as though he was withdrawing from the conversation.

In pain and restless Allen became even more troubled by Oliver's sullen silence. "God this leg kill's," he said, glancing indirectly at Oliver to see if there was a response. "How long do you intend standing there meditating and taking space up in my room. If you're going to say nothing or continue to babble nonsense you might as well go," he said with impatience.

Oliver ignored Allen's comments but seemed to wake and laughed. "The climate wouldn't suit me either - I hate hot and humid." He walked over and perched on the edge of the bed. "We can't pretend we haven't found a new species of humanoid type people – the evidence is glaring. On the one hand, we could become famous and on the other dead," Oliver's voice trailed off.

"I'm not saying we should disregard our discoveries. Just that we shouldn't panic. We need to go through all the proper channels," Allen said, fixing Oliver's attention with a strained and grave expression. "Things have changed greatly since the idea was previously put before the board. We need to find a sympathetic ear, which is high up enough to have an influence."

"Well I wouldn't be in a hurry to get back in the driving seat if I were you," Oliver said in annoyance. "You don't think it's suspicious the way the police dismissed the crash as an accidental loosening of a nut on the master cylinder? There's nothing more frustrating than seeing disaster and nobody believing you. We at least need to attack this problem away from Europe. For all, we know this could go as high as the Vatican."

"Oliver, your imagination is in overdrive, stop! I'm as scared as you, but we need to remain calm and restrained." Allen answered firmly.

"Don't go hopping on a plane at least wait until we can think it all over properly. Lie low for a while if you must but don't act on impulse."

"I know you don't like all the internet stuff, but I've been talking with people online, on the dark web – you know in secret," Oliver said in a lowered voice.

"Not those mad conspiracy theorists?" Allen said shuddering with disgust.

"No these are serious people, scientists, archaeologists and historians. They are in touch with the Ragliese and know about how dangerous the Manneband are."

"The what!" Allen laughed mockingly. "You've gone insane man. You should listen to yourself. My god, who are you trying to fool?"

"I'm not joking, they are organising an evacuation to safe houses in the US, and they plan to help the Ragliese infiltrate the system and gain positions of power. We're not dealing with bones here - these people exist and need help." Oliver was unable to prevent the fast-flowing words tumbling from his mouth.

Allen ran his hands over his red head and sighed. "You do what you want, but I'm going to do things the official way," Allen said, laying back and shutting his eyes. "I bet your spirit of adventure doesn't last long."

"We could both go. I'll wait until you are well enough to move."

"Oliver, you're being absurd. I'm not leaving my job or my gorgeous secretary," Allen said as he pulled a leaver, so the bed went flat. "You go on your crusade against the forces of evil and don't forget to send me a postcard."

"Okay, I can see you're tired but have a hard think about what I've said. I will leave you some reading material by your bed."

"What is it?"

"Roehampton's papers." Oliver got up and walked to the door. "I'll see you before I go."

Chapter Thirty-seven

Oliver retreated to the cottage his parents had downsized to when he'd left for university. His mum directed him towards an attic room, and he reluctantly followed, struggling up the narrow staircase with his suitcase and laptop.

"It's good that you're staying, as your father and I are going away for a few days at the weekend. A short break – a very nice hotel," she said as she rushed ahead. "You could look after the place, while we're gone." She paused on the tiny landing to wait for her son. "You said your tenancy agreement had finished and there's no point in renewing it. What have you done with all your things?"

"I left most of it at Allen's. I will slowly shift it over here if you don't mind."

"Of course not! It can go with the rest of your belongings in the cellar."

"I might only be here for a few days mum," he said, hoping his mother wouldn't pick up on his radiating anxiety as he reached her at the top of the stairs. "I have a new job in the US – it's a fabulous opportunity, but I'm not sure exactly when I'll be leaving."

"I know son. You told me on the phone," she said in her normally relaxed manner. "Your father and I are very proud of you and so pleased that all your years of hard work are paying off." Doris smiled kindly up at her son as she opened the door to the guest room. "Nothing very familiar, I'm afraid. As I mentioned, we had to put your things in storage."

Oliver poked his head into the room, "mum – a loft – spiders?" he said, shrugging his shoulders and scanning the effeminate looking room.

"I thought you'd have grown out of that by now, besides I've given it a thorough clean." She patted him on the arm and smiled again. "You'll be fine. I expect you'll have your head in your computer for much of your time," she chuckled. "I will leave you in peace."

Oliver dumped his bag on the floor and flung his laptop on the bed. He took his phone from his pocket and glanced at it to see if there were any messages from Allen. There wasn't, and he began to fret that he'd upset him during their last meeting. Restlessly, he moved around the small room, looked inside the wardrobe, the bedside drawers and under the bed. Oliver went to the window, expecting to see a stranger lurking below but only saw an expanse of yellow from the oilseed rape fields.

Eventually, Oliver settled on the flowery bed cover and took his laptop from its bag. Restlessly he tapped the keys and took his accustomed route back into a world of secrets and conspiracies. He watched the chat flying back and forth. A date and time of the exodus was being debated. Desperately, he watched aware of the frantic energy running through his veins. Finally, late at night, he received the news that a decision was, made and it filled him with alarm.

"A week! A frigging week," he muttered to himself and slammed the lid of the computer shut. *A week and then my route out of here will close,* he considered, drawing his legs tight into his chest as though the pressure would stop his rapidly beating heart. Other mutterings in cyberspace mentioned not having enough people in one place to lock the evil spirits back into the stones. They would soon escape and go on the rampage.

Oliver slid off the bed. He wanted to run but at the same time felt paralysed with anxiety. He paced to alleviate his distress, but it wouldn't pass. Trying to control his fear made him weary, but he was unable to sleep.

As dawn broke Oliver curled in a foetal position on top of his bed. He dreamt of witches gathered around a cauldron. They cackled together as they dropped snakes, lizards and spiders into the pot. Then his dream shifted into a darker realm as the hags held up torn human limbs. Curiously, he focussed on the hand of one and saw red hair sticking out between her fingers and looking down, he saw Allen's grinning head. Oliver jumped awake and uttered a prayer to any deity who would listen.

Taking sleeping pills, he'd found in the bathroom cabinet Oliver was able to manage his nights but spent his days confined to the house. Then after a week of dazed searching and looking for answers on his computer, he decided that he would go back to the hospital to speak with Allen and try to persuade him to move abroad.

After what felt to Oliver, like a long and perilous journey arrived at the hospital. He stood for a while, aware of the fist thumping in his chest and with his eyes darting in all directions, searching for any sinister figures, he took a few deep breaths. He composed his body and tried to still his mind. Consciously, straightening and swinging his arms casually as he walked, he entered and followed the green line on the floor, which led to Allen's ward.

At the counter, he saw two receptionists exchanging news and laughing. The older lady with the fuller figure seemed to be in charge and took the prime position to meet and greet visitors. Oliver rushed in her direction. She smiled automatically, but Oliver noticed it didn't reach her eyes, and he immediately felt uneasy. He watched dumbly as the woman tucked a stray strand of grey hair back into the blond. Then he noticed her long florescent green nails tapping impatiently on the counter.

"Can I help you?" she said, smiling her false smile.

Oliver smiled back and cleared his throat. "Yes, I've come to see my friend Allen Smith."

"You're not family? Visiting hours are from four to eight. You're welcome to wait."

"I'm in a hurry! I won't stay long," Oliver, said feeling derailed by the unexpected obstacle standing in the way of his plans. "It's urgent!"

"Sorry, what name did you say?" Her smile had faded, and she peered over her glasses and regarded Oliver sternly. "I'm afraid he's no longer with us," she said in a voice, which struck Oliver as being too light and airy for such a responsible job.

"What, he's gone home already." Oliver felt confused by the unanticipated event. "That's good – he's made a swift recovery." *Fit to travel,* Oliver thought with relief.

"I will get someone to speak with you," she said, looking flustered and hurried from her desk. "Sit down; there's a drinks machine if you want a tea."

Oliver remained standing and watched as the woman exited through a door at the back of the office space. Shortly after, she reappeared.

"The doctor won't be long."

"I don't need to see a doctor, and I'm in a rush," Oliver said, licking his dry lips. Then he spotted a tall congenial looking man in a white coat approaching him and smiling kindly.

"I'm Doctor Shaw," he said, holding out his hand. Automatically, Oliver shook it. "We can use the family room." Oliver saw the smile vanish from the doctor's face as he turned and led him down the corridor. An icy shudder ran down his spine as he realised something must be wrong.

"Please sit down, Mr..."

"Baker," Oliver added and sat.

"There's never an easy way to say this, but Mr Smith has passed away."

Oliver almost laughed, "No – sorry, but there has been a mistake. Allen only had a broken leg and whiplash. Smith is a very common name."

"No, I'm afraid there's no mistake," the doctor said, gravely. "His family have been informed."

Oliver was speechless as he grappled with the notion that his friend had died.

"How?"

"I'm not permitted to divulge that information, but I'm sure his family will fill in the gaps for you."

"Please, I'm going abroad tomorrow to start a new job."

"Under the circumstances and between these four walls," he said in a mellow voice. "It was a thrombosis in his leg, which travelled to his lungs."

Everything in the room merged into a fuzzy blur. Oliver leaned forwards and clasped his head in both hands.

"Sit here as long as you want. I will get one of the nurses to bring you some sweet tea – I'm so sorry for your sudden loss."

After the doctor had left the room, Oliver bolted to the nearest toilet and vomited repeatedly. Bent over the basin, his racing mind began to question Allen's diagnosis. *Wouldn't a hospital spot the symptoms early and be able to treat them? Was there an autopsy? Were there medications or chemicals, which could cause an unnatural thickening of the blood? Had he received any strange visitors?* He had an urge to walk straight back to the counter and confront the receptionist for more information but instead cleaned himself up and strode rapidly out of the building.

Chapter Thirty-eight

Kane hurried towards the light. Two days ago, he'd left his former self above ground and entered the cave system. Not since his army days, had he embarked on such a venture. The treacherous journey had been liberating and invigorating, the battle of his wits and mind against a harsh environment. Now he could see the brightness of his destination ahead.

Although separated, he felt the stamp of Poppy's love in his heart and their bond tightened with each careful step he took. As he'd descended sheer rock faces suspended himself from ropes, squeezed through narrow tunnels, stumbled over rocks and clambered over boulders, Poppy's words of encouragement continually splashed into his mind. The thought that she would be waiting for him on his return spurred him on.

Passing under an arch, he stood looking at the ground while his eyes adjusted to the sudden explosion of light. As he slowly looked up, he saw a vast space, a deep sinkhole. In the centre, a turquoise lake glinted like a giant gemstone surrounded by a profusion of bushes and flowers. Creepers tumbled, and silver strands trickled down the sheer cliffs, which reared up to a circular disk of blue sky. Kane found the peculiar landscape intoxicating and bewitchingly beautiful.

He had an impulse to jump into the refreshing water to cleanse himself of the accumulated dust, grime, guano and soothe the chewed-up flesh on his knees. Instead, he perched on a boulder and watched tiny swifts flitting after insects, listened to the birdsong in the otherwise deep silence and breathed in the seductive smells of the wildflowers. He watched for a long time and allowed tears of joy to run down his cheeks. *It's true, the garden's real,* he thought.

He took off his thick coat and t-shirt, went in search of dry firewood, and set about making a fire. He chose a sheltered spot under an overhanging rock to make camp. The twigs ignited immediately, and he felt pleased with himself for remembering what was, needed for such a venture. He'd obtained stored items from his father's house, army matches, a small gas stove, flask, a large serrated knife and even some old ration packs. Kane felt secure, confident and well equipped. The only thing he didn't have enough of was water.

Kane picked up his water bottle. As he crouched down to replenish his supply, he saw the lake was alive with fish. He remembered the tarpaulin folded up in his rucksack and decided to trap the writhing mass by slowly pushing them into the side of the bank. Thrilled at the thought of something more interesting for his dinner, Kane rushed back to his camp and retrieved the sheet. He tied rocks to the bottom corners and walked back to the lake.

He found a gap between a hedge and carefully stepped into the refreshing water allowing the weights to slip from his hands. A strong sun beamed down onto his back, and he heard insects buzzing. Kane sunk his feet into the sandy bed, corralled a shoal of fish and began walking into the shallows. Managing to scoop them up onto a patch of grass, he watched as they flapped and gasped. Not wanting to disturb the fragile balance or take more than he could eat he bent down and threw the smallest back into the water. Taking his knife from the pouch around his waist he gutted and washed those which remained.

Feeling satisfied he went back to the fire and placed the fish in his mess tin. While they cooked, he lay back on his rucksack, listened to the tiny sounds and watched the endless activity of the swifts.

By the time the fish was cooked, the disk of blue had darkened, and Kane could see points of light from the first stars. Thinking longingly of Poppy he began to pick at the flesh of the fish and thirstily drank the water, which he noticed had a sweet taste. He felt comfort in knowing that Poppy had once also walked under the arch and into the garden. *While places like this exist, I will not be tempted by booze,* he thought to himself, as he tried to recall when he'd ever felt so good.

After the last morsel, Kane licked his lips and stared up at the constellations. *Tomorrow I will search for flint and begin making my arrowhead;* he thought hoping it would be as easy as his other tasks. Finally, his eyelids felt heavy. Zipping his jacket up to his neck and covering, himself with the folded tarpaulin, he lay back down and quickly fell asleep.

In the thickest point of the night, Kane sprung into a sitting position aware that he wasn't alone – he'd heard something. Then he heard it again, a blood-curdling wailing echoing around the garden. He opened his eyes wide to see more deeply into the darkness. The air moved, and he heard a whooshing flapping sound.

Opening his mouth to steady his breathing, he picked a lighted branch from the fire and rose to his feet. His heart was loudly pounding as he took his knife from his pouch. Slowly he became aware of warm breath on the back of his neck and spun around to face the intruder.

Hovering like a kite before him was the most extraordinary creature, half-human and half-bird. Black feathers covered her body, large inky black wings flapped furiously, and she reached towards him with jet downy arms.

Kane shook his pulsating head. He felt dizzy; his vision was blurred and going in and out of focus. Suddenly the creature's face was in his, and he saw her gleaming red eyes and crow beak. The dreadful face pushed into his.

"Get out of our space!' she screamed in a cracked hysterical voice. "You don't belong here! Get out! Get out!" She pushed Kane hard, and he fell back against the jagged rock wall and felt a pain in his back. "You murderer! You murderer! Killer of children." The creature was bearing down on Kane again, so close that he was, forced to breath in her rancid breath. "You will feel the fires acid tongue." She grabbed the hot stick from his hand and pushed it into his cheek. Kane shrieked with pain.

Then he remembered the knife in his hand and furiously stabbed it into the mass of blackness. He felt slimy wetness and thought he saw a dark liquid spilling from the crow's body. The crow screeched, tumbled backwards and lay on the ground with her wings splayed out. Trembling Kane wiped the knife clean on his coat sleeve. When he lifted his head and peered back into the darkness, he saw the crow was gone. Clutching his weapon ready, he watched the space for a long time.

Eventually, he uneasily went back to his sleeping area by the fire and felt around the pockets of his bag for his torch. Waves of nausea swept over him, and he wondered if he'd been poisoned and was hallucinating. Feeling unsteady, he sat propped against the wall with his torch in one hand and his knife in the other determined to be on guard for the rest of the night.

After a few nervous hours, he noticed his eyelids sticking together like magnets, and he almost had to force them apart with his fingers. In this half-sleeping state, he became aware of rustling and noticed something moving out of the corner of his eye. Kane jumped into full wakefulness and looking down saw a mass of rats nibbling at his discarded fish bones. Relieved, he kicked them out of the way and felt grateful that they'd prevented him sleeping.

Above he saw the stars were beginning to fade, so he stood up and went down to the lake, scrutinising every shape to make sure there was nothing unfamiliar hiding in the shadows. He crouched down, threw water over his face and hair then, pushed his fingers hard over his head.

As he stood back up, he suddenly felt strong hands around his neck. Kane grappled with the invisible force. Struggling for breath, he collapsed to his knees. A crowd of ghostly shapes pushed him to the ground and pinned him down. Through his bulging eyes, Kane saw the painted face of a thickset man, the crow and other deformed figures both young and old, staring down. They tugged at his arms and pinched his flesh as though they all wanted a piece of his body.

The heavy weight on his chest released its grip on his neck and feeling half-dead, Kane gasped for breath.

"What brings you here?" A voice boomed and then shook him by the shoulders.

"Stop! I'm here with permission," Kane said and felt his words crumble away without being, heard. "I'm here to cut my flint spearhead." A sharp pain radiated out from his calf as teeth embedded into his leg.

"You are a persecutor here to destroy."

"I'm here for a miracle, to become clean and discover the secrets of who I am," Kane said, and tears trickled from the corners of his eyes and down his temples as he realised the truth of his words. He shut his eyes and focussed all his attention on his memories of Poppy. He was only vaguely aware of the grotesque creature's savage cries and insults and the repeated munching on his flesh.

The confusion abruptly ended.

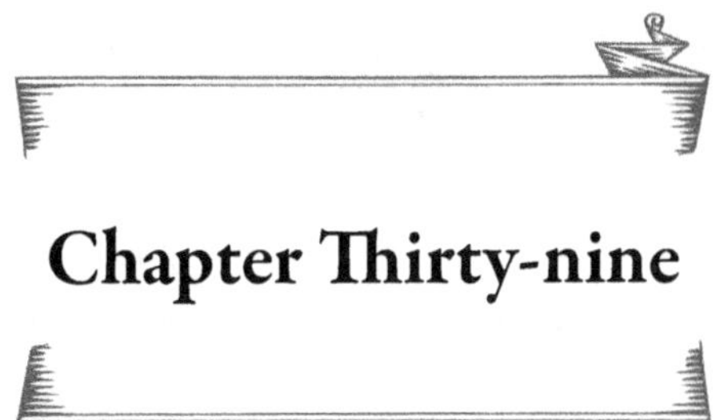

Chapter Thirty-nine

Kane slowly sat up and carefully moving his aching head, fearfully looked around. He scrutinised his surroundings for any signs of the phantoms from the previous night. It appeared that he'd fallen asleep by the lake, and when he checked his body, he found no indications of harm. Relieved he sighed and gazed into the glittering brilliance of the water, which was as blue as the disk above. Once, again everything was alive. Kane pondered his situation and watched the dragonflies flitting from one plant to the next, feasted his eyes on the bright hues of the numerous wildflowers and the various shades of bushes as they gently moved in the warm breeze.

There was an incongruity about the magical lilt of the place, by day it was a sublime oasis, but at night all his senses and emotions were thrust into an unknown dimension, which he'd always denied existed. He felt trapped in a crack between worlds. Above was his universe where the laws of physics applied and below was the solid sustaining earth, but here everything was unpredictable and permanently shifting. Kane decided that whatever else happened he wanted to have made his flint spearhead before dark and to begin the treacherous journey back to his world.

Suddenly, Kane's thoughts were interrupted by the sound of a rock tumbling down the cliff face. Startled, he glanced up towards the source of the disturbance. Straying silently along the edge of the cliff was a wolf or dog. It stood about thirty-three inches at the shoulder, had thick grey, white and black fur. Kane locked his eyes on the creature and uneasily followed its every move, hoping it wouldn't spot him and descend. After a few minutes of watching as it ambled along, the creature disappeared down a hole.

Kane froze and holding his breath listened intently praying the creature wasn't searching for a meal. Time lapsed, and he decided to arm himself ready for a fight. He took his knife from his pouch, crept back to his camp and took a chocolate bar from his rucksack. He crouched in the shadows and waited.

Kane's eyes followed down a curtain of rock, which stuck out from the cliff face and there at the bottom he saw the long snout, low forehead and furry ears. The beast had quietly settled on the other side of the protrusion. Kane stood up and cautiously walked to the opposite side of the lake. Here he found a well-trodden path, which led him into the shadows of the precipice. As he daringly approached, the wall reared up in height like a giant monster standing on its hind legs. He thought he was unseen, but the wolf-dog began to bark.

With his rations in his hand, Kane stepped out from behind the rock into full view. The wolf-dog was standing barking with his amber eyes staring straight at Kane. Then to Kane's surprise, he yawned, stretched and relaxed back down.

Kane sat down next to the animal and waited patiently, expecting an adverse reaction. Nothing happened, so he reached out with his hand and stroked the wolf dog's back. He felt an immediate attachment and understood that in some way, the wolfdog was there for him.

"What brings you here?" he said as the dog turned and sniffed at his coat. "You want some chocolate." Kane took the ration from his pocket, tore off the wrapper and offered the sweet substance to his new companion. The wolf-dog licked his hands. Without any restraint, Kane stroked and hugged the beast. Together they sat in the pervading peace looking out at the blissful scene. Finally, Kane remembered his purpose, and he felt a flicker of panic at how much time must have gone by.

"I'm going to have to leave you," he said, patting the wolfdogs soft head. "I'm here on a mission."

At these words, the wolf-dog rose, his body curled around, and his nose pointed at the cliff face. For the first-time Kane noticed a body-sized crack and looking at the ground saw that was where the path led.

"You think I should look in there," he said, smiling at the animal and noticing how now his emptiness was filled he once again felt whole.

Kane followed his guide and squeezed his body through the narrow space. To his surprise, there was a shaft of light coming from a hole in the roof and a slope of rocks, which led up to the higher ground. The floor was littered with fragments of stone. Kane bent down, picked up a splinter and examined it closely.

"Well it is flint," he muttered to the wolf-dog. "I will name you Flint. Is that okay with you?" he added, patting the beast on the head who'd drawn close to his side.

Searching further, he found a perfectly shaped stone to use as a chisel. "It's alright Flint, I know I must work my spearhead. There will be no cheating here," he said stepping into the cool shadows of the rock wall, where he began to hammer at a large lump of jutting stone. As he struck the smooth surface, splinters fired out in all directions. Kane hoped the loud banging wouldn't attract unwanted attention. He looked down at Flint and took comfort from the warm gleam of his amber eyes.

"This is dangerous work, my friend," he said, wiping his brow. "And hot," he added, becoming aware of his throat burning with thirst. He was fearful of drinking the water but knew he would have to relent at some point. Just as this notion crossed his mind, he heard Flint softly pad out of the cave and sometime later caught the sound of slurping water.

By about midday, the grey flint broke off into Kane's injured hand. He scoured the floor for a heavier rock, which he could use as a hammer. Then with his tools in his hand's, he pushed his way back through the crack and into the sunlight. Sweat was pouring down his back like treacle. He dropped the stones pulled off his coat and t-shirt and kneeling by the lake drunk heartily. The water was clean and trickled refreshingly down his throat.

Kane sat down by Flint and positioned the grapefruit-sized source rock on the ground. He lifted the hammer rock high and selectively struck the edges of his source stone. A large slab sheared off. Repeatedly he bashed the rock, sometimes missing and other times sending useless shards flying dangerously through the air. Eventually, the source rock lay in pieces much of which at first glance looked unusable.

"What next?" he muttered to Flint. The wolf-dog examined the pile and then, with his snout pushed at a larger slab. "Won't that be too big?" Kane said pondering over the stone. "It would make a good knife with its sharp edge." Kane felt that Flint was part of his pilgrimage, that their souls were, linked. "Okay I will trust your judgement, but this part will be awkward with my missing fingers."

Kane held the stone knife as best he could in his left hand and picked up a chip with a pointed tip. Pressing hard on the edge of the first rock caused flakes and chips to breakaway. Repeatedly he struck stone against stone until finally he was, left with a desirable shape. He felt proud of himself even with his deformed hand he was able to create an object of value.

"Look! This is it, Flint," he said, shoving his spearhead under the dog's nose. Then he shivered as a shadow passed over his back. He'd been so focused on his task he hadn't noticed the sun was setting. Making allowances for his left hand had slowed him down, and now the sun was sinking.

Chapter Forty

Panic rushed through Kane's head, crowding out all other emotions. He glanced up at the once blazing sky and saw it had dulled and was swiftly going pale like a dying man's eyes. Rapidly he pulled his t-shirt over his head and feeling disabled once again; he struggled to put his arms in his coat sleeves. Then he almost stumbled as he picked up his spearhead and dropped it in his pocket.

"We must leave straight away," he said, searching the ground for the path in the diminished light only to see many veins spreading in all directions. He felt lost and couldn't think straight. "I should have never come. This whole thing is mad." Glancing up he saw the red embers of his fire. Flint had also spotted them and led the way back.

Once back at his campsite, he opened his rucksack and dropped everything he'd brought into the bag.

"I must take back with me absolutely every scrap I brought," he muttered. Kane shone his torch over the ground, hunting for the tiniest thing he might have forgotten. Flint stood at his side with his ears pricked as though he was hanging on every word.

Kane dropped the last empty ration packet in his bag and satisfied he'd retrieved any signs of his existence slumped to the ground. The only thing, which remained out was his water bottle. He hadn't drunk from it since the previous night but automatically picked it up and placed it to his lips. After one gulp, he was choking and spluttering. Reaching into his mouth, his pincer fingers grasped the tip of the offending object. He pulled the half-swallowed foreign body and felt it dragging up his throat. He wanted to barf. When he glimpsed the long black feather, he shuddered with repulsion and threw it to his side. The quill wet with bile fell into Kane's open bag. Black on black was too hard for him to see.

Kane's attention turned towards Flint, who was growling low and looking in the direction of the lake. Paralysed, Kane held his breath and stared into the bushes. His senses sharpened he saw insubstantial shapes milling together and heard whispering. The volume increased in number and intensity. There was a plaintive wailing, angry moaning, arguing and cursing. Standing shoulder to shoulder, the black mass moved in Kane's direction. Kane drew his knees to his chest and covered his head with his hands to block out the hideous sight and noise. Flint stood guard barking and growling.

Glimpsing up Kane saw decomposing bodies, balls of pus, melting flesh, black and blue flaking skin and rag covered broken bones jostling closer and reaching out. The stench made him nauseous and repulsed as he pushed his body as far as he could into the cave wall. They leaned towards him their bony rotting fingers trying to touch his living skin. Shuffling together, stumbling over each other all hungry to grope at his body and bite into his flesh.

Kane squeezed his eyes shut, and his arms flailed as he tried to beat his ghostly attackers back. Briefly, he raised his lids and saw bulging bloodshot eyes staring back.

"Stay away from me, you motherfuckers!" he screamed as he felt tooth and claw pulling at his body. Tormented and restricted he thought it was his time to die. Suddenly he felt a release and peering into the middle of the tangled mass of decomposing flesh he saw Flint with his hackles raised, and his gums and fangs bared as he growled and snapped at the dead.

The tightly packed group loosened. They circled Flint their gaping jaws contorting and hissing while all the time edging backwards away from the angry beast. A message seemed to travel between them, and they retreated, back to the lake where they waited and whispered.

Slightly recovered, Kane called Flint to his side. The dog sat close still on hyper-alert. Kane flung his arms around the wolf dog's neck and buried his face in his soft fur.

"You saved me," he mumbled to his friend. "I suppose we all need saving sometimes he said in a cracked voice as a few tears dropped onto Flint's shoulder. Kane felt intimacy and unity like the tangled roots from two separate plants. These feelings grew stronger throughout the night as the appalling pale faces returned and attempted to take revenge on Kane for all the horrors perpetrated on them in life. Flint remained a steadfast barrier, protecting Kane until dawn. Kane woke uncertain as to whether he was a man or a wolf-dog.

Chapter Forty-one

This time Oliver descended the rope ladder, without hesitation. Normally, he wouldn't have ventured out in such a horrendous afternoon storm. Each time the air exploded, he jumped, fearing for his life, and he was relieved to be inside a Faraday's cage and out of the torrential of rain - anything unpredictable and uncontrollable filled him with dread. Glancing down, he saw the three familiar faces of the women staring up while the two children clung to Rosa's legs.

Cautiously he stepped onto the firm ground and left the ladder swinging gently. Oliver was aware of his state of high anxiety and his internal struggle with his decision to run away and to step into the unknown. He felt that his peaceful regular life had been violated and he'd been forced into a position not entirely of his choosing.

The women moved towards him, smiling, and Madeline held out her hand in greeting. Oliver felt far from cheery, and the corners of his mouth remained set and his face downcast. As a distraction, he shook the rain from his green waterproof coat and slipped his heavy rucksack off his shoulders.

"Welcome, I'm glad you've chosen to join us," Madeline said, scrutinising his face until Oliver felt uncomfortable.

"I didn't choose," he mumbled.

"I know this must be difficult for you, but a new and good life is waiting for us all," she released her grip and turned away. "I don't think you've met Poppy. Oliver watched a young girl of about Sarah's age step from the shadows of the tunnel entrance. She dropped her bags on the ground and strolled towards Oliver and extended her arm in greeting.

"Hi, I'm pleased to meet you," she said her hand lightly in his. "Don't worry, you're not the only man my boyfriend will be joining us soon," she smiled happily and went back to her belongings, bringing them further into the space.

Oliver felt the kinetic energy radiating from the walls and then with the boom, he automatically put his hands to his ears, echoing the children's actions. Sarah laughed, and Oliver felt his cheeks burning.

"The children don't like storms either, but it will probably have stopped by the time Kane arrives," Rosa's eyes shone with brightness and warmth. "You might recognise him he was the young man you and your friend saved the last time you were here. I think his name was Allen, was he unable to join you?" She looked at him inquiringly.

"No, he's been murdered," Oliver stated in a bitter matter of fact tone.

"That's terrible!" Rosa gasped, her brow creasing with anguish. "What happened?"

"I think we made too many enquiries to the wrong people." Oliver was uneasy and not sure if he should even trust these women.

"We're truly sorry for your loss," Madeline added. "At least you're safe now and will find us all caring and helpful company," she paused and looked down awkwardly. "I deeply regret that you've been drawn into all this," she mumbled and wiped the back of her hand under her hooked nose.

"So, we have to wait," Oliver said and walked over to the wall decorated with the handprints, where his journey had begun. He glanced at them briefly, but they didn't hold their previous allure. Sulkily, Oliver slumped down onto the damp ground with his back resting against the wall. He was thankful to be, left to his devouring despair and watched the strange women as in solemn silence they pulled their baggage close to their sides and sat on the hefty rucksacks.

After some time, Poppy walked over to Oliver and squatted at his side. Oliver remained silent and looked ahead.

"I know you probably don't want to hear this, but the place we're going to is vast and extremely organised," she said gently and putting her hand in her coat pocket pulled out some photos. "Look it's probably the largest bunker in the world," she said, handing him the pictures. Oliver flicked through them until he came across what looked like a battalion of soldiers each with a wolf at their side.

"Who are they?" he asked wearily.

"They're our guardians – we have a whole army there."

"And the dogs?"

"They're not ordinary dogs; they are their soul shadows."

Oliver breathed in the damp air and sighed. "Will I have to fight?"

"No, don't be silly, there are people there like you who are willing to help – scientists, doctors, teachers and religious leaders," she smiled kindly. "It's time we were able to live without being haunted by fear. We're not going to hide anymore," she said with resolve.

Oliver smiled at her falsely and handed back the images of their potential new life. He returned to his brooding and wondered if he would be, locked inside his nightmare for eternity.

An awkward silence built up between them as they waited. Oliver was wondering if he'd overreacted and whether to return to his parent's house when he felt a stirring in the air, heard a trudging sound, and an echoing voice calling Poppy's name. He watched as immediately the girl stood and rushed to the tunnel entrance. A tall, strongly built figure emerged accompanied by what appeared to Oliver to be a wolf at his side. The man dropped his bag to the floor, Poppy, rushed into his strong open arms, he lifted her off the ground, their lips touched, and they kissed tenderly, longingly.

"I did it, Poppy! I did it!" he said, reaching into his pocket for his spearhead. He held it up in the air, presenting his treasure to the smiling eyes, which were all looking in his direction. "Now we can truly be together."

Automatically, Oliver put his hand to his neck, fumbled for his chain, ran his fingers beneath the open zip of his coat, and felt the lump of his spearhead concealed beneath his clothes. Clutching the stone reassured him and generated a feeling of belonging. As he watched, the other man, his eyes so bright and anxious to be a part of a new life, he too relaxed.

Oliver stood and walked briskly over to Kane. He extended his hand and Kane took it in his strong grip and pulled him close.

"It's good to have another human on board," he muttered in Oliver's ear and patted him on the back. "This is a very female dominated society. Who knows who you might meet," he laughed and broke free. Standing back, Oliver was able to recognise his face.

"I'm Oliver, we have met before, but you were unconscious on that occasion," he said, smiling broadly for the first time since he'd arrived.

"I'm Kane, and this is my new friend Flint," he said bending and patting the wolfdog on the head. "Don't worry he's only half wolf – I've often admired such dogs on the internet."

Poppy crouched down and wrapped her arms around the beast's thick neck. "He's gorgeous – your soul shadow," she muttered. "You will be able to be within him and him within you."

"I don't want to break this reunion up, but we have a plane waiting to smuggle us out," Madeline called. "And I've just had a text saying that our car is already at the gate."

As they all hurried to gather up their belongings, Oliver saw Kane holding Poppy's shoulders, "I'm sorry, I've got more news," he paused and looked around uneasily to see who was listening. Oliver bowed his head. "I'm not going to be coming with you yet," he said. "I need to rescue my brother from those tyrants. I promise I will join you as soon as I can and will stay in touch all the time."

Still standing awkwardly close by Oliver saw Poppy's eyes staring up at Kane hot black and brimming with tears. "But he's a killer. Look what they did to you and your sister."

"I know but was that because of Adam's influence? I need to try and get my old brother back."

Poppy's face clouded with bewilderment as she tried to evaluate the situation. Then her eyes darted away, she turned from Kane and attended to getting ready to leave.

"I will join you, and we will be married," he said, rushing to help her attach her bags to a rope that hung down next to the ladder. "It's one last thing I must try. I murdered Jim, my brother – I have to try to save Joe. I promise after that we will be together forever."

"That was an accident. If you go back, you will be killed," she said wiping the tears away with the back of her hand. "Once a soldier always a soldier," she sighed. "We could help your brother as a team from a safe place." Oliver could see the girl steeling herself for a possible future alone. She kept her eyes cast down refusing to make eye contact.

Flint standing at Kane's side, began to growl, and the hair on his back bristled. Everyone froze and listened to distant demented wailing.

"You've brought them with you – they've been released from the garden," Poppy whispered. "You must have something of them in your possession." Poppy shot Kane a scowl, regarded the others with a stern expression and hastily climbed the ladder. "I will wait for you," she called down from the hole above. "So, you'd better come."

Oliver was staring up at Poppy's mournful face when the ground trembled. Immediately, he collapsed onto the cold ground. As it continued to quake, he scrambled towards the wall. He heard Flint howling and behind this, fearful shrieks and wailing rang out loudly. Shaken loose stones and boulders fell from the roof, and dust rained down then billowed in all directions.

Oliver curled into a tight ball, holding his head, praying for the alarming motion to stop while fearing that they would all be entombed.

"Get out now! Hurry!" Kane screamed as he frantically hoisted luggage and helped the women up the swaying ladder.

The shaking stopped, and in a moment of distilled peace, Oliver brushed the dirt from his eyes and glancing up, he saw Kane pushing the last figure through the hole. Then he watched as Kane turned and fastened his determined eyes into his.

"Oliver, hurry we must go," he said as wolf and man rushed in the cowering man's direction.

Oliver was reluctant to leave the shelter of the wall, but Kane grabbed his arms and pulled him to his feet. Then he grasped both their bags, flung them over one shoulder and half-dragged Oliver towards the exit.

As Oliver forced his leaden legs to move up the ladder, he heard disturbing cries, and twisting round saw the stumbling dead emerging from the tunnel. His stomach knotted, the ground rocked, and the ladder swayed like a pendulum. All that stood between the two men and the decomposing corpses was a viciously snarling wolf.

"Go, man! Go!" Kane said, grabbing the ladder to hold it steady. "For fuck's sake move," he roared at Oliver.

Without a second thought, Oliver raced towards freedom. Kane and Flint ran to his mother's derelict house as it was the nearest place to hide, where he slept hungrily on Joe's bed until the late afternoon.

Chapter Forty-two

Kane was at one within Flint and standing proudly on the height of the hill he looked at the valley below with the fearlessness and will of the beast. There was no sign of life, and in the half-light, the abbey wore an expression of serenity and stillness. As the wolfdog glided down the slope, the chestnuts in the woods to his left seemed to grow taller and darker.

Following his sense of smell, Flint skulked around to the back of the grey stone building. On the ground floor, a window was open. Without hesitation, Flint leapt into the air, through the open space and into the cool gloom of Joe's room.

Pressed against the opposite wall was a bed where Flint found Joe sleeping. The slack body lay on his back with his left arm hanging over the edge. Above on a shelf was a neat arrangement of toy trains.

Flint breathed in the scent of the child. His tongue flopped out of his mouth as he panted eagerly, and then he licked the blushed cheeks. Joe felt his presence, his lids fluttered and opened. Clear blue eyes fastened onto the wolfdog, he smiled and reached out with an adoring child's hand and touched the beasts head. Then fully awake he leaned over the edge of the bed and embraced Flint. His small, strong arms circled the wolf dog's neck, and he buried his face in the soft fur.

From deep within Flint, Kane, in this speck of time felt as though the whole world had unfurled revealing dazzling colours. The child was innocent, harmless and probably had been dreaming human dreams. Then the moment died as a wake of grief and regret for Jim's death surged through Kane. As he wept, he separated from Flint and found himself kneeling on the floor by Joe's bed. The boy had released his grip and was now sitting upright, staring bewildered at his brother and the wolfdog who was lying on the stone floor.

"Joe, we need to go home now," Kane said gently and reached out his hand. "This isn't a nice place. You need to be with your family." Kane smiled warmly and encouragingly. Still looking wide-eyed and bemused Joe gave Kane his hand. Then Joe wriggled towards Kane who swept him up into his arms. He hugged him close and then set him on the floor. Kane took a carrier bag from his pocket.

"We will take your trains," he said as he hurriedly took the prized possessions off the shelf. "You collect up anything you might want. Anything else you need I will buy for you, and when we get out of here the first thing we will do is go to the nearest sweet shop," Kane smiled down at the boy who was dropping his few belongings into the bag. "Get dressed now, and we can go."

As Kane watched Joe pull on his only pair of trousers and a faded t-shirt, he became aware that the old sense of danger had returned. He looked down at Flint who was still calmly lying on the floor with only half his attention on the proceedings.

"I think it will be more fun if we climb out of the window," Kane said the moment he saw Joe was dressed. Flint rose and waited obediently. Kane lifted Joe, so he could reach the window frame. Joe abruptly froze. Then he twisted the top half of his body around and listened as though he heard a calling travelling towards him through the corridors.

"Mathew! I forgot to get Mathew," He said with frightened, panicked eyes.

"Mathew must stay here." Kane felt his heart throbbing and sinking in the pit of his stomach. "I will get him for you. You go with Flint and wait for me outside." Before he'd stopped speaking, Joe had slid down the wall, wriggled out of his grasp and was running in search of his beloved doll. Joe's movements were quick and agile he slipped out of the room, slammed the door shut and, the instant Kane's hand rested on the handle he heard a key turning in the lock.

A pinprick of panic pierced Kane's heart, and he felt sweaty and sick. To relieve himself from the burden of human emotions, he merged with Flint. The beast leapt through the window and sniffing in the air tried to locate Joe's scent. Stealthily Flint rounded the building. At the front, he felt a strong draw to a particular place. A bank of smooth grass rose high and around the edge was a low wall. Placing his front paws on the cool surface, he was able to peer through the leaded window without difficulty.

Most of the small room was obscured by shadows but to the left of the window was an altar on which stood two large lit candles. In a draft, the flames flickered, and the light illuminated a familiar figure. Mathew was kneeling low to the ground in prayer and looming up behind him was a thicker, darker shadow. As the man drew closer, Kane recognised Anton.

Impotently, through Flint's eyes, Kane watched the proceedings with a cold fascination. Anton was covered in blood and raising his axe above Mathew's crouched body. The monk lifted his head, his lids flicked open, and he glared ahead with stony black eyes. Then he calmly rose and for a fraction of a second Kane was able to see, Mathew clutching the mimic doll in his hands and his eyes were equally cold and fiery. Together they turned to face Anton.

At the same moment, Kane saw Joe dash into the room and run towards Mathew. As he reached for the doll, Kane saw that Joe was already transformed his face in the candlelight was a mask of determined, icy willpower and around his head was a black halo.

It was clear to Kane that Anton had been caught off guard as his face clouded with confusion – he wasn't the type of man who would kill a child. Kane's blood chilled as helplessly he observed Anton reach down and lift the boy off the ground. As Anton stepped forward with resolve to complete his task, Joe kicked and wriggled.

In deep demonic voices, both doll and man hollered in unison, "he be the witch's guardian." Mathew stood tall and walked fearlessly up to Anton. "Brother, I see you have blood on your hands. The life of the innocent, taken while they slept, prayed or read God's words. I find you guilty." In one swift motion, Joe pulled what to Kane looked like a long hatpin from behind the dolls coat and thrust it in a gap between Anton's ribs. The giant of a man dropped his axe and crashed to the floor. Joe scrambled to his feet and stood beside Mathew while clutching the doll.

"Boy, you be my best witchfinder," Mathew said and ruffled Joe's hair. Child and man stared down at the helpless writhing hulk. "This Joe be my witless brother, his blood be from witches, and his heart be black like the devil's," he said, looking down at Joe with a fatal grin on his face. "Our work is not complete. The only way to destroy such a demon is to sever his head from his body." Mathew bent low and retrieved the heavy axe. "You can take the first blow. Hold it in both hands as it's weighty and aim for his neck."

Kane separated from Flint and in a desperate fury hammered on the glass until the lead bowed and the diamond shapes smashed onto the internal stone floor.

"Stop! Stop Joe!" he screamed repeatedly. "Don't listen to him, come with me!"

Mathew handed the boy the axe. Joe half-turned and looking over his shoulder directly at Kane shot him a look of horrendous evil. "Fuck off witch lover," he screeched in a sharp scratchy voice. Kane felt as though a fist had pushed into his chest, pulverising his heart and for a split second, it stopped beating. Everything froze as the axe fell with a hard thud.

Kane bowed his head in disgust and stepped back from the window. It all became clear at once. He realised in sharp detail that he'd deluded himself into thinking he could separate the good in his brother from the bad. There was no saving Joe, every cell in his body was, corrupted by Mathew. Nevertheless, part of him wanted to refuse to leave to keep fighting for his brother's soul, despite the evidence.

Kane glanced up to see if any more could be done, and to his horror saw Mathew and Joe standing at the window glaring at him. Hanging by a clump of bloody hair from Mathew's hand was the drenched scarlet head of Anton.

"Meet my new and best witchfinder," Mathew beamed his hooked nose almost touching his chin and wrapped his arm around Joe's shoulder. "Keep looking behind you brother," man and child laughed.

Flint growled and then pulled at Kane's leg, urging him to abandon his crusade. Kane and Flint blended into one, and the beast hurtled back up the steep hill.

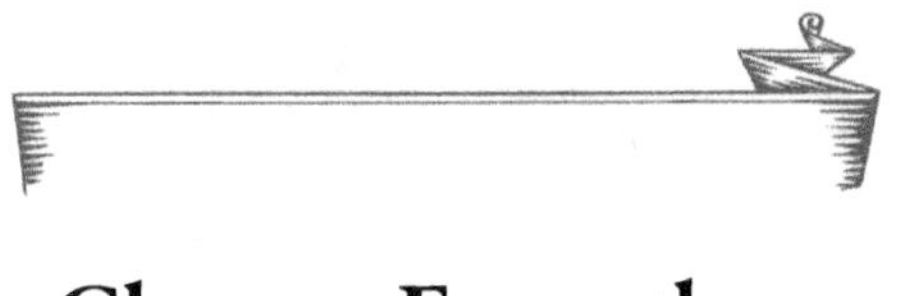

Chapter Forty-three

Kane had gone back to the park to retrieve his rucksack, which he'd hidden in a hedge. The night sky was dazzlingly clear, but all around the trees creaked unnervingly. He didn't need any more convincing the desire to escape and reunite with Poppy fed all his thoughts.

Urgently he and Flint rushed to his father's house to obtain his passport, to pack and make flight arrangements. It was late when he arrived. Quietly he pushed open his father's bedroom door and found him in a deep sleep.

"Goodbye, dad," he muttered and crept back downstairs and into the front room. Heavy with melancholy and exhaustion he slumped down at his father's desk and opened the computer, while Flint lay silently at his side. Instead of going on the travel sites he went onto Skype, he needed to see that Poppy was still real. He glanced at the time and saw that there was a chance that she'd arrived. To his utter surprise, she answered his call.

"I can't believe you answered," Kane said nervously as his heart fluttered into life.

"We've only just arrived, but this place is amazing," her alert eyes smiled, and she smoothed her long black hair into place. "Already, it doesn't feel like a sanctuary. Everyone here is pro-active."

Poppy's bubbling excitement sparked life and hope back into Kane. "I wish I could look at your face forever."

"Did you find your brother," she said softly. "When are you coming – waiting is unbearable – please hurry."

Kane fell silent and bowed his head as though in an act of devotion – longing for her to be at his side.

"It didn't go well, did it?" Poppy spoke soothingly – healingly. "I want to reach through the screen and comfort you."

"No, it didn't go well, but I'm not sorry I tried," he smiled. "I realise you can't save everyone."

"Promise you won't divert again - that you will focus on us. Remember you are a new man stronger and Flint, you and I will be welded together for eternity."

Alarmed, Kane put his hand on the screen. It was breaking up.

"There's something wrong with the computer; you're breaking up. I love you," he said hurriedly, hoping she'd heard.

"Kane, are you there? The screens crackling. Keep in contact – I will be waiting for you."

Poppy's face froze. Something caught Kane's eyes, causing him to scrutinise the image. It looked like a double exposure. He saw a tar-black shape mingling with Poppy's. The blurred edges seemed to be made of feathers and embed in her deep sockets were the round beady eyes of a crow. A black beak and mouth opened, and he heard a hoarse, grating caw. The more Kane looked, the worse, and more clearly, the double image appeared.

Kane felt a tangible dread, and a sob escaped from his throat. Then Poppy's perfect living picture re-appeared.

"I love you," she said, smiling sweetly.

Kane slammed the lid down, jumped up from the computer chair and went over to the rucksack he'd dumped on the floor with the purpose of sorting out the useless items from his journey to the garden and replacing them with particular things he would need for his new life. Madly he pulled his possessions from his bag and flung them on the carpet. At the very bottom, he found it, stuck on the side of a cooking pot – a long lustrous black feather.

Make sure you don't bring anything back from the garden. What belongs there must stay there. Poppy's voice rang loudly in Kane's head. He fell to his knees under the weight of sorrow and thumped the floor with his fists.

Flint came to his side and licked his face. Kane rose and with a fiery passion burning in his heart hastily packed.

"All the signs are pointing in one direction, Flint," Kane said, patting his companion on the head. "Come on comrade it's time to follow the others - to go on active duty."

This time Flint merged into Kane and became one with his soul. Kane felt possessed, his limbs filled with iron, strength; he noticed his senses were heightened, and a serenity flooded his mind with the knowledge that he was making the correct choice. Everything felt enhanced and doubly powerful.

Four hours later, in the damp morning, Kane was standing in line following people on a plane. A smiling attendant pointed him in the direction of his seat in the middle of the aircraft. He relaxed back in his seat, shut his eyes and listened to people boarding, laughing, chatting and reassuring the nervous. All kinds of smells surged through his brain, diesel fumes, food, people and perfume, building pictures of life from both the past and the present. The engine switched on, and people settled.

Kane felt content but feeling that he was on the edge of something huge was too excited to sleep. Two people sunk into the seats behind him and their whispering caught his attention. It sounded as though they were discussing a deep secret.

"Your talent will be recognised for eternity. You're already in magazines around the world. It's time to take the US by storm."

"You don't understand - I can't stand flying."

Kane immediately recognised the second voice, and his heart began pounding. He hoped Adam and his companion weren't aware of his presence. *Have, they been sent by Mathew to kill me? To, follow me and discover the whereabouts of the others?* Kane considered while continuing to listen and pretend sleep.

"We will start a new order – recruit willing monks from the needy. You won't have to worry about anything. I will do all the cleaning up for you."

The power of the plane's engines accelerated. "I hate this," Adam whined and fell into a focussed silence.

Well, this notches things up a bit Flint. Kane's internal voice explained. *I think they will be first on our hit list,* Kane said as his right hand reached up to the spearhead, which hung from a gold chain around his neck.

About the Author

Elizabeth Wixley was born in Hertfordshire in the United Kingdom but has moved many times during her childhood. She attended the Camberwell Art School and joined a design studio in Convent Garden. Moving to Bristol, some years later, she worked full time for the Local Education Authority supporting children suffering from emotional and behavioural problems whilst ensuring that the transition into a mainstream school was done in a supportive and nurturing manner. Whilst providing children with a haven for learning, she raised two sons as a single parent while studying for a degree in education at the University of the West of England.

Her love of fiction started at the age of six when Elizabeth's grandmother died of cancer and to ensure that the rest of the family was safe, she would spend the nights roaming the house looking for the" C" monster to make sure that he did not claim any more victims.

One sunny bright day, her sister told her that fork lightning would come and strike her down after which she would spend her days hiding in the garage, and when she heard that the sun was falling out of the sky, well, needless to say, she very seldom ventured out.

With trial and error, Elizabeth soon realised to fight her foes; she had to stare them straight in the eye, explore them and conqueror the inner demons to stand righteous. This helps fuel her love of horror and the many mysteries of the world. Creating a why and what-if scenario that runs prominently in her fascinating fiction.

Throughout Elizabeth's life, creative arts have been her passion, whether it is visiting galleries, painting or writing. She enjoys nothing more than sharing a compelling horror story with others and holding the sanity of her readers in the palm of her hand.

Other Books by E. M. G. Wixley

Adam's Cross

Book One of the Witchfinder Series

Kane's Cross

Book Two of the Witchfinder Series

Devil's Cross

Book Three of the Witchfinder series

Zach's Cross

Book Four of the Witchfinder Series

In the Devil's Own Words

Cathedral Chronicles

Blood Borne

Cathedral Chronicles

Reflections

Cathedral Chronicles

SECRETS AND SHADOW of the Missing

Living Dreams

The Warning

Living Dreams

The Tethered Unicorn

Living Dreams

Looking for Life

Email liz1949@hotmail.co.uk

If you enjoyed this book, please leave a review. Thank you!

Don't miss out!

Visit the website below and you can sign up to receive emails whenever E.M.G Wixley publishes a new book. There's no charge and no obligation.

https://books2read.com/r/B-A-IMIE-THNN

BOOKS 2 READ

Connecting independent readers to independent writers.